"The pressure inside Belle Terre's third moon is building and has been for some time. The moon will soon explode and, in the process, will destroy all life on this planet."

"Explode?" Kirk asked. "Are you certain?"

"Yes, sir," Spock said.

Kirk nodded. When Mr. Spock said he was certain, the event would happen. "How did we miss this?"

"The moon's crust makes scanning difficult," Spock said.

"How long?"

"So far I have been unable to ascertain the exact time of the explosion, again due to the nature of the olivium."

"A day? A week? A year?" Kirk demanded. "I've got over sixty thousand colonists to get off this planet and out of harm's way."

"My data is insufficient to allow me to predict the explosion exactly, sir," Spock said. "I may be able to give you a more accurate time frame after a few more hours of research."

"Do it," Kirk said. "And quickly. . . ."

STAR TREK®

NEW EARTH

BOOK TWO OF SIX
BELLE TERRE

DEAN WESLEY SMITH
WITH
DIANE CAREY

NEW EARTH CONCEPT BY DIANE CAREY AND JOHN ORDOVER

POCKET BOOKS

New York   London   Toronto   Sydney   Singapore   Belle Terre

An *Original* Publication of POCKET BOOKS

POCKET BOOKS, a division of Simon & Schuster Inc.
1230 Avenue of the Americas, New York, NY 10020

This book is published by Pocket Books, a division of Simon & Schuster Inc., under exclusive license from Paramount Pictures.

ISBN: 0-671-04297-1

First Pocket Books printing June 2000

10 9 8 7 6 5 4 3 2 1

POCKET and colophon are registered trademarks of Simon & Schuster Inc.

Printed in the U.S.A.

For Greg,
who gave it structure,
and
For Kris,
who kept it on track.

Part One

BAD NEWS

Chapter One

Countdown: 8 Days, 7 Hours

CAPTAIN JAMES T. KIRK dropped into the soft sand and leaned back against a large log of driftwood. In front of him the dune slanted down to the beach and the green-tinted ocean beyond. He tried to think back to the last time he had simply sat alone on a beach and relaxed. He couldn't remember ever doing that. But he also couldn't imagine this was the first time, either. He must have relaxed on a beach before, although he had no doubt Dr. McCoy would swear it had never happened. McCoy always said that James Kirk never relaxed.

Kirk supposed that was true. Maybe it wasn't too late to learn. Or more likely, it was time to learn.

He took a deep breath and looked around. There was a slight bite to the ocean breeze coming in over the waves, just enough to take the edge off the heat of the midday sun. The salt and brine smell drifted over the beach, strong enough to be enjoyed by a new arrival, but not overpowering enough to be noticed after the first few moments. The beach sand was almost a pure white, and stretched in a ribbon as far as he could see in both directions.

This planet Belle Terre was everything Governor Evan Pardonnet had said it would be. If this stretch of shoreline near the main colony compound was any indication of the rest of the planet, it was no wonder so many people were so willing to travel so far to get here. Even putting aside the governor's high-minded ideas of freedom of thinking, freedom from government, and freedom from the Federation, this place just might turn out to be the utopia Pardonnet had hoped for.

Below Kirk, ten children, chaperoned by Lilian Coates, played a game a few hundred paces down the beach to his right. The sound of children cut between the gentle slapping of the waves rolling up the sand, then retreating. The laughter and childish shouts of joy were wonderful reminders of the perfect afternoon he was having. As a starship captain, he hadn't had many like this.

He almost stood to go and see how the children were doing, then stopped himself. He had come here to relax.

Alone.

And relax he was going to do if it killed him.

He laughed to himself, the sound carried away on the slight breeze. McCoy would be proud of him. Shocked, but proud.

Kirk took another deep breath and stared ahead. The tinted green of the ocean spread out as far as he could see. The waves were no more than gentle rolling swells. The few clouds in the sky were white, puffy, and nonthreatening.

He took a third deep breath of the clean, fresh air and could almost feel the muscles in his back starting to loosen. It wasn't often that he took a few minutes to himself. And after getting the sixty-two thousand colonists and all their varied ships to this paradise, he deserved the time. If he had his way, he was going to take more time, as often as his Starfleet duties of protecting the colonists allowed.

At the moment a large number of his crew were scattered in twenty different groups over the planet, helping the colonists explore, carve out settlements, and load supplies and equipment to the surface. Every one of his senior officers except Spock had charge of a major operation. And from what he'd been told before he beamed down, everything was going smoothly. At this point, only two weeks after arriving, just about every one of the colonists was living on the surface of the planet, an unprecedented accomplishment.

The *Enterprise* was in orbit, standing ready to defend the colony ships from any more threats from the Kauld or their new Orion allies. A fleet of Kauld and Orions tried to keep the colonists from reaching this planet, but Kirk doubted they'd have much trouble from them again immediately. The *Enterprise* and the colonists defeated them handily, but Kirk had no doubt that the Kauld and their enemies the Blood would be back. The Blood leader Shucorion claimed to be a friend to the colonists, but Kirk wasn't so sure of that. The Blood/Kauld conflict would cause the colony trouble at some time in the future.

Just not now.

At the moment everything was going fine. There was time enough to get the colony started and get crops growing. And time for him to relish this beautiful new world just a little.

He reached for his communicator to check in with the ship, then stopped himself once more. There was also time for him to take a few moments to himself. They could find him if they needed him.

He ran his hand through the soft sand, then gazed off down the seemingly limitless beach. Belle Terre was just about as close to Earth as a colony could find. The climate here on the major continent was moderate and the growing seasons uniformly long, thanks to this planet's orbit around its sun. Pulling guard duty on Belle Terre for the near future wasn't going to be so bad after all. There weren't many better places he could think to guard.

But he couldn't imagine spending his life here, either, no matter how beautiful the place was. Space was too big, with too many mysteries to explore. He didn't mind guarding this colony for a while, as long as they needed him and the *Enterprise*. It was a challenge unlike any he had had before. But when this was done he wanted to get back into deep space.

Down on the beach a child laughed, drawing Kirk's attention that way. He smiled as the children all piled on each other, kicked up sand, laughed some more, then scattered, playing some game Kirk wasn't familiar with. Lilian Coates, her blond hair loose in the ocean breeze, her shoulders straight, her hands in the pockets of her light jacket, stood between the children and the ocean, watching, laughing along with them.

Kirk was amazed that she could even laugh at this point in her life. Her husband had been one of the many colonist casualties on the way here from Earth. With his death, her husband had left her far from home, alone on a colony world. Suddenly without a family, she had to take care of herself and their nine-year-old son, Reynold, in a very harsh and unfamiliar environment. That would be tough on anyone, and would destroy many. But Lilian Coates had just seemed to keep right on going.

He had met her a few times right after her husband had died. She was a strong woman, of that there was no doubt. She was doing just fine, or so it seemed at the moment. Maybe in a few months he'd make it a point to make sure that hadn't changed. Strong people like her were exactly what this colony needed for long-term survival.

He watched her guard the children for a moment, then settled back against the log, closed his eyes, and let the sun warm his face while the ocean breeze cooled him. If lucky, he just might be able to spend the entire next hour right here, undisturbed by the responsibilities of protecting an entire new world full of colonists.

"Captain?" Spock said from behind him.

It didn't seem as if the luck was with him.

Kirk sat up and opened his eyes. Below him Lilian glanced up his way, noting for the first time his presence, then went back to sharing a laugh with the children.

He turned to stare up at the Vulcan as he approached through the sand. "What is it, Mr. Spock?"

"The results of my tests, Captain," Spock said, handing him the scientific tricorder he carried.

"Couldn't it have waited?" Kirk asked without looking at the report. "I was enjoying a little time away from reports just like this."

Spock had been concerned about slight communication problems they'd been having when not in Gamma

Night. Before Kirk had beamed down, Spock had been focusing his attention on one of the moons of Belle Terre everyone called the Quake Moon, because it seemed always to be shaking with small quakes, more than likely caused by volcanic activity. Spock had a theory that the communication problems came partly from the moon and had been so intent in his project that he hadn't even wanted anyone talking to him.

"I'm afraid," Spock said, "that time is not something we have an abundance of, Captain."

Kirk stared into the expressionless face of his first officer, then turned his attention to the report. Two words caught his attention instantly.

"Quasar olivium?" he asked, glancing back up at Spock. "In the Quake Moon?"

"Yes, sir," Spock said. "It seems we have found the first naturally occurring deposits of the material."

Kirk shook his head, trying to clear it, then stood as he tried to remember everything he knew about the material quasar olivium. He knew it was named after the scientist Shultz Oliver, who first theorized that the material existed. According to all rules of physics, the material shouldn't exist. And just a few years ago the Federation had been able to construct minuscule portions of it at huge costs, by using factory-sized warp facilities.

Yet now Spock was saying the material existed inside one of the moons of this planet.

"Quasar olivium?" Kirk asked. "How is this possible?"

"I'm not certain, Captain," Spock said. "Olivium is formed in the heart of a quasar and rarely survives the process that creates it. It has never been found to exist in a natural state. Until now."

"Right," Kirk said, still trying to get the idea into his mind. "Until now. How much is there?"

Spock shook his head. "The material is in a constant state of quantum flux. I have no way of measuring the amounts accurately."

"An ounce?" Kirk asked. "A pound? Ten pounds?"

Spock shook his head. "Far in excess of hundreds of thousands of tons, if my readings are correct."

Kirk leaned back on the piece of driftwood he'd been sitting against earlier and simply stared at his first officer.

"Hundreds of tons?" Kirk said. "Spock, do you know what this means to science? To the Federation?"

"I do, Captain," Spock said.

Kirk nodded. More than likely his first officer knew even better than he did what such a discovery would mean. The technological advances that would be possible with just a few pounds of olivium were fantastic. Having tons of the material would change everything. More powerful replicators could be built that could make useless molecular structures into useful ones. Greater holographic technology, advances in medical science, advances in computers, more powerful weapons.

The list of advantages of controlling tons of olivium went on and on, and that was just what he knew about. He had no doubt the discovery would be far more important than he could even imagine.

The Belle Terre colony was just about to become the richest colony in existence. And the most sought after by every race in the sector.

And the most important colony in all of space for the Federation to defend against anyone who would try to take it. Governor Pardonnet had led these people way out here, in part, to get away from the massive restraints of the Federation bureaucracy. It seemed that now he was going to need the Federation and Starfleet even more just to survive. Kirk had no doubt that when word of this discovery got out, the Klingons, the Romulans, and just about everyone else would all try to gain some foothold in this pristine backwater.

Behind him the children laughed and the waves broke gently on the sand. Those kids didn't know how important to their future Mr. Spock's discovery was.

"There is another problem, sir," Spock said.

Kirk managed to force his thinking away from the possibilities and realities of olivium in that quantity and back to the passionless face of his first officer.

"I can think of about a thousand problems, Mr. Spock. What are you saying?"

"The quasar olivium is, by its very nature, unstable, existing almost more outside our space and time than in it. The center of the Quake Moon that seemed hollow to normal sensors actually holds the olivium in a very contained state."

"The bottom line, Mr. Spock," Kirk said.

"The pressure inside the moon is building and has been for some time. The moon will explode, and in the process will destroy all life on this planet, as well as vast quantities of the quasar olivium."

"Explode?" Kirk asked. "Are you certain?"

"Yes, sir," Spock said.

Kirk nodded. When Mr. Spock said he was certain, the event would happen.

"How did we miss this?"

"The moon's crust and the very nature of the olivium makes scans difficult," Spock said.

"How long?"

"So far I have been unable to ascertain the exact time of the explosion, again owing to the nature of the olivium."

"A day? A week? A year?" Kirk demanded. "I'm looking for a range, here." He was suddenly very aware of the children shouting below him in their play.

Kirk stepped closer to his first officer and lowered his voice. "You've got to give me an approximate time when the explosion might happen. I've got over sixty thousand colonists to get off this planet and out of harm's way."

"My data is insufficient to allow me to predict the explosion exactly, sir," Spock said. "But it is logical that at the rate of increase of pressure inside the moon, the explosion will occur between six days and one month from this moment. I might be able to give you a more accurate time frame in a few more hours of research."

"Do it," Kirk said. "Quickly."

Mr. Spock turned and moved away. After a few steps Kirk stopped him.

"Spock, can we stop the explosion?"

"I do not yet have enough information to give you an answer, or a possible method of doing that, sir."

"Then get it."

Spock nodded and moved away through the sand toward the closest beam-down point.

Kirk turned and looked back at the children below. One moment these colonists faced a future of vast riches, the next they faced death and being without a home. All in the same report.

Kirk snapped open his communicator. "Kirk to *Enterprise*. Come in."

"Go ahead, Captain," Ensign Jason said. Ensign

Jason was a young kid from Boise, Idaho, fresh out of the Academy. He was filling in for Uhura while she led a party working on setting up a communications base just south of Kirk's position.

"Ensign, find Governor Pardonnet and inform him that I need to speak to him at once."

Pardonnet, on the trip here, had often been hard to work with, but Kirk actually admired the young governor. Granted, Pardonnet's ideas of leading and Kirk's were vastly different. And they had often had discussions about decisions. Actually, they hadn't been so much discussions as Pardonnet talking on and on. But with this emergency the governor wasn't going to have a chance to have one of his discussions. He was going to follow Kirk's orders and be quick about it. They didn't have time to argue too much with the lives of the colonists at stake.

"Understood, Captain," Ensign Jason said. "Where would you like him to meet you?"

Kirk knew that if he had the governor meet him, it might take hours. And right now, as Spock had said, there weren't hours to spare. "Ensign, just get his location and give it to the transporter room. Then tell him I'm coming to talk to him. Tell him it's an emergency."

"Understood, Captain," the ensign said.

"And Ensign—have all the crew report back to the *Enterprise* at once. No exceptions. Kirk out."

Kirk glanced down at Lilian Coates and the playing children. She seemed to be watching him almost more than the children, as if she could sense that something was wrong. Maybe if they survived this, he'd explain to her what he had been doing here.

With one more deep breath of the fresh ocean air, he

said into the communicator, "Transporter room, do you have the governor's location?"

"I do, Captain," the answer came back.

"Then beam me there at once."

"Understood."

A moment later, while he was staring out over the ocean, the transporter beam took him. So much for resting and relaxing. He just hoped it wasn't going to be the last time he got the chance to look over this ocean on this beautiful planet they had come so far to find.

Countdown: 8 Days, 7 Hours

Lilian Coates watched as Captain Kirk transported away, not even bothering to take the time to go to a normal transporter location. She had a sense that something was happening, and that *something* wasn't going to be good for the colony.

As a child she had called her feelings before something went wrong "the fist." At the moment the fist was working full-time. It felt as if a deep sense of dread had clamped a hand around her stomach and was squeezing so tight that not even the beautiful day and the white sand of the beach could help relax it.

It was the same feeling she'd had just before her father had died of a heart attack. The same feeling just before her husband, Tom, had been killed.

Now it was here again.

She turned and looked out over the calm ocean, trying to let the waves soothe her fears. She was making up problems, she was sure. More than likely the captain had simply been called away by a routine action. This planet was so peaceful, so tame, what could be going dangerously wrong?

Maybe Kirk and Pardonnet were disagreeing on some way of dealing with colony protection again. She usually agreed with Kirk when she had heard both sides, even though Pardonnet was the reason she and Tom had signed up for this colony. And even with Tom dead, she still believed in the dream Pardonnet had for this planet. She loved the idea of less government, more freedoms. She could listen to Pardonnet talk for hours on those subjects.

But when it came to defense and protection of the planet and the colony, she had always agreed with Captain Kirk's ideas.

She stared up at the area near the log on the sand dune where he had sat. It seemed very empty without him there. And the fist holding her stomach wouldn't let go.

She focused her attention on the children.

Her son, Reynold, was playing with them. Since her background was in education, she had offered to watch the group of same-aged kids while their parents worked on setting up the colony. In a few weeks, they might even start some sort of formal school for all the children. But for the moment, she was just a glorified baby-sitter, and happy to be doing that much to help.

The children were done with their game, so she started them back up the beach toward the path to the main colony. Another hour and it would be dinner break and all the kids would join their parents. Maybe by then she would find out what was happening. And why Captain Kirk had to leave the beach so fast, before she had even had the chance to say hello.

In her stomach, the tight feeling of dread squeezed even harder.

Chapter Two

Countdown: 8 Days, 7 Hours

THE TRANSPORTER released Kirk in a large meadow that smelled of dried hay and autumn leaves, just the way the fall in Iowa smelled. As a kid, he'd always loved everything about the fall. The air here was crisp, much colder than the beach. Tall rock cliffs extended high into the air on his right, and the meadow was surrounded on the other three sides by what looked to be a thick forest of pinelike trees. The meadow was covered in a knee-high brown grass that rustled in the slight breeze. Kirk wondered which plant let off the dried-hay smell.

Near the base of the cliff a group of three men stood, talking, gesturing at the rock face. Kirk instantly recognized the tall frame and thick brown hair of Governor Pardonnet. He was wearing perfectly neat clothes and, as always, doing most, if not all, of the talking. The governor's pants looked as if they had just been pressed and the light blue jacket he wore was zipped halfway up over a matching shirt. Even the slight wind didn't seem to be bothering Pardonnet's hair.

The other two were colonists Kirk hadn't met before. One was tall with red hair and an angry appearance about him, the other stout, almost fat, and mostly bald. The short one didn't have an inch of space on his clothes that wasn't wrinkled, making him the perfect contrast to the governor.

Pardonnet ignored Kirk's presence in the meadow and kept talking to the other two as Kirk headed the twenty yards up the hill through the grass. The last time Kirk had talked to the governor, they had disagreed on how many of the colonists to send to the planet's surface. And how fast to send them.

Pardonnet was, of course, in charge of the colony, but Kirk was still in charge of the safety of the ships and the planet security itself. And Kirk had believed a slower, more paced flow of colonists to the surface would have been safer.

Pardonnet, younger and seemingly always in more of a hurry, had wanted everyone moved down as quickly as possible to get started on their wonderful new world.

It was only Spock's logical conclusion that colonists would be safer on the surface of a planet than in ships in orbit that had swung Kirk to Pardonnet's view. Now Kirk wished he hadn't caved in. Evacuating all the people and their belongings back to the ships was going to be a problem.

"Captain," Pardonnet said as Kirk approached. "The rock from this cliff face is perfect for building. And it's close enough to the main community that transportation will be easy." Suddenly the governor seemed to remember his companions. "Oh, this is geologist Whitby Sprague."

Kirk nodded to the tall, redheaded man who didn't bother even to nod or smile back.

"And this is Albert Cadmand," the governor said, indicating his short companion. "He's our best structural engineer."

"A pleasure to meet you, Captain," Cadmand said. "You did a great job getting us here."

Kirk shook the man's extended hand. "Thanks, but it was a group effort." Then Kirk turned to the governor. "We have a serious problem."

Pardonnet almost laughed, his dark eyes twinkling in the light. "Your crewman told me it was an emergency. I can think of at least a dozen emergencies I've handled just since breakfast and I've felt that was an easy morning. Actually, the worst was—"

"Well, I don't think you're going to handle this one before dinner," Kirk said, interrupting. He resisted the urge to walk right up into the governor's space. "The Quake Moon is full of quasar olivium."

The tall, red-haired man who hadn't spoken suddenly choked, as if he'd swallowed too large a hunk of meat. Then he said, "olivium?"

Even Pardonnet seemed to know what the material was as he stared at Kirk. The governor's face had gone white and he almost looked like he might faint. It was the first time since they left Earth that Kirk had seen Pardonnet completely speechless. If the situation hadn't been so serious, Kirk would have laughed.

"olivium," Kirk said, nodding, staring at Pardonnet, who was opening and closing his mouth like a fish out of water. "Quasar olivium. Hundreds of tons of the stuff, at least, from what my science officer tells me."

The governor moved over to a nearby rock and sat down, hard, as if his legs wouldn't hold him up anymore. The kid was stunned.

"Is this a good or bad thing?" Cadmand asked. The short engineer looked, in a puzzled way, first at the governor, then Sprague, then finally at Kirk.

"Both good and bad, I'm afraid," Kirk said.

"This is a joke, Captain," the red-haired geologist said, almost angry as he took a step closer to Kirk. "Olivium has never been found in its natural state."

"Until today," Kirk said, smiling at the man. "But that's not the problem."

"I'd say not," Pardonnet said. "With that much of the most sought-after mineral in existence, this colony will never want for anything. This is just too perfect to believe. How can we be so lucky?"

The young governor was quick, Kirk had to hand him that. But it was going to take him a little more time to realize that having the only supply of what was going to be the most sought-after mineral in the galaxy meant every race would be trying to get ahold of it. And that would make his peaceful, bureaucracy-light colony here on Belle Terre the hardest place in the sector to defend.

Assuming there was anything left to defend.

"I'm afraid the problem isn't owning, or what to do with, the olivium," Kirk said. "The moon that contains it is about to explode and wipe out this planet in the process."

"No!" Pardonnet shouted, jumping back to his feet and rushing back at Kirk. "When? Why? And what can we do to stop it? There has to be something we can do."

"My science officer tells me the explosion will be within six days to one month," Kirk said. "I have no real understanding of why it is happening, or how we can stop the explosion. I'll know more within the next few hours. But I wanted to inform you as soon as I learned about it."

"The Kauld?" Pardonnet asked, his question taking on a sharp edge of anger. "Are they behind this?"

"I don't know, Governor," Kirk said. "But I don't think so. I think we're just unlucky enough to be in the wrong place at the wrong time."

"This isn't the wrong place," Pardonnet said, his face red with anger. "Nor the wrong time."

"Olivium can only exist in a state of quantum flux," the geologist Sprague said. "If that kind of quantity of the material exists inside a moon, there's no telling what is happening in there. How can you be sure the moon will explode?"

Kirk looked at the geologist. "My first officer, Mr. Spock, told me it would happen with complete certainty. When Spock says complete certainty, you can count on it happening."

Sprague nodded, but still frowned.

"You and other colonist scientists are more than free to double- and triple-check Mr. Spock's findings," Kirk said to the man. "In fact, I'm counting on it."

"We will," Pardonnet said. "Oh, we will."

"Good," Kirk said, staring at Sprague. "I'll have him send you all his data as soon as I get back to the ship. The more input we have, the better I'll feel about whatever we have to do."

"So will I," the geologist said.

"At the moment," Kirk said, turning back to Pardonnet, "we need to focus our efforts on finding a way of stopping the explosion."

"If there is one," the geologist said.

"There has to be," Pardonnet said.

Kirk looked the young governor right in the eyes, holding his stare. "We have to be prepared in case we can't stop the explosion."

"He's right," Cadmand said, stepping up beside Pardonnet. "We'd better be ready to leave."

"And that's where I come in," Pardonnet said. The thought of losing Belle Terre seemed to deflate the governor. Over the long trip out here, Kirk had seen the young governor go through many emotional states. It usually only took him a few seconds to bounce back to his idealistic, never-say-die attitude. And this time was no exception.

"I agree with you on this one, Captain," Pardonnet said. He squared his shoulders and straightened his jacket. "We'll start the preparations for evacuation here on the surface and work to find a way to stop this explosion before it happens."

"Good," Kirk said. "Expect to hear from me within a few hours with more information. I'll keep you completely informed."

"Thank you, Captain," Pardonnet said. "We'll do the same."

Kirk flipped open his communicator. "Kirk to *Enterprise*. One to beam up."

As he waited the few seconds for the transporter beam to take him, he stared into Pardonnet's eyes. There was no doubt in Kirk's mind that the only way Pardonnet was ever going to leave this planet was kicking and screaming the entire way.

Countdown: 8 Days, 7 Hours

The inside of the small, plastic lab structure was deathly quiet, the air not even moving as Dr. Leonard

McCoy bent over the wide-lens scanner and studied the bacteria he saw enlarged there. Nothing dangerous to humans at all. He could tell that immediately. Not the type of bacteria that could even survive in a human body. He'd have to run a few more tests to be one hundred percent certain, but at the moment he'd bet anything these little green beasties were harmless.

But very, very important.

He studied the bacteria again. These were bacteria that, when introduced to the soil, had the wonderful ability to help break down organic compounds and convert them quickly to nutrients for plants.

This type of bacterium was native and original to Belle Terre. They had found it this morning while digging in an area of fast-growing brush. The bacteria seemed to increase the growing capabilities of soil and decrease the time it took a plant to come to full growth. If they tested out as they were indicating, the bacteria would be a good export to all farmers throughout the Federation.

Belle Terre just might have something very important to trade.

McCoy glanced up at the two faces waiting impatiently for his conclusion. The older woman with a head full of gray hair was named Dr. Audry. She was the colony's chief botanist and the hardest-edged woman McCoy had run into in a long time. The second person in the small lab was Dr. Henry Memp, also a botanist. Dr. Memp had focused his career on alien plants, at times working with different branches of Starfleet on specific projects. McCoy had known of both of them by reputation before ever learning they were to be among the colonists on this mission. During

McCoy's all-too-rare breaks on the long trip out, the three of them had gotten acquainted.

Now working with them was like a dream come true for him. He had spent the first week after arrival on Belle Terre working with the colony medical doctors to set up a central hospital and medical outposts in the different areas. He'd helped coordinate the emergency evacuation procedures and the assignment of medical doctors to the different colony regions on the planet.

But the colony medical doctors hadn't needed him much after that, besides an occasional inspection or advice on an injury, so when the two botanists contacted him for opinions, he was more than glad to go with them.

They had spent the last few days digging in the fields, all working side by side to make sure that what the colonists were going to plant would, first, grow, and second, not turn deadly to the colonists when eaten. McCoy had been called away a half-dozen times, but had always managed to return to help fairly quickly. Now he was suntanned and tired, but had never felt better. He wasn't going to mind at all spending time on this planet. There was certainly enough for all of them to do.

He gave the green-tinted bacteria one more quick look through the scanner. He had no idea where the green color came from—it wasn't chlorophyll, that much he knew. Still one of the mysteries of these little things. But they were harmless to humans, that much he was sure of.

He smiled at Dr. Audry. "Can't see a thing wrong. I'm betting it does exactly what we think it does."

"Great!" Dr. Memp said as Dr. Audry clapped her hands.

"I still want to do the series of tests we have outlined to figure out why it works," McCoy said. "And why they're green-tinted. But I think we just may have a gold mine here in these little devils."

"I think you just may be right," Dr. Audry said, her smile filling her wrinkled face.

At that moment his communicator beeped. He thought about ignoring it for the moment, then knew that wouldn't work.

He stepped back from the scanner and indicated that Dr. Audry should look, then flipped his communicator open. "McCoy here. What is it?"

"You need to return to the ship, Doctor," a young voice said. McCoy didn't recognize the voice, but that wasn't surprising at this point, with all the senior officers scattered over the planet. More than likely it was some young kid taking Uhura's place at communications and scared half to death.

"And just why in blazes would I do that?" McCoy shouted at the kid.

"Captain's orders," the kid said, not backing down at all. The youngster had nerve, McCoy had to give him that.

McCoy wanted to take another swipe at the kid, but stopped himself. No point in killing the messenger just yet. "Any idea what the problem is?"

"None at all, Doctor," the kid said.

"Understood," McCoy said and snapped his communicator closed. He was just about as annoyed as he got. They had just made a major discovery here and he was being called back to the ship, more than likely because of some minor cut or scrape a nurse could handle.

Both Dr. Audry and Dr. Memp were smiling at him. He knew that every time during the last day that he had been called away, he had gotten annoyed. But he had the right to be, he figured. This was very important work they were doing here.

"Don't worry, Dr. McCoy," Dr. Audry said. "We'll get some of the remaining tests done before you get back. Then when we're all one hundred percent sure of the use of the bacteria, and its safety, we'll tell the governor and go celebrate."

"Sounds perfect," McCoy said. "Just don't start drinking without me."

The other two both laughed and claimed they wouldn't think of it.

He turned and headed out of the small lab and across the edge of the bustling main colony toward the closest beam-down site. Whatever Jim had called him back to the ship for had better be good.

And important. Because what he was doing down here certainly was.

Countdown: 8 Days, 7 Hours

Captain Sunn of the pathfinder ship *Rattlesnake* was sprawled in his captain's chair, trying to kick the feeling that something really awful was about to happen. Up until a few minutes ago, he'd been sitting here bored out of his mind. Suddenly the uneasy feeling had hit him, a feeling he'd learned to trust over the years. But usually the feeling came up when exploring a dangerous area, or just before a flight. Not while just sitting in orbit.

There was no one else on the three-person bridge with him. There was no reason for anyone else to be here, with nothing happening for days at a time. He hadn't even bothered to shave in three days and his long black hair was tangled from his fingers twisting it. On the main screen in front of him was the planet Belle Terre, the destination of the colonial expedition.

As with a wagon train in the Old West, heading for parts unknown, they'd gone so far from Federation space that they had needed scouts to work the area ahead. So Pardonnet had hired Sunn and his ship to be part of that scouting trip, before Starfleet and Kirk had gotten involved. Granted, the trip out had had its exciting moments, but sitting here in orbit doing nothing was soon going to drive him crazy.

Maybe he was already going crazy and the feeling of dread was just the start of it.

He laughed and pulled himself up to a full sitting position, then quickly checked all the sensors.

"Empty, as expected," he said to himself, his words echoing around the empty bridge.

After the first three days of just sitting in orbit, he had tried to think of a way out of his contract with the colony, a contract which called for him and the *Rattlesnake* to stay near the colonists for at least another month, then explore the surrounding star systems before heading back.

Now only two weeks had passed, with two long, dull weeks to look forward to. He was going to be completely insane if he had to wait out the full month. There had to be a way to get the exploration started sooner, rather than later. Seeing what the surrounding systems were like excited him.

Originally from the wide-open plains of Texas, Sunn had grown up mostly bored, looking for adventure in any place he could find it as a kid. Back then he'd always dreamed about having his own starship, of exploring wherever he wanted in deep space. Now he had the ship, his own ship, and he was just about as deep into space as he had imagined getting. Maybe even deeper.

And he was again bored.

That was not what he had expected way out here. Something had to change and change fast. Maybe the feeling of dread was coming from that need for change?

He pulled his lanky, six-foot-six frame out of the chair and moved over to the main sensor station. He did a quick scan of the other ships in orbit, then the surrounding area of the system.

Nothing happening. Most of the colonists had already moved to the planet's surface and all attention was there.

"Except," he said aloud. His scans had noted that someone on the *Enterprise* had been doing an intense study of the Quake Moon. Why?

The feeling of dread seemed to increase as he turned the ship's best scanners at the moon. At first the readings he got made no sense. He'd gone to school for astrophysics and alien-planet geology, figured it would help him get off Earth. And it had, getting him a hitch right out of school on an exploration ship headed for an asteroid swarm in search of minerals for a nearby manufacturing planet. That kind of exploration had turned out to be more boring than sitting in orbit watching over colonists, so he had quickly moved on.

Now his college education was coming in handy again as he tried to adjust the instruments, always coming back to a setting that gave him the weird readings.

The inside of that moon wasn't hollow after all.

The entire inside was in an intense state of quantum flux. But that wasn't possible either.

For the next hour he did every test he could figure out to do, always getting the same answer, never letting himself believe the answer he got. Finally, he could think of no other test.

Finally he had to trust his findings.

The moon wasn't hollow. Far from it, actually. It was filled with quasar olivium, a mineral so desired that just an ounce of it would make anyone in the colony a fortune.

The Quake Moon was full of the stuff. By his readings, maybe hundreds of thousands of tons.

And clearly, from the scans the *Enterprise* was doing, they knew about it also.

Sunn moved back over and dropped down into his chair, smiling as he stared at the main viewscreen still focused on Belle Terre. The immediate future now looked far from boring. It seemed that this planet and its not-so-hollow moon was about to become the most desired hunk of ground in all the sector.

And the colonists and Starfleet were going to need all the help they could get.

And he was just the man to give it to them.

Chapter Three

Countdown: 8 Days, 6 Hours

KIRK HADN'T FELT this much silence and pressure on the bridge in a long time. In battle each member of the crew had something to do. Now they were simply waiting. As each of the bridge crew had come back, each had asked the same question: What was happening?

He had told them all the same answer: Give Mr. Spock a little more time and wait until everyone was back.

That left everyone wondering in a very thick, very heavy silence.

Kirk glanced around the bridge at his crew. Uhura at communications, Chief Engineer Scott at the engineering panel, Sulu at the helm, and Chekov at tactical. They were all trying to look busy at something, even though there was nothing to do. The only one missing was Dr. McCoy. Kirk knew he had beamed back on board, but had gone to sickbay first.

Kirk glanced around as the lift doors opened and Dr.

McCoy stepped onto the bridge. Now everyone was present. Time to tell everyone what they faced.

McCoy didn't look happy and Kirk had no doubt the good doctor was going to be even less happy when he learned what was going on. For some reason, McCoy had come to like many of the colonists during the trip here and seemed to be in his element working with them on the surface. Much more than many of the rest of the crew.

McCoy glanced around, obviously seeing that all the bridge crew had been recalled. Scott shrugged at McCoy, shaking his gray-covered head, clearly telling the doctor with his motion that he had no idea what was happening either.

"Well, Captain," McCoy said, moving down to stand beside Kirk's chair. "Would you mind telling me what was so all fired important as to drag me away from a fantastic discovery, one that just might, if it pans out, change the face of agriculture in all the Federation?"

Kirk just held up his hand for McCoy to wait a moment, then turned to his first officer, still intently bent over his scope. "Well, Spock? Anything more to report?"

Spock stepped back from the science station and turned to face the captain. Everyone on the bridge at the same time turned to stare at the first officer.

Kirk could tell that Spock knew that he was not only reporting to the captain, but informing the rest of the bridge crew at the same time. "The quasar olivium that fills the center part of the moon is difficult at best to measure, owing to its nature."

"Olivium?" Bones almost shouted. "Filling the moon? Poppycock!"

"No way, sir," Scotty said at the same time as Bones's explosion. Scotty stepped away from the station to the railing. "That stuff does na exist inna natural state."

"I assure you, it does exist," Spock said calmly in the face of the sudden onslaught of disagreement. "It fills the moon in its theorized state of quantum flux."

"The entire inside of the moon?" Bones asked, clearly shocked, from the tone of his voice. "Do you know what such a find would mean to medicine?"

"Yes, Doctor," Spock said.

Kirk glanced at his medical officer, who was looking stunned and pale. He had felt the same way when told the news. The repercussions of such a find were beyond comprehension all at once. This discovery would touch every aspect of Federation life and science.

"Go on with your report," Kirk said, turning back to his first officer.

"I have confirmed a more accurate time frame for the explosion," Spock said.

"Explosion?" Bones asked. "What explosion? Would someone please explain to me what in tarnation is going on?"

Kirk indicated for Bones to wait, and Spock went on.

"If left unchecked, and at the current rate of increase of pressure, and approximating the average crust density of the moon and its resistance to the pressure, the moon will explode in eight days and six hours. My margin of error is plus or minus three hours, but I should be able to refine that estimate within one hour, given a little more time."

"And the results will be as you predicted?" Kirk asked, stunned that the time was so much shorter than the one month he had been hoping for.

"Yes," Spock said. "All life on the planet will be instantly destroyed. And at least sixty-eight percent of the olivium will be destroyed as well."

"If this is some kind of Vulcan trick," Bones said,

"so help me I'll drain your green blood right into a jar."

"I assure you, Doctor," Spock said, "this is no trick. The moon contains, very securely it seems, a large quantity of quasar olivium. Due to olivium's unstable nature, and quantum flux properties of the mineral, the pressure inside the moon has been building for thousands of years."

"And it's going to explode in eight more days?" Kirk asked. "Why then? Why not eight more years? Or eight more centuries for that matter?"

"I do not have an exact answer for that, Captain," Spock said. "The pressure inside the moon seemed to reach a critical point some sixteen months ago, changing the gradual increase of pressure to a sudden and exponential one."

"So we have a moon full of the most priceless mineral ever known to civilized man," McCoy said, "inside a crust that's about to explode and kill sixty-two thousand colonists on the planet below. Right?"

"Doctor," Spock said, "you have an ability to summarize that seems beyond measure."

McCoy was so lost in his own thoughts that he didn't even realize Spock had insulted him. But Kirk laughed. "Spock, any leads on how we might stop this explosion?"

"None, Captain," Spock said. "I can think of no method that would drain the buildup of energy inside the moon without triggering the explosion itself."

"We canna just sit here and do nothin'," Scott said.

"Oh, we're not going to," Kirk assured his chief engineer. "I've already informed Governor Pardonnet and he's starting evacuation plans. You worked with the medical staff in that area, didn't you, Doctor?"

McCoy nodded. "I did, but more along the nature of

a medical-emergency evacuation under quarantine conditions. Nothing was ever done about trying to evacuate the entire population back to the ships. No one expected it would be needed."

Kirk nodded. "I want you back working with the medical staff to make sure that however the governor decides to handle this evacuation, it is done safely."

"Understood," McCoy said.

Kirk turned to his chief engineer. "Scotty, I want you working with Mr. Spock. I want the two of you searching for any method, no matter how far-fetched it might seem, to stop this explosion."

"Aye, Captain," Scott said.

Spock said nothing.

Kirk glanced around. "I'm going to be informing the other ships' captains of the problem we discovered. I'll tell them to send all ideas they might have through here. Listen to them, people. Who knows who might come up with the method of saving this planet. Now get to work."

McCoy turned and headed for the door while Scott moved over and joined Spock. Kirk stared for a moment at the scene of Belle Terre on the screen, then turned to Uhura. "Put a visual of the moon on the screen."

The ragged, cold image of the olivium-filled Quake Moon filled the viewscreen.

"Now," Kirk said to Uhura, "open a channel to all captains of all the ships in orbit around Belle Terre and let me know when they are all standing by. Tell them we have an emergency."

"Right away, sir," Uhura said, then set to work.

Kirk stared at the dark moon. Over the years his enemies had come in all shapes and sizes. But never one that looked quite like this. Or that packed such a punch as this.

Or had as many repercussions for the future of the entire Federation.

Countdown: 8 Days, 3 Hours

The domelike plastic structure that Lilian Coates and her son lived in actually seemed spacious compared to what their quarters had been on the ship. They now had one of a hundred "domes" made of blown plastic, form-fitted, that lined up through the trees just to the west outside the main colony, each spaced twenty paces apart. The "street" that connected them all was nothing more than a dirt-covered road where two tracks had been worn down in the slight underbrush.

Even though the row of domes looked the same, the interiors and sizes were different in many ways. Their dome actually had two small bedrooms, one for her and one for Reynold. Plus a bathroom with running water from a small storage tank, and combination kitchen and living area that was stuffed with most of the furnishings and personal possessions they had been allowed to bring with them from Earth.

And outside, around the row of domes, there was nothing but forest. It was heaven compared to how they had survived on the trip out.

If her plans worked as she hoped, she would stake claim to some land near the ocean, then over the next few years build her dream home. Actually it had been her and Tom's plan for a dream home overlooking this new ocean, but she was still going to build it anyway, she loved the plan that much.

Now all her dreams, and the colony's dreams, seemed to be evaporating like water on a hot sidewalk. From what she had heard, the Quake Moon, as people had called one of the planet's many moons, wasn't actually hollow as everyone thought, but instead held vast riches of an unusual mineral. And because of this mineral the moon was going to explode, destroying the planet.

Governor Pardonnet had called a large meeting in a few hours in the main colony center, broadcast live to every colonist on the planet and those few still remaining on the ships. At first she had considered going down into the center, to stand in the crowds in front of the newly built town hall, but then decided to stay right here and make sure she heard every word he said over the communication links.

Reynold came in from playing outside and sat down dejectedly at the table. His face was drawn and he looked like he was holding back tears. "Are we really going to have to go back into the ships? They're just kidding me, aren't they?"

"I don't know," Lilian said. "Governor Pardonnet will tell us tonight."

"The other kids say we are," Reynold said. "I don't want to go. I like it here."

She moved over and sat down with her son. "So do I," she said, putting her hand on his shoulder for comfort.

"So let's just stay," he said, his face brightening up. "I hate the ship. If you like it here and I like it here, why don't we just stay right here?"

She laughed at the simplicity of a child's logic. You wanted to stay, so you stayed. She wished it were that simple.

"We'll stay if we can," she said. "I promise you that."

"Good."

He jumped down and headed off into his room. Her promise had satisfied him for the moment, but if that Quake Moon was about to explode, she knew it wasn't a promise she could keep. And she knew that if they got back on those ships, Governor Pardonnet's dream of a colony was dead.

Her and Tom's dream would never come to be, and Tom's life would have been lost for nothing.

All of this would be for nothing.

She was so angry she wanted to slam things, break things, swear and cry. Instead she forced herself to just sit there at the table.

She forced herself to remember Tom and all the good times they had had planning this new life.

She forced herself to just wait until she had more information.

There was nothing else she could do.

Countdown: 8 Days, 1 Hour

Governor Pardonnet banged on the table in front of him and shouted over the roar of people talking. "Everyone please quiet down!"

He took a deep breath as the mass of people in the room broke off their conversations and either sat or leaned against the wall of the town meeting hall to listen. The building was the first one built on the planet, out of trees cut down here. It seemed an appropriate place to hold this meeting. This gathering was much smaller than the one to be held in the center area of the main settlement, in front of this building, in two hours. This was a preliminary meeting, with the leaders of all branches of the colony, to determine what he would say to all the colonists in the big meeting later.

He knew that talking to all the colonists at once was going to be difficult. He could feel the weight of that responsibility push down on him again, as it had done so often on the preparation and voyage here. He just hoped they had a few more answers by that point.

One hour ago he'd gotten the update and exact time of the explosion from Captain Kirk and passed it along to his scientists for confirmation. At the moment he had no idea what needed to be done, what needed to be said to the entire colony. He wanted the people in front of him to help on that score.

He looked around at all the familiar faces. They were the heads of all the different areas of the colony. Science, medicine, mechanics, agriculture, supplies, defense, and so on. With their help he had gotten them this far. Now they faced maybe the biggest challenge to the colony ever, and their settlement of the planet wasn't even two weeks old yet.

He waited until the room was almost quiet, then turned to Dr. Cullen Hayes, their chief physicist, and the man everyone seemed to turn to with most science-related questions. Hayes was a short man, middle-aged, with a bald head and thick eyebrows. He very seldom smiled and Pardonnet had never seen the man laugh.

"Have you confirmed the *Enterprise* findings?" Pardonnet asked.

"They are correct," Hayes said, his voice flat, but loud enough to carry easily to every corner of the room.

Instantly everyone in the room shifted, as if they had all been hoping, waiting for a different answer. Pardonnet could feel the depression settle over the room like a heavy blanket.

Hayes didn't seem to notice as he went on. "What we initially took to be a hollow moon is filled with olivium. And the moon itself is containing the olivium in such a way as to build up pressure inside. The pressure is increasing at an exponential rate and will cause an explosion in eight days, give or take a few hours."

The room now burst into talking. Some loud, some angry, some clearly just sad.

Pardonnet felt as if someone had pounded a fist into his stomach. He had clearly held out hope that the *Enterprise*'s findings were wrong. But Spock and Hayes couldn't both be wrong. The explosion was going to happen.

So now they had to face the next question fully. He pounded on the desk again until the room quieted. "Dr. Hayes, do you have a suggestion as to a course of action?"

"Yes. Get away from this planet inside eight days," he said flatly.

"No chance of stopping the explosion?" Pardonnet asked, holding up his hand to stop the room from erupting again.

"Let me explain what you are dealing with here," Hayes said calmly. "olivium exists in a state of quantum flux, meaning it lives both in this universe and in others, constantly and instantaneously moving in and out of our universe. It's that property that gives it its vast energy and makes it so valuable to all the sciences. It is impossible to pick up with a bare hand, yet with the right equipment, it will be possible to mine."

Hayes glanced around, then looked back at Pardonnet before going on. "The moon shell containing this olivium is a very hard rock almost three hundred miles thick at its thinnest point. The quantum shifts of the olivium have hardened the inner fifty miles of this shell into a substance far harder than anything we have with us on this mission. That's what's keeping the intense pressures that already exist inside that moon from coming out."

Pardonnet finally grasped the size and problem they

were facing. This wasn't like a child's balloon filled too full and about to burst. This was on a scale he had trouble grasping, involving forces he couldn't even imagine.

"Dr. Hayes?" someone in the back shouted in the silence. "What will happen to this planet when the moon explodes?"

Hayes shrugged. "The burst of radiation will kill every living thing planetwide almost instantly. The force of the explosion itself might tear chunks out of the planet at worst. At best, hundred-mile-wide hunks of hard moon rock will plow into the planet. There will be nothing left and nothing will survive it. It will be a million years before any life returns to this planet."

Now the silence in the room was so intense it felt like a weight on Pardonnet's shoulders, pushing him down, making it hard for him to breathe. This beautiful planet, destroyed. How was this possible?

"How about we drill a hole?" another person shouted. "We could drill a hole to the core of the moon to take off some of the pressure."

"Yeah, good idea," someone else shouted.

Hayes shook his head. "As I said, the inner fifty miles of the moon are fantastically hard, due to the quantum flux of the olivium. Not even the *Enterprise*'s phasers could cut through it. We have nothing to drill a hole with."

The silence came back like a hammer on the room.

Finally, after looking around at all the other shocked faces in the crowd, Pardonnet said, "Well, it seems we have no choice but to evacuate back to the ships."

"And go where?" Peter Daegal asked. "We don't have enough supplies to get even halfway home."

Pardonnet stared at Daegal, who was the person in charge of the colony's food and drinking water supplies. During the long trip out he and Daegal had met weekly to go over rations and consumption. Despite the troubles en route, when they reached Belle Terre, it was thought they would have enough to get to the first harvest with native plants and animals added in to supplement the diet.

Now there would be no first harvest. Or even a first planting. No hunting, no fishing.

"Is that true?" someone from the back shouted.

"I'm afraid it is," Pardonnet said. "But at the moment our first priority is saving all our lives. We'll have to deal with the problems that follow after we get out of the way of the explosion."

His answer was easy and dodged the question completely. It caused the room to again burst into talking, and this time he let them go. There really wasn't much more to discuss except the details of getting everyone, and as many of their belongings as possible, back on board the ships. Getting everyone to the planet had been easy by comparison to what they now faced.

He just wished they had a choice.

Any choice.

He moved back and leaned against a wall of the community center, letting the flow of talking and shouting go on around him. His way had always been to fight in the face of impossible odds. The only problem now was that the exploding moon was giving them no chance at all to survive here.

No odds. And no choice at all as to what to do.

They had to run.

And run fast.

In all his life, he'd never run from anything. He didn't like the feeling at all.

Chapter Four

Countdown: 7 Days, 23 Hours

SUNN SAT in his captain's chair, still alone on his ship's bridge, and watched as the image of Captain James T. Kirk came on the viewer.

Sunn and Kirk had spent a long time together on the way out here, yet had never met. Sunn had watched a dozen directives from the man, but had never shaken the man's hand. He only knew Kirk by his vast reputation as one of the Federation's best early explorers. And by what he had done to save the ships on this trip. So far, Kirk had lived up to his reputation.

At first, when he had heard that Kirk was going to be giving up his admiralship and coming on this mission, Sunn had doubted it was anything more than some stunt by Starfleet. Many people had thought the same thing. But after the trip here, Sunn no longer had those doubts. In fact, as far as he was concerned, it was just plain lucky Kirk had come along. They could all be dead by now if he hadn't.

And now this.

A few hours ago Kirk had announced to all the ships the discovery of the olivium, and the problem with the Quake Moon. Sunn had been stunned at the shortness of time involved. Sunn had also kicked himself for not going the next step in his sensory scans of the moon. He should have also discovered that the moon was about to explode. Of course, it made no difference, this time. But in Sunn's line of work, missing a critical element like that could cost him and his crew their lives.

Kirk and his crew hadn't missed the detail. Sunn would make sure he never did again, either.

Now Kirk was calling Sunn directly. Clearly Kirk needed something from him. It was going to be interesting what that something might be in these circumstances.

Sunn glanced at the time. Kirk didn't have long to talk. Gamma Night was scheduled to start in just ten minutes. Gamma Night was what the colonists called the disruption of all communication and transportation that occurred in this system ten hours out of every thirty. It was caused by a neutron star orbiting a black hole nearby, sending charged particles into the Belle Terre system with each revolution. So far no one had discovered a way to shield against it.

And flying in it was just stupid. Sunn supposed it was possible to do, at very low speeds, using dead reckoning type of flying. But that was just flying blind, and in a system cluttered with planets and moons and asteroids like this one was, flying blind was also suicide.

So Kirk had less than ten minutes and even less if he wanted Sunn to do something quickly.

The main viewer showed the bridge of the *Enterprise* and Captain Kirk. "Captain Sunn," Kirk said, smiling. "It's a pleasure to finally get a chance to talk to you."

"Pleasure is all mine, Captain," Sunn said.

"I need your help," Kirk said, getting right to the point. "Unless we can find a way to stop this explosion, the colonists have to be evacuated from the planet."

"And this entire system," Sunn said. "Let me guess, they don't have enough of anything to make it back to Federation territory. This was supposed to be a one-way trip."

"That's just about right," Kirk said, nodding. "Some of the ships were lucky to get here with the provisions they had."

Sunn had heard all that. It disgusted him that anyone could take ships into space for a voyage and not make sure they had enough provisions to get back safely. Seemed like a sure way to get killed out here.

"Since my ship's job is exploring ahead," Sunn said, figuring out where Kirk was going, "what do you need me to go searching for?"

Kirk smiled. "Glad you're ahead of me. I need you to find another planet, suitable for the colonists at least on a temporary basis. One that is unclaimed and preferably doesn't have an exploding moon."

Sunn laughed, even though he was somewhat surprised. "Yeah, I can see why not having an exploding moon would be nice. But you don't seriously think this bunch of colonists will just jump to another spot, do you?"

"Some might," Kirk said, "if you find a good enough

world for them. There's no telling what the boy governor can talk them into."

Sunn laughed. He was glad Kirk thought the same thing about Pardonnet as he did.

Kirk went on. "But if this colony fails, a large percentage of the people are going to want to head home. Either way we need another planet to stop at, gather what we can in food and provisions, regroup before the long trip back."

"Makes sense," Sunn said, glancing at the time. Only two minutes before Gamma Night cut this conversation off.

"You have less than eight days," Kirk said. "I know this sounds impossible, but . . ."

"Well, my job is exploring," Sunn said, interrupting Kirk before he could go on. "I usually don't have to do it that fast, but I'll see what I can find."

"Thanks," Kirk said. "I owe you one. The entire colony owes you one."

"Save the thanks for when I find a planet that will help."

Kirk nodded. "Good hunting."

Then the connection was cut.

Sunn sat there staring at the static-filled screen, thinking about the conversation. What Kirk had asked him to do was try to find a fall-back option. Clearly Kirk and the rest of the colony were going to focus on trying to stop the explosion, and if that failed, get everyone to safety. But getting the colonists a safe distance from the exploding moon wasn't a major problem. What followed the explosion was.

Sunn was smart enough to know that Kirk and the *Enterprise* weren't going back to Federation space with the colonists, not with a vast amount of olivium to protect. Even after the moon exploded and destroyed a large amount of it, there would still be enough of the important mineral here to start wars over.

The *Enterprise* and some of the other Starfleet ships were going to be forced to stay. And the best way to safeguard the olivium *and* the colonists at the same time was find them another planet close by for the colonists to "rest" on until help got here from Starfleet.

Sunn nodded in admiration at how smart Captain Kirk really was. No wonder he had the reputation of always being able to work himself and his ship out of any situation. The man covered all the angles way ahead of time.

Sunn had no doubt that his two crewmen would be as relieved to be moving again as he was. On the main screen he pulled up what few star charts they had of this area of space and started to study them. He was going exploring into totally unknown space. This was the very reason he'd left Texas all those years ago and gone into space. He could feel the excitement building in his stomach.

Now if they could just find the planet Kirk needed, this would be the perfect mission.

Countdown: 7 Days, 14 Hours

McCoy had beamed down to work with the colony's main medical staff right before the big announcement by Governor Pardonnet. So he stood and listened to it with them. He heard the governor tell everyone what McCoy had learned from Spock on the bridge. And McCoy heard the governor tell everyone they were working on ways of stopping the explosion. But just in case, everyone should be prepared to abandon the colony. And those personnel who were needed to get the ships ready for a long trip needed to return to them now.

"If the moon does explode," the governor had said, "nothing will survive on this planet."

The doctors who had worked so hard over the past few weeks to set up the temporary hospital were angry that they had to tear everything apart quickly and move back to *Brother's Keeper,* the Starfleet medical ship. McCoy didn't blame them, but there was no point in getting too angry over something no one could do anything about. Better to just accept and move on.

McCoy did what he could to get them started in the right direction, but after a while he had to admit he was angry too. And that they all had a right to be angry. The problem was, there just wasn't anyone to be angry at. This wasn't anyone's fault. It was just some sort of ugly cosmic joke that had sent all these people through the hazards of hostile space to be met by an exploding moon full of riches.

So, as most hardworking people did in a time of crisis, everyone let the anger show while they dug in and worked to get their minds off the problem. It wasn't until after nine long hours of work, packing equipment, organizing planet-to-ship scheduling, deciding when each detail of the evacuation needed to be done, that McCoy suddenly realized he hadn't contacted Dr. Audry about the bacteria. If the tests had panned out, it was critical they save samples of the little beasts.

He flipped open his communicator only to discover there was still almost an hour left of the Gamma Night.

So instead of waiting, he headed out across the main colony compound toward Dr. Audry's lab.

It was dark out, real night on this area of the planet, and the dirt streets and paths of the new colony were mostly empty. Only a few tired-looking stragglers moved about purposefully. He fit in with them perfectly.

The night air had a chill to it and a freshness that helped clear his mind. He could smell the nearby ocean and the pine on the gentle breeze. How could it be that such a beautiful place could vanish in just a little under eight days?

It wasn't fair. Nothing about this seemed fair. But when had he started expecting space to be fair? He'd been out here long enough to know better than that.

He stopped and glanced up at the clear night sky and the strange patterns of stars to where the *Enterprise* would be in orbit. He sure hoped that Spock and Scotty and Jim were finding a way to stop all this insanity. If anyone could do it, Spock and Jim could. Over the years they had beaten the universe more often than they had lost.

He took another full breath of fresh air and let it out slowly, using the moment to clear his mind. He didn't know if this was one of the more beautiful planets he'd ever been on, but after the long trip here, and the news about what was about to happen with the moon, it sure seemed that way.

He shook his head and started off again. As a doctor he'd seen a lot of injustices in his life. Young babies dying when they shouldn't have, husbands killed with young families waiting at home, his friends cut down in the prime of their lives. But never had he been witness to a planet destroyed far before its time.

Nope, there was nothing at all fair about the universe and the more he remembered that, the better off he would be.

He finally reached Dr. Audry's lab and knocked loudly on the plastic shell of the structure, expecting her to be asleep. Dr. Memp answered the door almost immediately and smiled at McCoy. Clearly Memp had been working since McCoy had left.

"Glad you could make it back," Memp said.

"The experiments?" McCoy asked, not even waiting to get completely inside.

"All tested out as we hoped," Dr. Audry's voice said from inside.

He went through the entrance and was greeted by her smiling face and a smell of something wonderful cooking. It was as if he'd walked into a kitchen on Earth, not a lab. On one small table there was a bowl and two plates, as if the two were just about to eat. McCoy's stomach rumbled at the thought of food, but he ignored it.

"The bacteria we found will be a fantastic boost to most Federation agriculture," Dr. Audry said. "And it seems highly adaptable to most soil types."

"If we can save enough of it," McCoy said.

Dr. Audry's smile left her face. "We heard the news and have been preparing ever since. We have to save enough. This discovery can't be allowed to die with this planet."

"I agree," McCoy said. "So let's get started digging more samples."

Dr. Audry held up her hand for him to pause. "It will be light in three hours. I think we can wait that long."

"All right then," he said, completely unwilling to stop and even take a break, "let's start setting up culture environments. Getting ready for morning. When the Gamma Night clears I'll contact some people in the medical units for their help. I want this stuff being kept alive on a dozen of the ships heading away from here."

"Environments are ready and waiting," Dr. Memp said. He put a hand on Dr. McCoy's back. "When was the last time you ate?"

McCoy shrugged. He couldn't remember anything but a few snacks at the hospital. His growling stomach was telling him it had been far too long.

"That's what I thought," Memp said to McCoy's shrug.

The young doctor gently moved McCoy toward a table holding two place settings and a steaming bowl of something that smelled wonderful.

"If we're going to be digging all morning, we need our strength," Dr. Audry said, moving over and putting down another plate. "Don't you agree?"

"If you mean getting strength from something that smells as good as that," McCoy said, sitting down and pointing at the bowl, "I completely agree. What is it?"

"It's a stew, made mostly from a plant we found the first week here," Memp said. "Tastes like a combination of fresh-cooked bread and chicken."

"Everything tastes like chicken," McCoy said.

Dr. Memp laughed. "Maybe, but not *this* kind of chicken."

McCoy took a tentative bite, then a full mouthful. "You're right," he said, savoring the wonderful flavor. "I've never had chicken taste this good before."

Dr. Audry dug into her own bowl. "I agree. And don't worry, we're going to make sure this plant gets saved, too."

McCoy had another spoonful of the wonderful stew filling his mouth and could only nod his approval of that idea.

Countdown: 7 Days, 13 Hours

Kirk sat in his command chair, watching the fuzzy picture on the main screen. He could see some of the nearby ships, but this static-filled picture was the best they could do so far against the Gamma Night. He hated sitting here, mostly blind for ten out of every thirty hours. For the past two weeks he had tried to be somewhere else during the ten hours, including eating and sleeping, just so he didn't have to be aware of how helpless they were.

But this Gamma Night he had stayed on the bridge the entire time, waiting, while Spock and Scotty went over and over the information they'd scanned from the olivium moon before the Gamma Night set in. It had done him and the crew no good for him to stay, but he couldn't leave, even to eat. He just felt his place was on the bridge.

As the Gamma Night started to clear and the image on the main screen sharpened, Uhura turned to him. "Incoming call from Governor Pardonnet."

"On screen," Kirk said. He knew exactly why the governor was calling. If he had been in Pardonnet's shoes, he would have done the same thing.

"Any ideas on stopping the explosion, Captain?" Pardonnet asked. It was the exact question Kirk had expected.

"Nothing yet," Kirk said. "But we might have more information after getting some preliminary readings on the moon's pressure after the last ten hours. Have *your* scientists come up with any ideas?"

"Nothing," the young governor said.

Kirk could tell Pardonnet wasn't happy about that either, so he changed the subject. "How are the preparations for evacuation coming?"

"No one is happy about them," Pardonnet said. "I'm certainly not. But we seem to have no choice, do we? So we're getting ready as fast as we can. We'll start moving the first wave of personnel back to the Conestogas in the next hour to get them ready."

"You know how important it is to get as many supplies stocked on the ships as possible?" Kirk asked. He didn't want to tell the governor that he had sent one of the pathfinder ships in search of another planet close by. There would be no point, since that had only an outside chance of success at best.

"I understand, Captain," Pardonnet said, coldly. "I prepared for the mission here, I understand what it will take for us to return. I am very clearly aware we will not have enough provisions starting out."

"Good," Kirk said. "I'll keep you informed as to our progress here."

With that he motioned for Uhura to cut the connection, then stood and moved over beside Spock. Scotty had left a short time ago to check out a problem in Engineering.

"Any changes?"

Spock turned from his station. "None, Captain. The explosion will still occur at the time predicted."

Kirk nodded. For some reason he'd been half hoping that the pressure inside the moon would just suddenly drop during the Gamma Night. Of course, he knew that wasn't going to happen, but a part of his brain had hoped it would.

"However," Spock said, "I may have discovered one

possible method of causing a contained explosion, to release the pressure inside the moon."

Kirk could feel the energy of hope surge through him. "Show me," he said.

Spock brought an image of the moon up on the screen above his station, then cut the moon in half, leaving a cross section. The interior olivium was shown as a bright red, almost angry-looking area, constantly in motion. The crust was black and thick and very solid-looking.

Spock pointed to one area of crust near the upper-right-hand corner of the screen. "This area is on the side of the moon away from the planet."

"What's special about that area?" Kirk asked, not seeing anything different at all.

Touching a switch on his station, Spock magnified the area of the crust, and it instantly became clear to Kirk what he was talking about. In the cross section he could see a decidedly thinner area of the moon's crust right at that point.

"At one time in the past," Spock said, "this area appeared to be one of many vents from the core of the moon that released pressure into space. These release passages were what kept the moon from exploding for so many centuries. But they have become plugged, as they all did. This plug would be the weakest area of the moon's crust."

"It's still over three hundred kilometers thick," Kirk said.

"Three hundred and sixty-four point one-six-four-nine-seven-zero kilometers thick," Spock said.

"How do you propose we break through that?"

"I don't propose we break through the plug, Captain," Spock said. "I'm suggesting we might be able to loosen—so to speak—the plug and let it push outward, with help, of course, from the pressure building inside the moon. Such a release would not cause the major explosion we are trying to avoid."

Kirk looked at his first officer, but as always Spock showed no emotion at all. The Vulcan was being completely serious, as always. Somehow Spock thought it might be possible to pull a two-hundred-mile-thick plug of dense rock out of a pressurized moon.

"Okay," Kirk said. "Explain how this might be done."

"A specialized tractor beam, focused at a certain point, pulling on the interior of this blockage, would create friction along the static points of the rock plug, causing the rock on the edges to heat to a point where it would become liquid."

"Thus allowing the pressure from inside the moon to push the plug in that vent outward," Kirk said. "Like a cork popping from a champagne bottle."

"Simply put," Spock said, "but yes."

Kirk stared at the massive hunk of rock shown in the cross section. "How many tractors would we need?"

"I calculated that if every ship in the fleet, including shuttles outfitted with special tractor beams, focused a tractor beam at a specific point, the chance of success would be five point two percent."

"That's not very high, Spock," Kirk said, staring at his first officer.

"It has a significantly higher chance of success than any other option."

Kirk nodded. He was afraid of that.

He stared at the screen for a moment, then turned to face his first officer. "So what are the downsides of this idea?"

"This action will consume much of every ship's energy supplies, as well as put extreme strain on each ship's systems. I calculate that a number of the ships would be destroyed in the attempt."

"That's a high price to pay for such a low chance of success," Kirk said.

"Granted," Spock said. "There is also a two point three percent chance of our actions triggering the major explosion."

"And killing us all," Kirk said.

"Basically," Spock said. "Yes."

"Wonderful," Kirk said. "This is just getting better and better all the time."

Chapter Five

Countdown: 7 Days, 10 Hours

THE SILENCE in the large meeting hall seemed heavy, as if the entire roof were pressing down on the hundred or so colony leaders and top citizens that had crammed inside. Governor Pardonnet forced himself to take a breath. He was standing in front of the group, on a slightly raised stage, with Captain Kirk and his first officer, Spock.

For some reason, all Pardonnet could do was stare at Captain Kirk and the Vulcan as if they had both gone crazy. They had found a slim chance of keeping the moon from exploding, but by attempting it, they were asking him to put every man, woman, and child in the colony at risk. Sixty-two thousand lives.

"Excuse me!" someone shouted from the back. "Did I hear that right? You said there was only a five percent chance of success with this idea?"

"Approximately five point two percent," Spock said.

"Oh, that makes it better," the person in the back said, clearly disgusted.

A few people laughed, but not many.

"And this is the best idea anyone has come up with?" Pardonnet asked. He glanced at Kirk, who nodded. Pardonnet then turned to the group of his top physicists. "Do any of you have any better ideas?"

None of them spoke.

Again the silence around them seemed to grow heavier, the room smaller, the air harder to breathe. Pardonnet couldn't believe this was even happening. It seemed that Belle Terre, with its exploding moon, was offering them very few choices, and none of them good. They either packed and ran for home, or stayed and took a very slim chance of saving their new world by risking their lives.

Neither option had much chance of success, as far as Pardonnet was concerned. Too bad they couldn't try both. Or just maybe they could.

Pardonnet turned to Spock and Captain Kirk. "If we're to try this uncorking of the moon, when is the best time?"

"As soon as possible," Spock said. "It will take some time to modify all the tractor beams, but that should be accomplished within twenty-four hours."

"The best window would be immediately after the next Gamma Night," Kirk said. "About twenty-seven hours from now."

"So we continue the preparations to head home," Pardonnet said. "If the idea does not work, we've lost nothing. We'll still have time to evacuate and get out of range of the explosion. Am I right?"

The audience seemed to like his idea as the silence turned to murmurs of agreement. Pardonnet watched as

Captain Kirk glanced at Spock, clearly uncomfortable, then turned back to face Pardonnet.

"What am I missing, Captain?" Pardonnet asked before Kirk could say anything.

"Remember, there are many risks involved with this," Kirk said. "As I said before, there is a chance the attempt may trigger the explosion earlier than expected."

Now the people were back deadly silent.

"And we'd all be killed," Pardonnet said. He so wanted to forget the chance of that happening, but Kirk wasn't letting any of them forget it.

"Exactly," Spock said.

"But we might all be killed on the way back to the Federation," Pardonnet said. "So go on."

"True," Kirk said. "The good side of it is that the chances of our attempt triggering the explosion are less than the chances of our saving the moon. However, I don't know how much you would be damaging your chances of making a successful evacuation if this is attempted."

"I'm not following you, Captain," Pardonnet said. And he could tell from the looks of some of those close by, neither were any of the others.

"The attempt to pull the plug out of the moon will drain every ship's energy reserves. It may cripple or possibly even destroy some ships."

Pardonnet nodded. Now he understood. There was even a higher price to pay for this attempt. "Will there be enough energy left to get most of the ships outside the explosion range if this attempt fails?"

Kirk glanced at his passionless first officer, then back at Pardonnet. "We should be able to get the surviving ships out of range in one way or another. But you will not have enough energy to start home immediately."

Pardonnet nodded, but he could tell there was one more thing Kirk wasn't saying that needed to be said. "Go on, Captain."

Kirk stared at Pardonnet for a moment, then glanced at the gathered colony leaders. "I've been direct with all of you since the beginning," Kirk said. "I need to do that now, even though I do not want to, or even like what I'm about to say."

Pardonnet had never heard Captain Kirk talk like that before. The entire room was deathly still as Kirk went on.

"Explosion or no explosion, the *Enterprise* will not be returning to the Federation."

"The olivium," Pardonnet said, instantly understanding what Kirk was saying. "It's far too valuable to Starfleet to let it fall into anyone else's hands. I had suspected as much."

"Far too valuable to all of science," Kirk said. "To all of the Federation. To every citizen of the Federation, not just your colony. So if you decide to not try stopping the explosion and just head back, you will be doing so on your own."

"So you are willing to let sixty-two thousand people travel defenseless?"

"You have the privateers—the original plan was for you all to come out here with just them, remember. And if your choice is to head for home I'll do what I can to help you. You will be far from defenseless. But you will not have the *Enterprise*."

"I don't see where there is anything else we *can* do but head back," Pardonnet said. "That moon isn't giving us much of an option."

Kirk faced Pardonnet squarely, clearly not caring who was listening in the audience. "You and your people have lots of choices." His voice was low and controlled and Pardonnet could feel the anger just under the surface. "You all risked your lives, and your children's lives, to come out here. There may be other planets worth colonizing nearby. There is still a remote chance of saving this planet. Or if the moon explodes, you can remain close by until an escort arrives from the Federation."

Kirk stepped one step closer. Pardonnet kept his gaze firmly on the captain as Kirk went on. "There are options, Governor. You have more options than just cutting and running for home. I'm just trying to be clear with you how I must stand on that one choice. I want you to have all the information."

Pardonnet held Kirk's stare for a long few seconds, time that seemed to stretch even longer with the intense silence in the room full of people. He didn't like Kirk's attitude, he didn't like what Kirk had just implied about him, but he understood why Kirk had said it.

Pardonnet let himself smile, still not looking away from Kirk. "So let me get this straight, Captain. You are willing to risk your crew, the *Enterprise,* and the other Starfleet ships and crews to help us save our new world?"

"I am," Kirk said. "I was willing to do that when I signed onto this mission. Nothing has changed."

"And if we fail, and something goes wrong, you will be killed along with us, leaving the olivium defenseless?"

"That is correct," Kirk said. "Saving this planet is a risk I'm willing to take in exchange for that. I am not willing to risk the olivium falling in the wrong hands just because you chose to head home."

Pardonnet nodded and after a few long seconds broke away from Kirk's stare. He turned to face the colonists gathered in the room. "The captain is right. We took many risks to come here, knowing this wouldn't be an easy path to follow. We should not turn away from another risk now. I suggest we try to pull the plug on that explosion. But I'm open for other ideas. Or ways to accomplish that task as safely as possible."

A voice from the back said, "Put all the children in one Conestoga and move it out of danger before we start."

Pardonnet nodded. "Good idea," he said. Everyone murmured their agreement.

"It will greatly reduce the chances of success," Spock said. "Every ship will be needed in the effort. Especially the ones with the large mule engines."

"Surely we can spare one ship for the children?" Pardonnet asked.

"No," Spock said. "We cannot."

Pardonnet stared at Spock as the meeting broke down into loud chatter. Kirk was right. There were lots of choices, there just weren't any good ones.

Countdown: 7 Days, 10 Hours

Lilian Coates began packing, not exactly sure where to start. She could remember her and Tom packing and then repacking back on Earth, throwing away things they wouldn't need, discovering items they couldn't live without. But back then they had many more personal possessions than they would have been allowed to take. It had been hard to pare down everything, but at the same time it had been exciting and often fun. The prospect of a new life ahead of them kept them going, energized.

Now she had no idea what lay ahead for her. There was nothing back on Earth to return to. She had never expected to need to go back.

She had to do all the packing herself, with only what she had brought from their cabin and storage on the ship. Yet this time it seemed harder, slower going. She found herself moving away from the task often to do anything else. But there just wasn't much else to do but get ready to leave the home they had known for only a few weeks.

Reynold came into the room and saw the packing containers. His nine-year-old face seemed to drain of life as he stared at her. "You promised we weren't going to have to leave."

She dropped the sweater she'd been folding and moved to him. He didn't want to be held, so she knelt in front of him and looked him right in the eyes. "I know I did. And we still might not have to. Tomorrow they're going to try to stop the moon from exploding."

"And if they can't stop it?" he asked. "Then we have to leave, don't we?"

"I'm afraid we do," she said. "There's nothing I can do to change that."

"Well," he said, looking at her with his stubborn frown, the same look his father used to get all the time. "I'm not leaving. You can't make me."

With that he turned and went out into the other room.

She sat on the bed and stared at the door. How she wished it were that easy. How she wished that they didn't have to leave. Maybe they would all get lucky and the attempt to stop the explosion on the moon would work. Maybe this was all just a false alarm.

She glanced around at the packing containers and her clothes laid out on the bed and knew deep in her stomach that wasn't going to be the case. This next day or so would be the last days they would spend in this home.

Countdown: 7 Days, 9 Hours

"You're in my light," McCoy said gruffly as a shadow covered the hole he was working in. He had just managed to fill two containers completely full of rich dirt containing the bacteria. He knew he could get at least two more full containers out of this hole before he'd have to move on.

"Sorry, Doctor," the voice of Jim Kirk said from above, almost as if it were coming out of the blue sky.

McCoy sat up and wiped his dirt-covered hands on his pants. He could feel the pain in his back from bending over so long, and his arms were going to ache from the digging, he had no doubt about that. But it was all worth it.

He eased himself over a few feet and sat down with his back against a rough rock, then took a drink from his water bottle. He hadn't done this much manual labor in years and years. Luckily he was a doctor, not a farmer.

"What are you doing here, Jim?" McCoy asked, squinting up into the light as Kirk studied the hole in the rich dirt of the field.

"Actually a better question," Jim said, "is *what* are you doing here?"

McCoy tapped the sealed containers. "Bacteria," he said. "A very special bacteria. Most important discovery this planet has to offer the Federation beyond the olivium. It's going to change agriculture, save millions of lives on other colonies. We can't just leave it."

Kirk glanced across the field where six others were working. McCoy could see Dr. Audry's form taking a rest from digging.

"So you are all making sure samples and cultures are saved," Jim said. "Good work."

"Thank you," McCoy said. "Figured this was more important than helping the medical people pack instruments."

"If it's half what you say it is," Jim said, smiling as he kneeled beside McCoy, "you were right. You need more help?"

"We've got crews working all over the planet," McCoy said. "And we're going to make sure samples are stored on every ship leaving this system. Unless that damned moon kills us all, this discovery will get back."

Kirk nodded, but didn't say anything.

"So what's the problem?" McCoy said. He'd been around his friend for too many years not to know when Jim Kirk was struggling with something.

Kirk shook his head and picked up a handful of the rich soil. "All these months coming here, my responsibility was protecting the colonists, getting them across hostile space to this planet. Now a few hours ago I told them I would no longer be responsible for them if they headed back."

McCoy looked at his friend. "You're having problems with the fact that a mineral is more important than sixty-two thousand lives? Right?"

Kirk nodded. "Spock was right. You have a knack of summing something up just about perfectly."

McCoy laughed. He didn't mean to laugh, but it just sort of came out and Kirk looked at him puzzled.

"First off, Jim, if the colonists head back on their own, that's their decision."

"I know that."

"Good," McCoy said. "Secondly, even if they do head off on their own, there is a good chance they'll make it to a point where Starfleet can escort them the rest of the way."

"I know that, too," Jim said.

"So let's get right to the point," McCoy said, pushing himself away from the rock to get a little closer to his friend. "If the mineral in that moon, exploded or not, gets into the wrong hands, all the billions and billions of lives in all the Federation would be at risk."

"Which is why I have to stay here," Kirk said. "I understand that also. I just can't get over the feeling of not doing my duty to the colonists."

"Then do your duty to them," McCoy said, a little gruffer than he wanted to, "And to the entire Federation in general. Do both."

Kirk looked at him.

"Come on, Jim," McCoy said, laughing again. "I've seen you bend people around your finger."

"And how would that help?" Kirk asked.

McCoy stared his friend right in the eye. "Quit playing by the gentleman's rules with Sir Evan, the boy governor. Quit giving him choices you don't want him to make. Give him only choices that you can live with."

Kirk smiled.

McCoy could see that his comments had helped. The captain had just needed permission in his head to take the gloves off, to control the colonists in this situation. And McCoy had no doubt Jim Kirk could control the boy governor without even trying. It wouldn't even be a fair match.

"Thanks, Bones," Kirk said, patting McCoy's leg and standing.

McCoy stood with him, stretching muscles he couldn't remember using before. "That's what friends are for."

"You sure you don't need extra help?" Kirk asked, glancing at where the others were digging.

"Thanks," McCoy said. "I think we have it covered on the digging side of things. You just make darn sure the colonist ships don't leave this area until they are guarded, no matter what happens to the planet. I don't want to have done all this digging for nothing."

Kirk laughed. "I will, if you make sure these containers are on all the ships before we try to pull the plug on that moon. We don't want this discovery lost any more than we want the olivium in the wrong hands."

"It will all be safely tucked away," McCoy said. "You can count on that."

"And you'll be back on board, right?" Kirk asked. "We might need your services."

"Wouldn't miss the giant moon-pull for the world," McCoy said. "You can count on that too."

Kirk turned and headed across the field toward the beam-down point outside the colony.

McCoy watched his friend walk for a moment, noting that Kirk seemed a little more determined than he had a few minutes ago. And when Jim Kirk got determined, the universe needed to watch out.

With a loud groan, McCoy got back down on his knees and started digging again in the hole, carefully filling a container with bacteria-filled dirt. He was far, far too old for this type of labor.

But in this case, it was worth it.

Part Two

DO OR DIE

Chapter Six

Countdown: 6 Days, 8 Hours

CAPTAIN SUNN stared at the star system appearing on his main viewer. Yellow sun, Class-M fourth planet. Maybe they could get lucky right out of the box.

He doubted it. He was of the belief that he and his crew could search systems at this speed for months and not come across something that would work for the colonists. But he had promised Kirk he would do what he could do. And that was exactly what they were doing.

So far, on their short and very rushed exploration, they'd dropped out of warp at twelve promising systems just long enough to take a look around and jump back up to speed. Three systems with nothing hospitable to humans, eight with planets that were more like Mars than Earth, and one that held a pre-warp culture on the only good planet.

Twelve down, who knew how many more to go.

When Kirk had asked him to try this, he had given no real instructions as to one direction over another. And since there were a thousand directions Sunn and the *Rattlesnake* could head in, he had narrowed the choice down with a few criteria.

First, the direction had to be generally, but not directly, back toward Federation space. That way if he found a marginal planet, the colonists could use it as a stopping point. That eliminated half the possible directions.

Secondly, it should be away from the homeworlds of the Blood and Kauld. No point in asking for trouble when they didn't even need to be in the fight.

Third, the new planet needed to be outside the sphere of the Gamma Night problem. That really wasn't a hard and set criteria, but Sunn was so tired of sitting around for ten hours, he had made it one.

And fourth, there should be a large number of possible star systems along the route.

That had narrowed Sunn's choices to almost a hundred different paths away from the Belle Terre system. At that point, looking at the star charts of this small area of the galaxy, he had gotten a true realization just how large the universe was, and how packed it was with stars. Up until that point, he'd never really given it any thought one way or another.

He had picked the path with almost two hundred stars along a four-day flight, and they had set off, right after the Gamma Night released them.

Four days out he planned on turning the ship in a wide arc and heading toward Belle Terre, checking planets on a new course on the way back. A course that had another one hundred and twelve possible systems. They were going to try to at least check out over three hundred systems in under eight days. How impossible a task was that?

"Captain," Roger said, lifting his gaze from his scope and staring at Sunn. "We might have a good one here."

Sunn just stared at Roger, not believing he had even heard those words.

Roger Utlilla, a stout, black-haired man with a steady smile, had been with Sunn for almost five years as his second-in-command. Roger was from a small island in the Pacific and loved to explore almost as much as Sunn. All three of them on the *Rattlesnake* loved the thrill of finding new planets, seeing the new sights the universe had to offer. Otherwise they wouldn't be on this ship.

"You're kidding," Dar Longsun said, leaning forward.

Dar was their pilot and the only other crewman on the bridge, or the ship for that matter. Dar was from the desert area of Arizona. He was shorter than Roger and rail thin. His bald head, combined with his thin shape, often got him called "Pool Cue." The last guy who had called him that had needed two days on the medical ship.

"Put it on the main screen and tell me what you've found," Sunn ordered. "You know I don't want to waste any time on any false alarms."

A blue-green planet filled the screen, looking similar to Earth in basic color and cloud cover. Sunn studied the image. One pole had a small ice cap, the axis of the planet was clearly tilted slightly, and oceans covered a large percentage of the surface. Sure looked promising.

"There's massive evidence of a past humanoid civilization here," Roger said. "Now there are no signs of life above small animal stages."

"So what happened to them?" Sunn asked. "And how long ago?"

Over the years he and his crew had stumbled on a number of dead planets where civilizations had once thrived and then were wiped out for one reason or another. Usually the civilizations had been pre-warp and had destroyed themselves. Earth had come darn close itself to being one of these dead planets at different times in its history.

Sunn stared at the screen. This kind of planet just might be perfect as a stopover point for the Belle Terre colonists, giving them a place to hold up and get supplies, or wait until supplies came from the Federation.

Or maybe it might even be a good place to form a new colony. That had been done lots of other times on planets where earlier civilizations had existed. Why not this one? That was one of the questions he and his crew needed to answer before they reported back.

"No idea what did them in," Roger said. "No evidence of bomb craters or high radiation of any type. Looks like it was fairly recent, too. I'd say within the last one hundred years."

"Well, something wiped them out," Dar said.

Now Sunn was really interested and excited. Who knew what kind of discoveries a recently lost civilization might have to offer to the Federation. Who knows, maybe one race's tragedy could be the lifesaver of a colony.

"This system on any charts?" Sunn asked.

"None that we have," Roger said. "From the size of their cities and road system, they were at least space-flight level when they went missing. But no leftover energy sources at all. Maybe they just packed up and left the neighborhood."

"Air breathable?"

"Perfectly," Roger said. "I'll need to test for contaminants down closer, but basic balance seems good. Gravity just slightly less than Earth standard."

Sunn looked at the planet now filling the screen. It looked so tame, so beautiful from orbit. But something had wiped out the civilization down there just a fairly short time ago, as far as the universe was concerned. And before he reported back to Kirk on this planet, he needed to find out what had caused the disappearance of an entire race.

"Okay, Dar," Sunn said, "take us in for a closer look. Near one of their bigger cities."

"You got it," Dar said.

Sunn could hear the excitement in Dar's voice, and could feel it in his own stomach. This kind of thing was why he was out here in space. He'd have to remember to thank Captain Kirk for the chance.

Countdown: 6 Days, 7 Hours

This Gamma Night, Kirk had actually managed to get some sleep, mostly because there was just nothing else for him to do. And McCoy had suggested, not exactly subtly, that a rested captain making decisions was better than an exhausted one.

So he managed to sleep for six hours of the Gamma Night and now strode onto the bridge ready to do what they needed to do: Pull a plug out of a moon. Kirk had to admit, McCoy had been right. He did feel better.

Spock was at his station and McCoy stood beside Kirk's chair. Sulu and Chekov were at their stations and Uhura smiled at him from communications.

"Did you follow your own suggestion, Bones?" Kirk

asked as he sat down in his chair and glanced at the static-filled screen.

"Slept like a baby wrapped in cotton," Bones said. "I can see you did as well."

"Not sure about the cotton," Kirk said. He turned and looked back at his first officer. "Spock, how long until the Gamma Night clears?"

"Less than two minutes, Captain."

Kirk nodded and tapped the communications button on the arm of his chair. "Scotty, are the tractor-beam modifications finished?"

"That they are, Captain," Scotty said.

"Shuttle ready to fly as well?"

"Just sittin' there," Scotty said.

"Stand by," Kirk said. He turned to Uhura. "When the interference clears, check with all the other ships as to their tractor-beam modification status and tell them to stand ready to move into position on my order."

"Understood, Captain," Uhura said.

McCoy moved in a little closer to him. "Jim, you really think it's wise to leave most of the colonists on the surface of the planet for this? There's still time to get them on board the big Conestogas."

"It would make no difference, Doctor," Spock said. "If the moon explodes while we are making this attempt, all ships including the *Enterprise* will be destroyed along with all life on the surface of the planet."

"I don't think having them anywhere near this system is wise," Kirk said.

"That's my point exactly," McCoy said. "Get them loaded up and away before we try anything."

"If all the ships do not participate, Doctor," Spock said, "there will be no point in, as you put it, trying anything."

"And where would they go, Doctor?" Kirk asked, staring at his friend. "To the Kauld? I'm sure they'll welcome them with open arms."

Kirk had had this discussion before he beamed up with Governor Pardonnet. It had finally been the governor and his top people's decision that the risk should be everyone's risk. Every man, woman, and child. They had all come here, taken a massive chance at finding a new home together. They would stay together in the attempt to save their planet.

Kirk had understood, to a point. Maybe even admired them for doing it. But he and the governor both knew there really wasn't any other choice. The colonists had nowhere to go and not enough of anything to make it back to Federation space. Saving this planet was just about their best hope. And, as Spock had pointed out, they only had slightly over a five percent chance of doing that. At the moment, everything seemed stacked against the Belle Terre colonists.

McCoy stared first at Kirk, then at Spock, but said nothing more as he moved back out of the way and stood, holding on to the railing.

The screen cleared of static as the Gamma Night passed. Kirk glanced at Spock as he immediately checked his readings, then glanced at Kirk. "No change in the moon, Captain."

"Understood," Kirk said. Again he was disappointed. He wasn't sure why he was always hoping the situation would change just because they couldn't follow it with their sensors.

"I keep hoping this is all just goin' to go away," McCoy said.

Kirk knew exactly how he felt. But it wasn't going to

until they forced it to go away. "Move us into position, Mr. Sulu."

As he watched, the *Enterprise* broke orbit and moved around to the far side of the large moon. The surface wasn't as big as that of Earth's moon, and it was far more ragged. But considering what was in the center of this moon, it was far more valuable.

"All ships report in ready, sir," Uhura said.

"All ships are moving into positions, sir," Sulu said, "behind and around us."

Kirk nodded as Sulu stabilized the *Enterprise*'s position far too close to the jagged surface for his liking. Since the *Enterprise* had the more powerful tractor beam, it was going to be the center of all the ships. Each ship had been assigned a specific area of the two-hundred-mile-thick rock plug to try to pull out. The *Enterprise*'s job was to try to make all those individual pulling tractor beams act uniformly on the entire two hundred miles.

If this worked, the area between the plug and the rock walls would slowly grow hot from the tension, eventually turn liquid, and allow the plug to move outward. More than likely far faster than a cork out of a pressurized bottle.

"Sulu, I want you ready to move us out of the way instantly if that thing lets go," Kirk said. "You understand."

"Course plotted and laid in, sir," Sulu said. "Standing by."

Kirk glanced at Uhura. "Make sure every ship has a plotted escape route, also."

"Understood, Captain," Uhura said.

Kirk sat back and waited as on the screen ships from the wagon train took their positions above the moon.

Conestogas with their big mule engines, transports, industrial, and cattle barges. Even the hotel vessel *Uncle Jake's Pocket* moved in beside the coroner ship *Twilight Sentinel.*

Only two ships from the original fleet weren't in the mass formation above the moon's surface. The hospital ship *Brother's Keeper,* since it had no tractor beam and one would have been nearly impossible to install, and the small pathfinder ship *Rattlesnake,* that Kirk had sent looking for another safe haven.

Every other ship was going to take part in this attempt.

"Open a channel to all the ships," Kirk said after the last had moved into position. It was the most mismatched group of ships he'd ever seen in such close quarters.

"Open," Uhura said.

"Okay, people," Kirk said, "this is going to take some time if we do it right. Slow and steady wins this one. Set all tractor beams and wait for my mark to engage engines at one-tenth impulse."

He motioned for Uhura to cut the communications line to the other ships, then said, "Set the beam, Mr. Chekov."

"Done," Chekov said.

"All other ships are reporting they are ready," Uhura said after a moment.

"Open the channel," Kirk said.

"Open."

"Good luck, everyone," he said to the other ships. "Start pulling, one-tenth impulse. Now!"

Kirk felt the *Enterprise* jar slightly as it began to pull against the rock. Then nothing. The engines at this speed didn't even seem to strain.

He watched the screen, but nothing changed.

"Is that it?" McCoy asked.

Kirk felt the same way. He knew this was going to take some time. But he was used to going into a battle quickly, with action. Well, they were acting now, and nothing was happening, or so it seemed.

He glanced over at Spock, who didn't look up from his station. Too soon to tell if it was working at all.

Kirk tapped his communications button on his chair. "Scotty, how are we doing?"

"Purrin' along like a kitten," Scotty said.

Kirk glanced back at McCoy, who only shrugged, then turned to Uhura. "Any problems on any of the other ships?"

"Nothing, sir," Uhura said. "All report green."

Kirk again glanced at his first officer. "Spock, how's it looking?"

"There is a slight rise in temperature along the desired fault lines in the rock," Spock said, not turning from his science station. "In two hours I should know more."

"Two hours?" Kirk said, staring at the jagged rock face of the moon in front of him. He knew this was going to take a long time, but not that long! Could the tractor beams of all the ships hold up against such a steady pull for two hours? Or the engines? Many of the ships had barely limped into the Belle Terre system as it was. Two hours of pulling at one-tenth impulse against a moon was going to strain every system on every ship.

"This is going to be like watching mud dry," McCoy said.

"Worse," Kirk said, forcing himself to sit back in his chair and take a deep breath. Much worse.

Chapter Seven

Countdown: 6 Days, 5 Hours

GOVERNOR PARDONNET stood behind Captain Chalker of the *Mable Stevens* and stared at the rough surface of the moon and all the other ships in formation around them, all pulling with tractor beams on a two-hundred-mile-thick section. In his worst nightmare Pardonnet couldn't have imagined something like this happening to his colony. He had prepared for problems on the way to Belle Terre, and had prepared for every problem he could foresee facing on a new world. Food, housing, politics, weather, you name it, he had worried about it and planned for it.

But not this.

How could anyone have ever planned for a moon exploding, let alone two hours and thirty minutes of tug-of-war with rock?

It had seemed as if the time had stopped. He kept glancing at a clock, thinking at least ten minutes had gone by, but each time only a minute or two had passed. And worse yet, nothing seemed to be happening. Over sixty thousand lives hung in the balance and time had slowed to a crawl.

On the screen the rough, uneven surface of the moon seemed almost to laugh at them. If something could be moved with the simple power of the mind, that hunk of rock would already be flying away into space. That was how hard Pardonnet had been staring at it the last two hours.

Ned Chalker, a very heavyset man with pale skin and pasty-blue eyes, shook his head. Hours ago he'd started sweating and now his shirt was completely wet and his thin, blond hair was hanging down the side of his head. Chalker stared at readouts on the arm of his command chair. "We're starting to overheat," he said. "And we're draining energy faster than a broken dam."

"Can you put me through to Captain Kirk?" Pardonnet asked. He had wanted to talk to Kirk a dozen times during the slow two hours and thirty minutes that had just passed, but had resisted until now.

"On screen," Chalker said, pointing to a position beside his chair where Pardonnet should stand.

"Captain Chalker, Governor," Kirk said.

Pardonnet could tell Kirk hadn't had the best few hours either. He looked drained and was moving with jerky, impatient motions.

"We're starting to overheat here, Kirk," Chalker said before Pardonnet could get in a word. "And getting close to our reserves as well."

"I'm afraid you're not the only ship," Kirk said. "We've heated the fracture lines between the rock plug and the rest of the moon, but not enough to turn them molten."

"So we've failed?" Pardonnet asked. It felt as if the weight of the world had smashed down on his shoulders simply by saying those words. He couldn't fail. The colony had to go on. Too much was riding on it.

"Not yet, Governor," Kirk said. "Stand by for further instructions."

The connection was broken.

Pardonnet stared at the rock surface of the moon. Kirk had said "Not yet." What did that mean?

"That crazy Kirk is going to get us all killed," Chalker said, shaking his head.

"Or save us," Pardonnet said. He had to believe Kirk could do that.

Chalker looked up at Pardonnet. "You trust that cowboy from Starfleet?"

Pardonnet shrugged. "At this point, do I have a choice? For that matter, do any of us have a choice?"

Countdown: 6 Days, 5 Hours

Sunn watched as Dar, his pilot, flared the ship out flat and eased it gently down into the green-covered meadow near one of planet's cities. With only a slight bump the *Rattlesnake* was resting on the soil of another new planet. And one of the more interesting ones Sunn had ever seen.

"Nice landing," Roger said, as the landing gear adjusted the ship to a level position.

"All in a day's work," Dar said.

"Yeah, right," Roger said. "Do you remember the last time you landed on a planet surface?"

"Actually," Dar said, "no I don't."

"Nice landing," Roger said again, smiling.

"Thank you," Dar said, laughing.

"Run full scans," Sunn said to Roger, then glanced at Dar. "Keep us ready to lift off on a moment's notice. I don't want to be caught here with our pants down until I find out what happened to all the local residents."

"You got it," Dar said. "But it sure is a beautiful place, isn't it?"

Sunn had to agree with that. The main screen was showing a sight right out of some storybook imagination. Tall, graceful spires of buildings shot hundreds of stories into the sky, framed and supported by smooth-cornered lower buildings. The city seemed to just sort of ease itself down into the rolling green hills around it as if it had actually grown from the soil. For all Sunn knew, maybe it had. He'd seen stranger things, especially from an advanced civilization as this one had clearly been.

They had landed near one of the major roads leading out of the city and Sunn could tell, even in the road's overgrown state, that it once had been well maintained. But there were no signs of the types of vehicles that used the road.

He studied the green carpet of plants they had landed on. From what he could tell, the field they were in had once been some sort of agricultural area. He could still see patterns of ancient crop rows.

"These people really knew their architecture," Roger said, glancing up at the viewscreen, then back at his scanners. "Those buildings are perfectly solid. Full of garbage, but solid. The place is totally dead. A few rat-sized creatures, a lot of small birds, nothing more."

"Radiation? Contaminants in the air?" Sunn asked. "Any indication of what happened?"

"Nothing," Roger said, clearly amazed. "Freshest air

I've ever seen on a reading. More than likely because there's no civilization left to contaminate it."

"Man, this place would be better than Belle Terre for the colonists," Dar said. "All they'd have to do is clean up a little and move in."

"And die from whatever killed the previous tenants," Roger said. "I don't think we should be too hasty here."

"I agree," Sunn said. He was thinking back to how he'd found the olivium in the Quake Moon, but hadn't taken the next step and discovered that the moon was about to explode. Maybe there was something out there that just wasn't reaching their first scans. Something had to have happened to all the people who had built this city and the others around this planet like it. And before he went too far, he was going to have answers.

"Okay," Sunn said, "before anyone steps one foot out of this ship, I want to run every test we can think of, and a few we haven't thought of yet."

"You got it," Roger said. "Already started some of them."

"Stay alert and ready to move us, Dar."

"You say boo and I'll have us in orbit," he said.

"Good," Sunn said. "Keep a good eye on the surrounding space as well. Maybe these people, or what killed them, are still out there somewhere."

With one more look at the beautiful scene on the main viewer, Sunn moved over to an empty science station and started some basic scans. Just as he'd done with analyzing the hollow moon, he was going to peel back the layers of this world one at a time until he found the truth.

And then this time, he wouldn't stop there. This time, as Kirk and his people had done, he'd look one layer below the truth.

Maybe then he'd find the answers he needed instead of the ones he wanted.

Countdown: 6 Days, 5 Hours

Kirk stood beside the science station, waiting for his first officer to do one final check before reporting. The last few hours had seemed to stretch forever. But now they were at the breaking point of this entire attempt. It was either going to work, or fail, and now was the time to finally find out which.

"If this is to succeed," Spock said, turning away from his instruments to face Kirk, "the pressure must be increased at this point in time."

"Increase it?" McCoy said. "Have you gone batty?"

"How much?" Kirk asked. He didn't like the idea of increasing pressure on the moon, either. Many of the ships were already having troubles and if strained any harder, there would be no doubt they would have failures.

But at the same time, nothing had really moved inside the moon in the last two and a half hours. Their pulling had managed to do most of what they had hoped for, by heating up the border between the plug and the rock walls of the moon. But the plug was still firmly in place. Those borders had to become molten rock before that two-hundred-mile-thick plug was going to move. So something had to change.

"Every ship must increase the pressure to one-quarter impulse," Spock said.

"Now I know you're nuts," McCoy said from where he stood near Kirk's command chair. "That much force will pull some of these ships apart!"

"I am perfectly sane, Doctor," Spock said. "I am just

attempting to accomplish the task we have set for ourselves. Nothing more."

"And might that task be killing us all?" McCoy asked, glaring at Spock.

Kirk didn't need his two officers bickering at this point. "Spock, is there any chance that maintaining the current amount of pull will succeed?"

"No," Spock said flatly. "Only a force of one-quarter impulse will increase the pressure enough to turn the rock walls between the plug and the moon's crust molten."

"Well, that answers that," Kirk said.

Kirk moved over and sat down in his command chair. The rough surface of the moon dominated the main viewer, its sharp crags and black rocks looking more and more alien with every passing hour. On the screen above the moon he could also see many of the ships. They were ships he was very familiar with during the long journey here. He knew that most of them were not built to withstand what he was about to ask them to withstand. But they were also not able to withstand the long trip back to Federation space at this point.

"Jim, break this off now," McCoy said, "while the colonists still have ships to get away from here in."

"They won't need ships if this works, Bones," Kirk said.

"Bah," McCoy said. "We're just signing death certificates for thousands of colonists."

"I hope you're wrong, Bones," Kirk said. He turned to Uhura. "Open a channel to all ships."

"Open, sir," she said.

"On my mark," Kirk said to all the ship's captains, "increase the pull on the moon to one-quarter impulse and hold it as long as possible."

He took a deep breath and paused, giving the captains time to inform their helmsmen of the change. Then he said, "Now!"

Unlike the first moments of the pull against the moon, this time Kirk could feel the difference instantly. It was as if the entire ship swayed in space, then settled in. Joints creaked and a circuit popped, making both McCoy and Uhura jump.

Around them the engine sounds were much, much louder, filling the bridge like a roaring waterfall, vibrating the decks, shaking even his chair.

If it was doing this to the *Enterprise,* what was it doing to the rest of the fleet?

Maybe he could speed this up some. There was no doubt most of the ships wouldn't last long at this speed.

"Spock," Kirk said, "would increasing our pull above the others help? The *Enterprise* is built to withstand more than the other ships."

"It would," Spock said. "Considering the location of our tractor-beam hold, it would have the effect of increasing the others as well. A booster effect."

"Sir," Uhura said, "reports are pouring in. Engines are overheating, a few tractor beams are about to fail."

"Tell them to hold on!" Kirk said. "As long as they can!" Then he turned back to the screen. "Increase speed to one-half impulse, Mr. Sulu."

"Increasing, sir."

Around them the *Enterprise* started to rattle as the forces pulling at it tried to rip it apart. It felt as if a monster were shaking the ship, roaring as it went.

"Are we getting close, Spock?" Kirk shouted over the noise.

"Impossible to tell, sir."

"Go to point six impulse!"

"Point six!" Sulu shouted back, confirming he had done the order.

The rough surface of the moon below didn't seem to be bothered.

"Come on," Kirk said, under his breath. "Let go."

"No movement yet!" Spock reported.

The shaking and rattling now was almost so loud Kirk couldn't hear Scotty shouting from Engineering over the communications link. "Captain, she canna take much more of this!"

"How long, Scotty?" Kirk shouted back.

"A minute at most!"

"Hold her together!" Kirk shouted.

On the main viewer one of the big Conestogas suddenly veered away wildly. Kirk watched as the crew of the big ship valiantly tried to get control, but without success. The huge ship, with its two mule drives shoving it, smashed into the moon's surface and exploded.

"That was *Hampton Roads*," Sulu shouted.

Captain Nickle had been in charge of that ship. A good man. He and his crew would be missed. But thank the heavens it also hadn't been full of colonists.

At that moment the coroner ship *Twilight Sentinel* broke off and shot away so fast it seemed as if it had disappeared. Clearly its tractor beam had suddenly failed.

"Spock?" Kirk shouted over the roaring and shaking.

"Rock is becoming molten," Spock shouted, "but the plug is not moving."

Two more ships suddenly broke away and shot into space. One was spinning, clearly out of control.

"This isn't working, Jim!" McCoy shouted. "Call it off!"

Near Spock one panel exploded in a shower of sparks, filling the bridge with acid-smelling smoke.

"Engine failure in thirty seconds!" Scotty shouted over the communications link from Engineering.

Two more ships broke free and shot off as their tractor beams failed.

And then one of the mule drives of the Conestoga *Yukon* exploded, sending debris swirling in all directions. A large hunk of the engine smashed into one of the smaller private ships, destroying it instantly.

"Spock!" Kirk shouted. "Tell me that thing's about to break loose!"

"It's not!" Spock shouted back.

"Send word to shut down!" he ordered. "Mr. Sulu, back us off to zero!"

Slowly the noise and shaking around them reduced until finally only the silence and the smoke remained.

"Captain," Uhura said, "I'm getting reports in of widespread damage to most ships. We lost two of the Conestogas and four smaller ships completely."

Kirk stared at the screen for a moment, then said, "Order the remaining ships that can to return to planetary orbit. Set up search parties for survivors of the destroyed ships and damage-repair crews for the others."

"Yes, sir," Uhura said, turning back to her communications board and starting to work.

"Spock, what happened?" Kirk said, turning to his first officer.

"We were unable to generate enough force, Captain," Spock said plainly.

Kirk slumped into his chair. They had failed. For some reason, over the past few hours, he had thought they just might pull this off, save the planet, save that beach that just a short time ago he'd been sitting on.

"Well, it was worth the try, Jim," McCoy said.

Kirk shrugged. "I hope those who gave their lives for it thought so."

"If they didn't," McCoy said, "they wouldn't have been here."

"I know that, Bones," he said. "It doesn't help."

The silence on the bridge suddenly seemed to be louder than the shaking and engine noises had been a few moments before. The wreckage of the Conestoga was like a scar on the surface below them.

"We tried, it didn't work," Bones said. "Now it's time to focus on getting the colonists to safety before this monster blows completely."

Kirk nodded, staring at the rough surface of the moon below. McCoy was right. It was time to get the colonists the hell out of there.

He hated to lose, hated to be beaten. There had to be something they were missing, some way to stop this explosion from destroying so many dreams. But at the moment that seemed as impossible as stopping a sun from going nova. Sometimes in the universe, there were just events too big for man to control.

But that thought did nothing but gall James Kirk.

Chapter Eight

Countdown: 6 Days, 3 Hours

LILIAN COATES stared at the half-packed containers. Now it looked as if she had no choice. The attempt to stop the moon explosion had failed. Governor Pardonnet had announced they had no other options but to leave Belle Terre at once. She had less than a day to get everything she and Reynold owned together and ready for transport back to one of the ships. She didn't know which ship, but that really didn't matter. One cramped room was like any other. She and Reynold would survive the trip back to Federation space, but it wasn't going to be pleasant.

In fact, from what the governor had said, the trip wasn't going to be easy for anyone. The attempt to stop the moon explosion had destroyed a number of the colony's ships and left others useless. Conditions on the way back were going to be crowded and slow going.

Lilian had to give the governor credit. He hadn't pulled any punches, but told them exactly how hard it was going to be. The only way the Belle Terre colony was going to make it back to Federation space was with a rescue mission from Starfleet meeting them partway with repair parts, dilithium crystals, and empty ships. And he was considering having the colony's ships move out of the danger zone and just wait, meaning that the length of time they might be on the crowded ships would be longer than even the trip here.

On the way to Belle Terre she would have met such challenges head-on. But now, without Tom, and with no plans for a better future, she didn't have much energy to meet anything.

Of course, at the moment she really didn't even have the luxury of time to think about her future, or feel sorry for herself. She had to get packed and ready to transport back to the ships when their turn came.

"Reynold!" He was big enough to help and right now she needed his help.

The silence in the small dome-house suddenly caught her attention. She hadn't seen Reynold since just after the governor's speech an hour ago. He had sat and listened to it with her, then gone into his room. She assumed he had stayed in there, so why wasn't he answering?

"Reynold, honey," she said, moving toward his room. "I know you want to stay. So do I."

She opened his half-closed door and realized she had been talking to herself.

With a quick glance into her room and then the bathroom, it quickly became clear that he wasn't in the house at all. Yet he hadn't told her he was leaving, and he always told her when he was going outside. That was the agreement they had made.

She tried to push down the sense of panic filling her thoughts. The "fist" that always warned her of something bad about to happen was again gripping her stomach.

She went quickly out the front door into the fading light of the evening. A few people were walking toward the main part of the colony, but no one else was in sight.

"Reynold!" she shouted as she moved around their dome, looking down the road and off through the trees in all directions.

Her call echoed for a moment in the forest and around the other dome-houses, then faded to silence. Reynold was nowhere to be seen.

And he wasn't answering even if he could hear her.

She quickly went back inside and checked every inch of their house, leaving his room for last. When he wasn't hiding in his closet, she forced herself to stop and take a deep breath.

"What are you doing, Reynold?" she asked out loud. "You're only nine years old. Where could you go?"

Then she noticed what she should have seen earlier. His coat was missing. And his favorite hat. And the pack that he had used when he and his dad had gone hiking just before leaving Earth.

Clearly he had decided to run away. She knew he didn't want to leave Belle Terre, and this was his way of deciding he wasn't going to be made to leave. A child's logic.

But where would he have gone?

She moved quickly back through their living room and outside, turning right and walking up the slight incline of the dirt road. Three domes from hers was

Reynold's best friend, Danny Laird. She knocked loudly and insistently on the door and after a few seconds Kathy Laird appeared.

Kathy was a short, thin, and attractive woman who enjoyed laughing. She and her husband both were geologists. At the moment Kathy looked as tired and upset as Lilian felt.

"Lilian?" Kathy said. "What's wrong?"

"I think Reynold's run away," Lilian said, "since he doesn't want to leave Belle Terre. Have you seen him?"

She shook her head. "No, I—"

Lilian could see the sudden worry and panic creep into Kathy's eyes as she turned away from the door.

"Danny?" Kathy called out as she moved back into the dome. "Danny?"

Lilian stood, the tall trees around her swaying gently in the evening breeze, the fist around her stomach clamping up even harder.

"Danny!"

A moment later both Kathy and her husband, Estes, came to the door. Between them they had their younger child, JoAnne. Both looked panicked.

"He's not here," Estes said. "And his favorite pillow is missing."

Lilian nodded. "I was afraid of that."

She scanned the trees and domes around her. Nothing at all to be seen. Reynold had run away, and he hadn't gone alone.

At that moment, three domes away, Judith Whitney came to the door of her home and shouted, "Diane! Time to come in."

Diane was Reynold and Danny's age. And one of their best friends as well.

91

"Diane!" Judith called out again, the panic clearly starting to fill her voice.

Lilian glanced at Estes and Kathy, knowing instantly that it hadn't been just their two kids who had taken it upon themselves to stay on Belle Terre. As she started up the street toward Judith, Lilian wondered how many other kids had gone with her son.

And just where had they gone?

The problem was, on an unexplored planet, how far *could* a bunch of nine-year-old kids go? And how should she and the other parents go about finding them?

By dawn she wasn't asking those questions anymore. Over five hundred people had stopped packing and joined in the search and no one had found even one sign of the six nine-year-olds who were missing. It was as if they had been beamed right off the planet.

Countdown: 6 Days, 2 Hours

Captain Sunn glanced at the time. They had been on this planet now for almost twelve hours. Half a day on one stop that they still hadn't determined would help the Belle Terre colonists. If this planet turned out to be bad, they had wasted a large percentage of their total search time.

But so far none of them could find one thing wrong with this planet. And that was exactly what was driving Sunn crazy. There had to be something wrong here. Or had to have *been* something wrong. Otherwise, why weren't the original residents still here, filling their beautiful cities, tilling their fields, traveling on their roads?

Something killed them or chased them away. And

before he could tell Captain Kirk this was a good place for the colonists to come to, Sunn needed to know what happened.

But the answer to that question wasn't coming easily.

They had tested the soil for any signs of past contamination. Negative.

They had run extensive tests on the air. Same result. Nothing to indicate any past problems.

Now Sunn and Roger were doing complete scans of the areas under the city and fields. Nothing there but a fairly extensive subway system and sewage-removal system.

"You know," Roger said after they had finished the last scan, "I'm starting to really hate this place."

Sunn laughed. "Too perfect for you?"

"Exactly," Roger said. "No pollution, no big predators, no crowds of natives. Just empty cities and beautiful landscapes. Ughh."

"So where haven't we looked for problems yet?" Dar asked.

Sunn pointed upward. "An exploding moon is about to wipe out Belle Terre. Maybe something natural in the nearby arca got these people."

"Like what? A giant solar flare?" Roger asked. "We'd have seen evidence of it in the soil."

Sunn knew that. Anything really major or poisonous coming from space and killing the population less than one hundred years ago would have shown up instantly in the soil and air samples. Or stuck to the outside of the buildings if nothing else.

"I got it," Dar said. "Neighboring aliens abducted them all? Had them for lunch."

Sunn laughed. "Let's check anyhow. And then go over everything again."

"And if we can't spot anything then?" Roger asked.

Sunn shrugged and glanced at the screen, at the beautiful and very empty city spread out in front of them. "We'll cross that bridge when we come to it."

Countdown: 5 Days, 23 Hours

"I want to find another solution," Kirk said, staring at the Quake Moon on his screen. "And I want to find it fast."

None of the bridge crew said a word. Sulu and Chekov both sat studying their instruments, McCoy stood behind Kirk's chair to his left, and Spock worked at his science station.

Kirk and the rest of the crew had spent the last few hours dealing with all the problems caused by the attempt to pull the plug on the explosion. Casualties had been great. Sixty-seven colonists dead, a hundred more injured. All crew of different ships. Eight colony ships either destroyed or completely beyond repair. Another thirty ships damaged.

All for nothing.

The failure was going to make leaving Belle Terre even more difficult. Now not only were they short of provisions, but they were short of ships.

Kirk studied the moon as he would study any enemy. He didn't like failing, and right now this entire wagon train to the stars was failing badly. He had gotten all these colonists to this planet; he wasn't going to leave without a fight. And as far as he was concerned, trying to pull that plug had just been round one. They still had just under five days to figure out another solution.

"Someone needs to find a giant pin and just ram it

into the moon like popping a balloon," McCoy said, breaking the deadly silence on the bridge.

Kirk glanced at McCoy, who was standing behind him. McCoy was clearly just as upset as anyone at the entire prospect of losing Belle Terre.

"A three-hundred-mile hardened crust of a moon is not a balloon skin, Doctor," Spock said from his science station.

"To a big enough pin it is," McCoy said, glaring at the Vulcan.

Kirk was just about to tell his two senior officers to quit bickering and come up with an answer when he suddenly realized that McCoy just might have the answer in his joking comment. They did need something to pop the pressure building inside the moon and just maybe they could find a pin large enough.

"Spock," Kirk said, "the doctor just might have something there." Kirk jumped to his feet and patted the puzzled-looking McCoy on the shoulder on the way past.

"It is highly illogical to think that 'popping' this moon would be a solution," Spock said.

"Thank you," McCoy said. "I'll take that as a compliment."

Kirk waved Spock's comment away and faced his science officer. "What would be the result of something large hitting the thin plug-area of the moon's crust?"

"It would depend on the factors involved," Spock said.

Kirk, annoyed, again waved his science officer's answer away. At times getting a clear answer from the Vulcan was all in how Kirk asked the questions.

"Let me try this again," Kirk said. "What *amount* of force at impact on the plug area of the moon's crust would cause that area of the crust to rupture without setting off a chain reaction that would explode the entire moon?"

Kirk figured that was about as clear as he could put that question.

Spock looked at him for a moment, then nodded, clearly thinking, showing no outward sign at all of the intense calculations Kirk knew were going on in that head.

Kirk glanced back at McCoy, who was still looking puzzled, then at his first officer. Finally Spock said, "My initial calculations will only be estimates, sir. It would take three hours to get you exact numbers."

"I'm willing to take your estimates, Spock," Kirk said. "As a starting point."

Spock nodded. "It would take a mass approximately five percent the mass of the Quake Moon, impacting at ten times a standard orbital velocity over the plug area, to rupture the crust of the Quake Moon."

"And what would happen then?" Kirk asked. "Would the expected large explosion occur?"

"No," Spock said. "The pressure would be released at the rupture, stopping the chain-reaction larger explosion that is building now."

"Great!" Kirk said.

"However," Spock said before Kirk could even turn away, "the smaller explosion from the collision and rupture, even on the far side of the Quake Moon, would blanket the exposed side of Belle Terre with radiation."

"Leaving it lifeless?"

"Possibly," Spock said. "I would need more time to do the calculations. And that would depend on the type of explosion that would occur."

Kirk could feel the faint tinge of hope building. There was a way to save the planet, and half the life on it. That might be enough. Just barely enough.

"How big an object is five percent of the Quake Moon's mass?" McCoy asked, moving up and joining the discussion.

Kirk could tell that the doctor clearly wasn't happy with this idea, but going along with it.

"A smaller moon, Doctor," Spock said. "Or an extremely large asteroid, depending on the physical makeup of the body involved."

"So, Jim," McCoy said, "what you are suggesting is ramming one small moon into this larger moon to cause a smaller explosion that will destroy only half of Belle Terre?"

"Doctor," Kirk said. "What I'm suggesting is that we keep looking for answers. And this is one possible one."

"Just like pulling the plug was an answer," McCoy said. "Spock, what are the odds of this idea working?"

"At the moment, Doctor," Spock said calmly, "less than one per cent."

Kirk watched as McCoy glared at him for a moment. The tension was so thick on the bridge again that Kirk wondered how anyone was breathing. They were all upset and clearly getting desperate. Maybe he was getting so desperate to save the colonists and Belle Terre and the olivium that he wasn't thinking clearly.

"Point taken, Doctor," Kirk said. "So let's keep looking for ideas."

"Captain, I think this idea may be worth investigating further," Spock said. "If you'll allow me?"

Kirk waved Spock toward his science station. "Be my guest. Until we come up with another idea that sounds better."

Spock nodded and turned to his scope.

"Well, Doctor," Kirk said, moving back and dropping down into his chair, "any more ideas?"

"You'll be the first to know," McCoy said.

"Anyone else?" Kirk asked, glancing around at his bridge crew.

No one said a word, so Kirk sat back and stared at the Quake Moon's rough surface filling the screen. Two hours later he was still sitting there.

Staring. And he wasn't one inch closer to solving the problem.

Chapter Nine

Countdown: 5 Days, 20 Hours

SUNN STARED AT the beautiful alien city on the viewscreen, then pushed himself out of his captain's chair. "Well, we're getting no answers in here. Time to go exploring."

For over a day they had searched for any clue to what happened to the residents of this planet and had gotten nowhere. Period. As far as they could find out, this city should still be crawling with the original residents.

Now it looked as if their only hope was to find some sort of record in the dead city. Maybe the former inhabitants of the place left a forwarding address.

Dar and Roger moved with him to the hatch, then watched, laser rifles in ready position, as the airlock cycled and then opened. Sunn stepped forward and stood at the top of the short ramp, looking around. The air had a crisp bite to it, but as their readings had told them, it smelled clear and fresh.

"Wow," Dar said, taking a deep breath and releasing it. "After all the months in the ship, this is great."

"I'll second that," Roger said.

Sunn had to agree that being outside felt good. Very good, in fact. In the short time they had been over Belle Terre, none of them had taken any time on the planet's surface. At the moment he couldn't remember the last time he'd stepped onto the surface of a planet. Too long, he decided. After they got done with this he was going to make sure they saw a planet's surface a little more regularly.

"Keep a constant scan going all around us," Sunn said. "I don't want us surprised out here."

Roger nodded and glanced down at his Starfleet-style tricorder. "All clear. Just like it has been every other time I've checked."

"Keep checking," Sunn said. "Dar?"

Dar indicated that he was ready, laser rifle up and hot.

Sunn patted his hip to make sure he had his weapon, then headed down the short ramp toward the ground. In front of him stretched the green field for about a hundred paces before being cut by one of the roads that led into the city.

He hit the bottom of the ramp and set off through the knee-high grass toward the road and the city beyond. There was no wind at all. The sun felt warm against his face, but the crispness of the air was going to be enough to keep the heat down. If this placed turned out to be as good as it looked, the Belle Terre colonists were going to have a new home, cities already built and just waiting.

But that was a big if. And right now this planet scared him more than he wanted to admit. Something had happened here not that long ago and he wasn't that sure he really wanted to find out what.

Yet to do his job right, he had to know.

The road was some sort of hard, almost black surface that up close showed cracks of aging and weathering. The grass had grown up over the edges and through some of the cracks, but mostly the road was perfectly flat and still in good shape. Considering that no upkeep had been done on it for almost one hundred years, Sunn was impressed. The residents of this planet had known how to build to last.

With Sunn walking up the middle, Roger along the right, and Dar on the left and behind, they headed for the tall spires that towered in the center of the city in front of them.

Beautiful brown and tan and white buildings seemed almost to glow in the sun, welcoming them with their beauty and perfect lines.

It was the last place Sunn wanted to go.

Countdown: 5 Days, 18 Hours

Governor Pardonnet stopped among the tall trees and stared at the hundreds of people moving ahead and around him, spread out through the dark forest no more than a few arm-lengths apart, searching. Each had a flashlight, the beam like a long, white sword cutting the blackness. Every so often a call would ring out in the darkness. "Reynold?"

Or "Danny?"

Or "Josiah?"

Or any of the six children's names. Otherwise only the sounds of twigs snapping and branches being pushed aside marred the night quiet.

Where could six kids have disappeared to? He just couldn't imagine. No one seemed to know. And there was barely five days left to get everyone back into the remaining ships, all the supplies loaded they could carry, and away from this planet. The thought of leaving made him sick, yet he had no choice at all. Five days to save sixty-two thousand lives, yet right now hundreds were looking for six lost children.

And he was helping them look.

When the problem of the children had been reported to him, he'd had his ship move to a position in orbit to do a scan of the area. Nothing was found, but his ship's scanners were pretty basic and couldn't even do much to penetrate effectively a forest like this. Plus it couldn't tell who were children and who were adults out looking for the children.

He watched the searchers move up the incline and through the dark forest. Walking with them, he was just one more searcher covering a few feet of forest floor. There had to be a better way for him to help find the children and get everyone back to packing and getting ready for the long trip back to Earth.

He turned and moved back down the hill toward the main colony lights in the distance, trying to keep his mind on the path ahead and not on the coming destruction of this planet.

When he finally reached the edge of the colony he opened his communicator and called to his ship. "Put me in touch with Captain Kirk. At once."

A moment later Kirk's voice came back strong and sounding impatient. "Kirk here. What can I do for you, Governor?"

"I've got a problem you might be able to help me with," he said. "I've got six children who have run away and been missing now about nine hours. We could use a Starfleet-level scan of the area to see if they could be spotted that way."

"Not a problem, Governor," Kirk said. "I'll have the *Impeller* help you. Expect Captain Merkling to contact you in a moment."

"Thank you, Captain," he said.

"Keep me informed. Kirk out."

Pardonnet held the communicator in his hand, waiting. A few days ago this would have been a small problem, easily handled. The kids would have been found and everyone would have moved on with their lives. Now, with the failure to stop the explosion and the million details he faced trying to evacuate and get enough supplies for a trip back, this problem seemed immense, almost impossible.

Yet this gave him something to focus on for the moment. The whereabouts of six children instead of the overall concerns of sixty-two thousand colonists.

He knew he should be somewhere else, working to find solutions that might save all their lives in the coming months. Yet right now, here on the edge of this forest, he needed to solve one problem at a time.

He needed to start somewhere, and finding six missing children was exactly the solution he needed.

Countdown: 5 Days, 18 Hours

Kirk finished asking Captain Merkling to help the governor find the missing children, then turned back to where Spock was working at his science station. Dr. McCoy leaned on the rail, waiting. Chekov, Sulu, and Uhura were at their stations, but all were turned facing Spock.

The Vulcan had just said, "Captain, I think I might

have a solution," without looking away from his console.

For the past five hours they had come up with, and then rejected, at least half a dozen ideas for stopping the moon from exploding. They had rejected them all simply because it became clear that none of the plans would work.

Kirk was angry and frustrated, but not yet willing to give up. Not by a long ways. They still had over five days before the moon exploded, and if it took every hour of those five days to find an answer, he would keep searching.

Now Spock had an idea.

Spock looked away from his station at everyone staring at him. "Dr. McCoy's original idea of plunging an object into the thin area of the moon crust may have more merit than I first thought. And a higher chance of success."

"That's not my idea," McCoy said.

"I think you called it a giant pin," Sulu said.

McCoy scowled at Sulu, but said nothing.

"Explain," Kirk said to his science officer. At this point he was willing to listen to just about anything that might work to save this colony.

"My initial calculations showed there was a ninety-nine percent chance of the planet being completely destroyed from the rupture caused by an object crashing into the moon at the location of the plug we tried to remove. That was the question you asked me. Correct?"

"It was," Kirk said.

"Would you get to the point?" McCoy asked, clearly more annoyed than Kirk was feeling.

At the moment, Kirk was beyond annoyance and into the edges of anger. He was going to have to keep that under control. Right now he needed to make clear decisions, not decisions based on desperation.

Spock went on. "In those calculations I did not take into account the shielding effect of the crust of the moon itself."

"I'm not following you, Spock," Kirk said. "Why didn't you calculate that effect?"

"Yeah," McCoy said. "And what in the world would it change, anyway?"

"Quite a bit, actually, Doctor," Spock said. "And I did not calculate it because it did not apply in the question you asked me, Captain."

"Explain," Kirk said.

Kirk watched as Spock's long fingers keyed in commands on his science station. Then the Vulcan indicated the main screen. The image switched from a live image of the moon to a graphic one showing both the moon and Belle Terre. Everyone on the bridge turned to look.

"The plug is here," Spock said.

A blue mark appeared on the moon showing the location of the plug they had tried to remove.

Spock went on. "An object crashing into that area would cause a rip in the moon that would release the pressure inside, but would also send an explosion of rock and olivium outward in this fashion."

Kirk watched as the illustration on the main screen showed the moon rupturing outward. Even though the plug was more on the back side of the moon, and the moon remained intact, part of the spreading debris trail hit Belle Terre. It was clear that Spock had been right. The planet would not have survived such an event.

"However," Spock said. "The very slight rotation of the Quake Moon causes a second thin area of the crust to be almost directly on the back side of the moon one hour before the explosion is set to occur."

"A second area?" Sulu asked. "Like the plug?"

"Similar, but not as thin," Spock said.

"Directly on the back side?" Kirk asked, glancing at his first officer. "Away from Belle Terre?"

"Only two point three degrees off center, Captain," Spock said.

"Close enough?" McCoy asked.

"Yes, Doctor," Spock said. "Close enough."

The image on the main screen showed the moon rupturing again, only this time the debris from the moon missed Belle Terre. So the planet didn't get destroyed right in the first bang, but Kirk had a dozen problems with this idea.

"If we wait until one hour before the explosion," he said, "won't a collision with another object just set it off?"

"There is a twenty-four percent chance of that occurring," Spock said.

Kirk nodded. That meant it was a seventy-six percent chance it wouldn't happen. And since the explosion was going to occur an hour or so later anyway, it made little difference that he could see, unless they were still too close.

"Wouldn't a collision like you're talking about knock the moon out of orbit?" Sulu asked.

"It will alter the orbit of the moon," Spock said, "and cause massive tidal disturbances on the planet's surface for a number of years. But it will not be a severe enough orbital shift to cause undue destruction on the planet's surface."

"So Belle Terre will survive?" Kirk said.

"Yes," Spock said. "But the exposed side of the

planet will be exposed to an extreme dose of radiation lasting sixteen point three seconds."

"How extreme?" McCoy asked.

"Enough to kill humans, Doctor," Spock said. "And most plant life."

"But only on one side?" Kirk asked. "The other side will be safe?"

"Yes," Spock said. "Shielded by the bulk of the planet itself. However, at the time of the explosion, the planet's main continent will be exposed. Only the small island chains will be on the safe side."

"So the operation could be a success, but we lose the patient anyway?" McCoy asked. "How much sense does that make?"

Spock only looked at him.

"Actually it makes a great deal of sense," Kirk said. "It gives the colonists a place to live, at least until they get the supplies and equipment to get back to Federation space safely. And it gives us some choices in how to protect the olivium."

The bridge around him was silent.

He stared at the graphic on the screen. For the first time in hours it felt as if they had found something that just might work. It had its downsides, clearly. But at least it was better than sending over sixty thousand colonists unguarded into hostile space. He wasn't going to let that happen, yet he also couldn't leave the olivium unguarded.

So the best solution was to save the planet.

"There is one other problem with this idea," Spock said.

"No pin," Sulu said.

Kirk glanced at Sulu, then back at Spock.

"Mr. Sulu is essentially correct," Spock said. "There

is no object in the orbit of Belle Terre of a size sufficient to cause such a rupture in the Quake Moon."

Kirk stared at Spock, then back at the screen that
was again showing the real Quake Moon. Then he took
a deep breath. This was the best chance they had. He
had to run with it.

He turned and faced Spock. "I want you going
through every calculation as many times as is needed to
make sure this will work. Understand?"

Spock nodded.

"Mr. Sulu, you and Mr. Chekov get scanning for any
moon or asteroid the size Spock tells you to search for.
There's got to be one out there somewhere in this system."

"Yes, sir," Sulu said.

Kirk turned to Uhura. "Patch me through to the other
ships. I want them searching, too."

"Even the *Impeller?*" she asked. "It's helping search
for the children."

"Yes," he said. "I want them helping on this as soon
as they find the children."

Kirk moved over and sat back down in his chair as
his crew went silently and efficiently to work around
him. The Quake Moon filled the screen, almost taunt-
ing him. But at the moment it didn't have the power it
had just a short time ago. They had come up with a way
to tame it.

If they could just come up with another moon to
tame it with.

Or, as McCoy had said, a pin.

Chapter Ten

Countdown: 5 Days, 17 Hours

REYNOLD COATES pulled his jacket tighter around himself and then hugged his knees to his chest. The dark shadows of the big cave seemed to wave back and forth in the light from Danny's small fire. They had built the fire between rocks just as Reynold's dad had taught him to do, but the rocks kept him from getting close enough to the fire to get warm. He hadn't been warm since they had come into the cave.

The other kids were sleeping around him, in sleeping bags, as if nothing were going on. But Reynold couldn't get to sleep. Not only was he scared, but he was starting to regret leaving his bed.

Then he remembered that his mother and the governor were going to make them all leave the planet tomorrow. He was going to make them all get back into the ships and go back to Earth.

Reynold and the rest of the kids liked it here too

much. And none of them believed that a moon was going to explode. They all knew it was because the parents didn't want to stay, so they made up the moon story to tell them.

On the way here from Earth some kids' parents and ships had wanted to turn back. They all wanted to go back to Earth. But Reynold didn't want to go back. He wanted to stay right here, on this planet. And if he had to stay in this cave for a while to prove to his mother he wanted to stay, then he would.

He tossed another few sticks on the fire and watched the sparks flare up toward the high ceiling of the cave. It was lucky for them that Diane and Gary had found these caves, tucked into the side of the hill above the colony. Even though there were no big animals in the forest, he didn't want to stay outside all night. This was better.

The mouth of the cave was like a small black dot in the far wall. Every so often he imagined something coming through the opening, but the hole was so small, he'd had trouble getting through. Nothing really big could come in. That thought made him feel safe.

He shivered once, then forced himself to lie down and curl up in his sleeping bag. It was warmer. His dad said it was made out of a special material. He had liked sleeping in it when he and his dad had gone camping before getting in the ships. Maybe after they stayed here, he could talk his mother into going camping with him like Dad used to do. That would be fun.

His mother was going to be mad at him, but at least she would know he wanted to stay. He didn't want to ever leave Belle Terre. He liked the trees and the beach and all the great sand. This was much better than he remembered Earth ever being.

Maybe tomorrow he'd go tell his mom that.

He watched the fire for a few more minutes before the tiredness finally forced him to close his eyes.

Countdown: 5 Days, 17 Hours

Sunn couldn't remember being this tired or hot before. Around them the alien city's buildings towered into the sky, giving some shade from the heat, but not much. For three hours they had walked, first through the fields outside the city, then through the lower buildings, then into the taller structures.

Three long hours of finding nothing.

Three hours closer to having to report back to Captain Kirk. They had to solve the questions of this planet and either consider it a find for the colonists or move on and look for something else. Time was running short.

He signaled that they should stop as he leaned against a wall in the shade. The street between the buildings was cluttered with small debris, a number of transport machines, and nothing else. At least the walking had been smooth so far. Just long and hot.

The buildings like the one he leaned against were made up of a fine-textured, rocklike material, obviously manufactured. From a distance all the buildings looked to be of the same design, smooth, with no windows. But up closer there were clear differences. Every building had windows, but they were mounted flush to the surface and tinted to match the structure.

And every building had types of doors leading out into the street. The doors were where the real differences could be seen. Some were tall, narrow, and plain. Others were huge and decorated in ornate patterns. As they went by, almost every door to every building was closed up tight. At first Sunn hadn't thought that odd, but now he did.

The ground vehicles they had passed seemed to have worked on some sort of air cushion or magnetic cushion to keep them off the surface when moving. There wasn't a wheel on anything in sight. And no dead passengers, either. Just parked vehicles.

"Nothing, Captain," Roger said, studying his scanner and sounding disgusted. "This city is just completely dead. No energy signs, nothing moving. Dead."

Sunn nodded. It was just as their scanners had shown from the ship. Nothing in here except the empty shell of a past civilization. They hadn't even found any clear signs of remains of the inhabitants. Of course, they hadn't gone in any buildings yet, and after one hundred years, the weather would have scoured anything left outside, at least along the path where they had walked.

He stared up at the tall buildings above him. He really wasn't looking forward to going inside. But it seemed they now had no choice. They weren't finding any more answers out here on the street.

He pushed himself away from the wall, wiped the sweat off his forehead with the back of his arm, and looked for the closest door. Directly across the street the building looked sealed, the tall, wide door seemingly still shut tight.

"Let's give that building a try," he said.

He moved across the street with Dar and Roger following. At the door he pushed the ornate handle, but nothing moved. He shoved harder, but the thing was solid. Locked or jammed. It hadn't been opened in a hundred years and either way it wasn't going to come easily.

"Roger, get us in."

Sunn stepped back and watched as Roger trained his

rifle on the middle of the door and fired until the door basically turned red, then vanished in a sour-smelling smoke.

The inside was pitch dark, the light from the street only penetrating a few feet inside the room. Sunn pulled out a flashlight and with it in one hand, and his other hand on the phaser at his hip, he moved in.

The main ground-floor area was large. Huge, actually. So big it swallowed the beam of his light into the distance. Large enough to serve as a hangar for their ship, that much was for sure. And the contents of the room were very different from what they had seen in the street. In here debris was everywhere. Much of it smashed and piled. It took him a moment to realize that this must have been some large store.

And the smell was one of old and rot. A dry smell that seemed to cling to everything. Not at all the fresh smell of the streets and meadows.

"What happened in here?" Roger asked, moving in behind Sunn and panning his beam over the huge space.

"Looks like a riot took place," Dar said.

"Spread out," Sunn said, "and let's see if we can find an answer to that question."

Sunn went straight ahead, Roger to the right, Dar to the left. Slowly Sunn picked his way through what had clearly been a path from the main door through the head-high piles of debris and furniture. He couldn't imagine a culture that could build such beautiful cities having such debris-filled interior rooms. Clearly something or someone had moved all this around. But who? And why?

Smaller trails led off through the piles in both directions. For the moment he was going to stay on the main path that led across the room.

"Captain," Roger shouted out, his voice echoing. "I think you need to see this."

Sunn could barely see across the room where Roger was waving his flashlight beam to show his location. Sunn glanced in the other direction. Dar wasn't that far from him. "Dar, join us."

"On my way," Dar said.

Quickly Sunn went back down the main path through the piles of debris toward the bright light of the door, then turned and headed toward where Roger was signaling.

It was clear that Roger had taken one of the side paths and was now standing almost inside one of the piles of debris. He stepped back as Sunn approached and pointed to an opening in the pile.

Sunn bent down and for the first time came face-to-face with the skeletal remains of one of the planet's past residents. It shocked him and he almost jumped back. But he'd seen hundreds of skeletons and this one was no different. Clearly humanoid, double rows of teeth, wider forehead than a human's, short body. Rags of some sort of cloth covered most of the bones, but Sunn couldn't tell if the person had been female or male from the dress.

Sunn poked his head farther into the hole and saw two other bodies sprawled together farther in. Clearly they had been living in here, in the remains of this store.

He stepped back and let Dar look inside as he shined his light over the vast space and the hundreds, maybe even thousands of piles of furniture and debris that filled the vast space.

"What would cause a culture that was clearly advanced, that could build buildings like these, to die like this?" Sunn asked.

"Not a clue," Roger said.

"They were afraid," Dar said, backing out of the small entrance. Dar pointed around the room. "Inside, nothing at all outside. These people were afraid of something outside. I'm betting we'll find scenes like this in most of the buildings."

"Are you saying these people retreated into this and died?" Roger asked.

"Makes sense," Dar said. "I'll bet they died from lack of supplies. Too afraid to go outside and get them. I didn't see any remains of food around those bones."

"You're right," Roger said. "If it had been disease that killed them, they wouldn't have bunched up together like this. They would have run from the cities and the roads would have been jammed solid with debris."

Sunn had a hunch they were right. Everything outside was neat and clean. Something had driven this advanced civilization indoors to die. But what? And would it be dangerous to the Belle Terre colonists?

"Let's look at some more buildings," Sunn said, turning toward the door. "We need more facts."

After looking in five more buildings, he knew their theory was right. This entire culture seemed to have retreated indoors and died there. They had solved the question of where the residents went. Now they just had to know why before they reported back to Kirk.

What had these people been afraid of?

Countdown: 5 Days, 13 Hours

"Two hours until Gamma Night," Kirk said. "Come on, people, we need to find something that will work."

Kirk paced back and forth in front of his chair. For five hours his crew and three of the other Starfleet ships had searched this system and outside this system, looking for any object large enough to smash into the Quake Moon, yet small enough for them to move. It was turning out not to be such an easy task. Every solar system was full of millions of asteroids, small moons, and comets. Leftover junk from the forming of the system. This one was proving to have even more than normal, but most of it too small.

It had been five hours of "almosts" and "false alarms." Five very long hours.

Spock had worked out the exact details of what needed to be done. And the exact size of the asteroid or moon needed to smash into the Quake Moon to get the best results. They had found two objects that were close to the perfect size. One was a large asteroid outside the system just beyond the sixteenth planet. The other was a small moon in orbit around the gas-giant eleventh planet. The asteroid was slightly too small, the moon slightly too big.

So, after finding each one, Kirk had ordered them to keep looking. But if they didn't find another possible item in the next few minutes, he was going to settle on the moon. They were running out of time with Gamma Night coming on.

Spock said a slightly larger object would be better than smaller by at least two percentage points. To Spock that was a significant difference, so the moon it would be.

Kirk forced himself to stop pacing and sit down just as McCoy entered from the lift. The doctor had convinced Kirk to take a break and get some food two hours ago, and was coming back from doing the same thing.

"I can tell the luck is continuing to be bad," McCoy said. "Just from the look on your faces."

"Luck has nothing to do with it, Doctor," Spock said. "The search continues in a systematic fashion."

Kirk turned to his science officer. "Spock, have you done all the calculations on getting that moon from the eleventh planet into position to hit the Quake Moon?"

"I have," Spock said. "It will be a complex series of events requiring a great deal of force."

"Are you sure it can be done?" Kirk asked. He needed his science officer to be exact. It was what he trusted about him. When Spock said something was possible, it was.

"It can be done," Spock said. "But not easily. We must be in position to begin in six hours, seven minutes, and forty seconds. If everything goes as necessary, the moon would hit the desired location on the Quake Moon exactly sixty-four minutes before the explosion."

"What?" McCoy asked. "You mean to say we're going to be trying to shove a moon out of orbit during Gamma Night?"

"Yes, Doctor," Spock said.

"It's a *small* moon," Sulu said, smiling at the doctor.

Kirk smiled, but McCoy clearly wasn't amused. The problems with sensors and communications during Gamma Night had plagued them since they got within range of the neutron star that was causing it. They were just going to have to deal with it again.

"Spock, will we be able to do what is necessary during the Gamma Night interference?"

"Yes," Spock said flatly.

Kirk wanted one more question answered before he gave the order to try this. Since this was the only attempt they would get at stopping the Quake Moon from exploding, he wanted to make sure everything was thought of.

"What is the largest problem you foresee in moving the moon into position?" Kirk asked, trying to be as exact with his questions as he wanted his first officer to be with his answers.

Spock nodded at the question. "It will take the combined force of several ships, in exact positions, to get the moon moving and out of orbit around the gas giant."

"Understood," Kirk said.

"We will then need the extra force of further colony ships to get the moon to a correct velocity and on the intended line toward Belle Terre and the Quake Moon."

"How many of the colony ships?"

"For the acceleration stages, at least ten of the larger ships," Spock said. "Twelve would be more desirable. However, for slowing and turning the moon into the needed angle and speed to hit the Quake Moon with the desired results, it will take the combined force of every ship."

For a moment there was silence on the bridge. Then McCoy asked, "You're kidding, right?"

"Vulcans do not 'kid,' " Spock said.

"Those ships will be full of all the colonists," McCoy said. "Sixty-two thousand people."

"Possibly," Spock said. "Unless they elect to stay on the far side of the planet."

"And be killed if we fail," McCoy said.

"If we follow this course and the moon explodes instead of ruptures, Doctor," Spock said, "most of the ships involved will be destroyed, including the *Enterprise*. There will not be sufficient time to get out of the danger zone."

The silence on the bridge was the loudest Kirk had ever heard it.

Sulu, Chekov, Uhura, and McCoy all stared at Spock. It seemed that they had not realized this attempt at stopping the Quake Moon from exploding was so risky. There was no doubt it was going to be. The *Enterprise* was going to be connected to the ramming small moon almost right up to the point of impact. If the Quake Moon only ruptured as they hoped, the *Enterprise* would have time to get out of the way. But if it exploded, no ship still inside the inner solar system would survive.

Kirk didn't mind risking the *Enterprise*. And risking the other Starfleet ships. It was part of the duty they all agreed to perform. But he didn't have the right to put the lives of all sixty-two thousand men, women, and children on the line. Only they had that right. It was their colony. And they would have to be told of the risks and the reward to make that choice. That was going to be up to the governor to do. There was time for that.

Kirk glanced around at McCoy, who seemed half stunned at the idea of risking all the colonists. Then Kirk turned to his first officer. "Can it be done?"

"It can, Captain," Spock said.

"That's all I need," Kirk said.

And it was. Right now it was the only option they had, and they had to get it started or even that option was going to pass them by.

He turned to Uhura. "Have all the other Starfleet ships meet us at the eleventh planet at once. Spock will relay details."

"Captain, the *Impeller* has not reported in," she said. "Those children are still lost."

Kirk glanced at Spock. The Vulcan nodded.

119

"The *Impeller* too," Kirk said. "Find the governor and tell him I will be joining him in two minutes. Emergency."

"Yes, sir," Uhura said.

Kirk stood and headed for the door. "Spock, you're with me. We've got a governor to inform about what we are doing."

"Mind if I join you?" McCoy asked.

Kirk glanced at his friend. McCoy had come to love these colonists more than any of the rest of them. It might be a good idea to have him in on this discussion.

"More than welcome," Kirk said. "Mr. Sulu, you have the bridge. Just make sure we're back on board before the Gamma Night sets in."

Countdown: 5 Days, 12 Hours

The transporter beam took Kirk, Spock, and McCoy back to the *Enterprise*, leaving Governor Pardonnet standing alone on the edge of the forest, in the shade of the pine trees.

He felt stunned, almost as if he were sleepwalking, after the conversation with the three men. Kirk had an idea to save Belle Terre. There was a price to pay, and there were high risks, but at least it was an idea that both Kirk and Spock thought might work. But the plan left him with a decision he couldn't shoulder alone.

He took a deep breath of the warm afternoon air, trying to clear his head. There were so many things that needed to be done in the next five days before leaving. So many thousands of details to focus on, yet since last night he'd only been able to focus on the safety of six children. They'd been missing now for over fifteen hours. Adding the *Impeller*'s sensors did not help as much as they'd hoped, as the starship reported that many of the hills around the colony were laced with Kelbonite, which sensors could not penetrate. Those areas could only be searched on foot.

But they *had* searched the hills. Repeatedly. And there was still no sign of the children.

What could have happened to them?

He stared back up through the trees, then shook his head. He had to focus on all of the colonists, not just six. He had been excited when Kirk had first proposed the idea of crashing a small moon into the Quake Moon to rupture the moon and release the pressure. It was a solution.

Then Spock had outlined the results of the rupture. This entire continent would be leveled, massive floods and winds, extreme radiation over this half of the planet. Nothing would survive on this half of the planet and it would be decades before the weather on this continent would settle down to what it was now.

Pardonnet had been shocked, but knew that half a planet was better than no planet. They could survive on the island chains on the other side of the planet long enough to get a foothold back on the main continent. They had come to this planet for the long term. Ultimately, if the planet survived, the weather and replanting would be a short-term problem.

Then Spock had explained what would be needed of the colonist ships.

And McCoy outlined the chances that the moon might explode instead of rupture, giving the colonist ships no time to get out of range.

It had become clear right at that moment that to save this colony, every man, woman, and child would have to agree to risk their lives.

"It's a big decision," McCoy had said.

"It's not my decision to make," Pardonnet had replied. And it wasn't his decision. It was everyone's decision.

But before they could make it, they would have to understand it. The *Enterprise* and the other Starfleet ships were going to set the moon in motion during the Gamma Night. He needed to call all the leaders of the different areas of the colony together for a meeting before the Gamma Night set in. Then afterward they'd present the idea to everyone and see which way the decision went.

He opened his communicator and told his ship to tell all the area leaders and top scientists to meet him in the town hall in two hours. "Tell them it is a critical meeting. Tell them there is a new idea on how to save Belle Terre."

He flipped the communicator closed. That would get them there. Now the question was, where were the six children?

Around him the forest, and one of the last beautiful afternoons of Belle Terre, kept silent.

Part Three

NO TIME

Chapter Eleven

Countdown: 5 Days, 11 Hours

ROGER GOT to the top, looked around the large room, then shouted back down the incline to Sunn. "Found it!"

Sunn, with Dar right behind him, ran up the wide incline that led from the lower floor of this building to the next level. It seemed that not only had this culture shunned wheels on things, it had shunned stairs, preferring instead to build wide, gently sloping ramps that twisted and wound their way through every large building like snakes. Actually, such construction was brilliant in that it allowed for plumbing, electrical, and heating ducts to be built into the ramps, instead of having huge utility cores in the center of every structure. There was no doubt these people were master builders.

What Sunn had been looking for was a communications building of some sort. Basically a news room, where there might be some sort of indication as to what had happened in the end to these people. Some sort of clue as to what had scared them so badly that they had retreated indoors to die.

Sunn, Dar, and Roger had ducked in and out of buildings for the last hour until finally they found this room. And Sunn could see why Roger thought they had found what they were looking for. The room was a mess, as every interior of every building was. The only skeleton here was one slumped over what looked to be a desk in the back. The rest of the room was cluttered with equipment. Massive amounts of equipment on and around all the desks. But the key was the false-looking setlike areas with garish writing and maps of the local area on the wall.

Light was coming in through the dirty windows. It seemed that every ground floor had no windows, but from the second floor upward, every building was mostly windows. Sunn guessed that was why every skeleton they had found had been in the dark, lower levels, since these aliens had clearly been afraid of something outside. This planet had hosted some strange people, Sunn was starting to decide. Especially at the end of their lives, when they chose to live it in the dark.

Sunn moved through the clutter to the skeleton. The entity had clearly been working on something, writing in a type of ink that had long since faded. Sunn pointed to the tabletlike item the entity had been writing on. "Take that back with us. Maybe we can recover enough of it to read."

"Sorry, old friend," Dar said, pushing the skeleton gently aside and putting the tablet in a pouch. The bones held together and a slight dust drifted from the body.

Roger was already bent over one of the machines on

the dead alien's desk. "It's a computer, like others we've found. Completely powerless."

"Can you get it started up again?" Sunn asked, staring at the exposed mass of circuits and boards. Another strange trait of these people had been their desire to leave all working parts right out in the open. Most cultures covered their machinery with boxes, hid it behind walls, or decorated it with something to change its nature. This race had seemed to love the working parts of something left right out in plain sight. It sure made working on them easier, that was for sure.

"I think so," Roger said. "If I can cross-connect my sensor's power source like I did on the other one, it should be enough to run the thing, but not blow the old circuits."

"I wonder why this guy wasn't afraid of the light?" Dar said, pointing to the skeleton. "First one we've seen on an upper floor."

"Maybe we'll find out right now," Roger said, patting the mass of circuits. He tapped a button on his sensor and there was a slight pop and a small screen in the middle of the parts came to life.

Roger watched the snow on the screen for a moment, then said, "So far nothing shorted out. Let me see if I can recover some memory from the storage bank on this thing."

Sunn nodded. What had sent them on this search for a news room of some sort in the first place was the discovery that these machines sitting on desks throughout the city had memory that wasn't dependent on energy to maintain. This culture had discovered a way to store bits of information on the molecular structure of a silicon substance. Since that was the case, Roger said he could recover some of the memory, even after one hundred years of no power to the machines. He had proved that by recovering what looked to be accounting information from a machine in one building.

At this place they hoped for news.

After a moment Roger said, "Here we go."

A creature's face appeared frozen on the screen. Humanoid, close-set eyes, no hair, wide forehead. It was talking, showing the double row of teeth Sunn had seen so much of over the past few hours in all the skeletons.

"This is the last image on the memory," Roger said, "I figured it would be best to start here and work backwards."

"Good idea," Sunn said. "Run it."

Roger punched a button and the alien started talking and moving, clearly not happy with what he was saying. It took the Universal Translator a moment to catch up; then the words the alien was saying became clear.

"The massive blackness that is passing through our sky is not pausing or taking any prisoners. It is our judgment day. It is the time of the passing as we all knew was coming."

The alien took a deep breath **and** went on. "Our planet's entire space fleet has been lost. In the last hour the area of the planet closest to the blackness has lost all communications. We have been unable to contact anyone. The blackness does not kill, but takes all energy from every source. No machines will work after it has passed. It is the judgment."

Again the entity paused. Sunn didn't know what to think. He almost had Roger stop the recording and start it again, but then the entity went on.

"Our area of Nevlin, our city, will be drained into the blackness within a few minutes. Take shelter! Fear the sky! The foretold time of blackness is upon us at last. This is all Elah's time of judgment and we have been judged lacking. The entire surface of Nevlin will soon be black. May we all meet in the next life where the sun always shines upon our people."

The small screen went dead.

Sunn felt stunned.

He glanced at the skeleton of the creature slumped over the edge of the desk in the sunlight. Now he knew their names, the planet's name, and what happened to their civilization. All its energy was sucked from it, literally.

"Why did they all die?" Dar asked. "It was only their energy that was taken from them? They could find new energy sources."

"They all died because they all thought it was their duty to die," Roger said. "Religion of some sort, more than likely."

Sunn glanced at Roger, then at the skeleton. Well, they had answers. These Elah had died of fear after something black in the sky took their energy. Sunn could just hear Captain Kirk. "Do you know what the blackness was?"

It seemed that by finding these answers, they now had another larger question. And a question that had to be answered before this planet could be deemed safe for the colonists.

Countdown: 5 Days, 10 Hours

Pardonnet had just finished explaining to the other leading members of the colony what Captain Kirk had proposed to do. The room was silent; all hundred or so people who had come seemed stunned. He took a drink from a glass of water on the table beside him, letting the coolness of the water calm him. He'd talked about thousands of different things over the years preparing to lead this colony. But nothing had prepared him for this kind of decision.

"Any questions at all?" he asked, finally breaking the silence.

"After the Gamma Night," Dr. Connie Baxter said from the back, "are you going to tell all the colonists?"

"I will," Pardonnet said. "We'll set a time here, in this meeting, and hope that everyone can get to a communications screen or a central location somewhere. Then for the three hours following the announcement, I propose everyone vote."

"Majority wins?" someone asked from the back.

"Do you see another way?" Pardonnet asked. "All the ships need to be involved in the effort, and we all need to be on the ships. Majority on this rules and there's not time to take the dissenting voters anywhere safe, even if we had someplace safe to go."

"And we can't spare one ship to take all the children to safety?" someone asked.

Pardonnet shook his head. "I asked the exact question of Kirk. Every ship is needed, especially the large ones, or everything might fail."

He took a deep breath and squared his shoulders. "Look, people, we are in this colony together. Captain Kirk has found another way to save our planet and this colony. I think the chance is our best hope for a future. Any future, to be honest with you. I know I have no future back on Earth. My home is here now."

Around the room heads were nodding. Almost everyone in this colony had never expected ever to see Earth or Federation space again.

"Okay, then," he said after another long moment of

silence. "The evacuation needs to continue at full pace. Everyone has to have all the supplies and personal belongings on board their ship in thirty-six hours whether we vote to try this idea or not."

That deadline seemed to take energy out of the air as people slumped and a few groaned. Pardonnet ignored them and went on. "Pass the information from this meeting to as many others as you can over the Gamma Night and stand ready for my general announcement and then the vote. We have a chance to save our planet. I am hoping we all vote to take it."

With that he stepped away from the table, indicating that the meeting was over. The room filled with talking, but he didn't stay to get involved. He headed for the door. He could spare a few more hours right now helping in the search for the children and he was going to take them.

Those six kids were out there somewhere, and if it were up to him, they would be on board the ships in thirty-six hours, no matter what the decision was about the moon.

Countdown: 5 Days, 9 Hours

Reynold looked at the entrance to the cave. From what little light was coming through the brush, he could tell it was starting to get dark again. His mom was going to be really, really mad at him after this. And he knew she was worried. But as Danny had said, if they went back now, they'd still just end up on the ships going back to Earth.

Reynold knew that Danny was right. Danny was usually right.

All day they had spent playing games and eating.

Each of them had brought lots of food, and the caves were pretty big, so it had been fun exploring and eating. But now it was getting dark and he missed his mother. He'd never been away from her this long before.

And he really missed his dad.

He tossed a few more sticks on the fire and rubbed his hands together to warm them. He'd gotten warm during the night in his sleeping bag, but now was cold again.

"Hey!" Diane said, appearing out of the dark in the back of the cave. "Come look. I found a new cave!"

He jumped up, taking his flashlight and a candy stick with him. Finding new caves was always fun.

For the next few hours of exploring, he forgot about leaving Belle Terre and going back to Earth. Looking through new caves was just too much fun.

Countdown: 5 Days, 5 Hours

Kirk stared at the fuzzy screen. He could barely see the small moon they were about to knock out of orbit around the gas giant. The moon was so small, and this system so uncharted, that no one had bothered to name it. Sulu was calling it the Needle and so far, much to McCoy's annoyance, the name was sticking.

Gamma Night blocked most of the sensors and communications with other ships. They had managed to rig a tight-beam system that allowed him to communicate with the other Starfleet ships near the small moon. The system worked on relays, one ship to the other, and remained constantly open, in case it was needed. That way if something went wrong, he could at least call off the attempt.

But all the preparations for moving the moon had been done before Gamma Night had set in six hours ago. Tractor beams had been calibrated and set, each ship attached by tractor to the small moon. Timing had been worked out to the second. Since then they had just done more waiting.

Kirk tried to stare through the fuzziness of the screen. It seemed that since this fleet had left Federation space, he'd done more waiting than any other time in his career. Space always was basically long stretches of boredom punctuated by short moments of activity. But for some reason, on this mission, with this colony, he'd noticed the waiting more than usual.

"One minute," Spock said.

Behind them the lift door slid open and McCoy joined the bridge crew.

"All systems ready, sir," Sulu said. "Tractor beam still locked and holding."

"Stand by," Kirk said. He hoped the rest of the ships were ready as well. Nothing was coming across the tight-beam emergency frequency, so he was assuming they were. He had no other choice at the moment. They were mostly blind and basically deaf out here, trying to shove a moon out of orbit. A thousand things could go wrong. He just hoped none of them did.

"I see I'm just in time for the big show," McCoy said, moving down to stand by Kirk's chair.

"Let's hope there's not much to see," Kirk said.

"On that screen, how could we see if something did go wrong?" McCoy asked.

Kirk didn't even want to think about that.

"Fifteen seconds," Spock said.

"On Spock's command, Mr. Sulu," Kirk said.

"Aye, sir," Sulu said.

"Five," Spock said.

"Four.

"Three.

"Two.

"One.

"Fire engines."

"One-quarter impulse now!" Sulu said.

Around Kirk the *Enterprise* shook and the noise level increased to a dull roar as the ship struggled to push on the moon. He could feel the deck under his feet shudder slightly.

"Seven minutes and sixteen seconds to shutdown," Spock said.

"Status, Mr. Sulu?" Kirk asked.

"Tractor beam holding firm. Engines overheating slightly as expected, but nothing more."

"Good."

He sat, watching the fuzzy image of the moon on the screen, waiting again.

Waiting for something to go wrong.

Waiting for the time to pass.

Waiting.

Maybe it was getting older that was causing him to notice the waiting more. Time seemed more important and waiting more worthless. But at times there was just no choice. They all had to just wait.

No one on the bridge, not even McCoy, said anything.

Seven minutes of silence, seven long minutes of waiting later Mr. Spock said, "Cut engines now!"

"Engines cut," Sulu said.

"Release tractor beam," Kirk ordered.

"Released," Sulu said.

Kirk looked around at Mr. Spock. "Let's hope that worked."

"We'll know in three hours and forty-two minutes," Spock said. "I will be able to take accurate readings at that point."

"Well, I'm glad I didn't miss that," McCoy said, the sarcasm clear in his voice. "You up for some dinner, Jim?"

Kirk nodded. No point in sitting up here waiting for three more hours. He stood and smiled at Bones. "Only if you're buying."

Bones laughed. "You think your company is worth that much, huh?"

"Would you rather eat with Spock?" Kirk asked as they headed for the lift.

Both of them laughed as they entered the lift and turned to face the clearly puzzled look of the Vulcan.

Chapter Twelve

Countdown: 4 Days, 19 Hours

LILIAN COATES stood outside her dome home, brushed her hair back out of her eyes, and stared up into the trees. Another night had come and gone and still no sign of Reynold or the other children. Almost a thousand people at different times had spread out around the main colony area, searching, calling, walking. The children had just vanished. Even the Starfleet ship *Impeller* had used its powerful scans to cover as much of the area within one hundred miles as they could. And the parts the *Impeller* couldn't cover had been searched on foot dozens of times. Nothing.

Yet in her heart she knew Reynold was alive. But her heart wouldn't lead her to him. It just kept pushing her to keep searching and searching.

Slowly, others who had been searching had stopped and gone back to packing, promising if they had time they would return. And right now she'd heard there was a vote going on. Captain Kirk had another idea to save the colony, but it would risk the life of every colonist. Governor Pardonnet had given a speech and then called for a vote. It would be over shortly, or maybe it already was. It didn't matter to her at the moment. Only finding Reynold mattered.

Over the last few days she had come back to her home, to her and Reynold's home, every few hours to see if he had returned. She also used the time to freshen up, get a small bite to eat, and then return to the search.

Around here people were moving belongings out of their domes, taking them to beam-up points. She knew that many of the homes along the two-week-old road were already empty. But she had no doubt that six were not.

Six families were staying, at least until the very last minute. She doubted if she'd be able to leave at all without Reynold. The other families had other children to think about. They would have to go. With Tom dead, Reynold was all she had left. She'd either find him or die trying.

She stared at the tree-covered hill above the colony. For some reason her little voice kept pulling her back to that hill, even though it had been completely searched. At this point, she had nothing else to lose, so she might as well follow her little voice.

It couldn't lead her any farther off track than she had already gone.

She started up through the trees alone. The few searchers who were left were scattered far and wide. There was so little time left. At this point, it was going to take a miracle to find Reynold.

And she had never been one to believe in miracles. Maybe it was about time she started.

Countdown: 4 Days, 19 Hours

"In six hours we're going to need seven colony ships, Governor," Kirk said. "At least three of them must be the Conestogas."

Governor Pardonnet's face filled the main screen. To Kirk, the young governor was starting to look older. He had bags under his eyes and for the first time that Kirk could remember, his jacket seemed wrinkled. The fire that usually lit Pardonnet's eyes wasn't there at the moment.

"I know, Captain," Pardonnet said. "The vote will be over and counted shortly and I'll let you know the results. If the people don't want to take the chance, there will be no point in sending the ships. There will be time."

"Thank you, Governor. I'll be standing by. Kirk out."

The image of the governor was replaced with a small, pitted moon that everyone was now calling the Needle. Its entire size fit on the viewscreen, unlike the images of the Quake Moon Kirk had been staring at for days. This moon was only a fraction of the size of the Quake Moon, which was why they could move it. And why it would only rupture the skin of the Quake Moon instead of causing the complete explosion.

Their push during Gamma Night had gotten the Needle started right on track, and given it enough velocity to escape the orbit of the gas-giant planet. In the last two hours the Starfleet ships had already nudged it three times, helping it gain speed, slightly changing its course. But the crucial first course change and acceleration was going to need the colony ships to help. If the colony voted to go back to Earth, it wasn't going to matter.

And if that happened, he'd be faced with the problem of what to do with the colonists. He doubted he could let them head off unprotected, yet at the same time he really couldn't stop them. His duty was to protect them, and to protect the vast importance of the olivium. Millions would die if he lost control of the olivium. But sixty-two thousand colonists might die if he let them leave unprotected.

He stared at the Needle on the screen, its pitted surface rotating slowly. He hoped the colonists went for this idea and it worked.

The other option was not something he wanted to face.

Countdown: 4 Days, 19 Hours

Pardonnet paced in the small room as the electronic votes were verified with each colonist's personal identification number, then recorded. Judith Short and Harvey Ray Johns, two of the colony's official treasurers, were doing the work. Judith was a short, young woman with three children. Harvey was tall, thin, and had a skin condition that caused his face to always seem sunburned.

Pardonnet watched them for a moment as their fingers flew over the keys, working. They were both so intent on their work, he didn't want to even ask how it was going. There was nothing he could do to help. In a few minutes he would know the results. But there was no way he could sit still.

He paced and thought, the only sound in the small room the clicking of computer keys.

Off and on over the last few hours he'd gone out searching for the children. Twice he'd promised parents of one or another of the children that everything possible was being done. And he hadn't been lying to them. Everything was being done. There just wasn't that much anyone could do.

And now, with this vote, either way his free time was ended. It was going to take every waking minute left available to get supplies loaded, people loaded, and ships either out of danger or helping with the moon. But he wasn't going to forget the missing children. He'd make sure the search continued with as many people as possible, for as long as possible.

"Governor," Judith Short said.

He turned to see her smiling face. He had no idea what the smile meant. Harvey was also smiling, his face even redder than usual.

"The vote is finished," she said. "Overwhelming to try to save the colony. Almost unanimous."

"You're kidding?" He was so stunned, that was all he could think to say.

"I'm not," she said, smiling even harder.

He could feel the energy coming back into his body as if someone had opened up the flood gates. He squared his shoulders, brushed a hand through his hair, and then said, "Great!"

What else could he say?

He reached into his pocket and pulled out his communicator. "Put me through to Captain Kirk. We've got a planet to save."

The voice of Captain Chalker on the other side said, "Hot diggidy dog, we're staying."

Pardonnet smiled, then glanced at the still smiling faces of Harvey and Judith. It seems he wasn't the only one who didn't want to leave.

Countdown: 4 Days, 17 Hours

Reynold Coates stared at his friend Danny.

Danny was mad, both at Reynold and at Diane. That much was clear, even in the light inside the cave from the fire. Reynold had said he thought it was time to go back. It was starting to get dark again outside.

Diane had agreed and Danny had gotten mad. The others had said nothing. Danny was sort of their leader and none of them liked it when he got mad.

"It won't do any good if we go now," Danny said.

"Why not?" Diane said.

"We need to wait one more night. That way they won't leave at all."

"How do you know that?"

"I just know," Danny said. "I heard my dad say that today was the day they all needed to leave. If we go back tomorrow, he won't be able to go."

Reynold stared at Danny. Danny was usually right about things, but Reynold didn't know anymore. He missed his mom.

"Look," Danny said, "we just eat, go to sleep, and it will seem like almost no time has passed. Then we can go back in the light."

Reynold liked that idea. Coming up here in the dark had been scary. The cave was safe and fun, but the forest scared him a lot at night.

"Going through the trees in the light is better," Reynold said.

Diane glanced at the fading light coming through the

brush-covered entrance to the cave, then nodded. "Okay, in the light is better."

"Great!" Danny said.

Reynold sat down on his sleeping bag and pulled it over him. One more night wouldn't be too bad. Then he could go home. It would be good to see his mother again, even though she was going to yell at him something awful.

Chapter Thirteen

Countdown: 4 Days, 14 Hours

SUNN SLOUCHED in his captain's chair, very glad to be back in the *Rattlesnake* again. This planet Nevlin, as the past residents had called it, was beautiful, of that there was no doubt. And those Elah cities were wonderful to look at from a distance, but walking around for hours inside those buildings, among the skeletons of the Elah, had gotten on all their nerves. Especially after they had learned that the entire race had basically committed suicide after an unknown black object from space sucked all the energy from all their buildings and equipment.

Why a smart, advanced race like the one that had built those cities had decided to stay inside and starve to death was beyond Sunn. It was clearly one of the more alien things he'd seen in all his years of exploring. There had clearly been something about that black thing from space that had scared them not only once, but at another time far in their past. That meant it just might live around this system somewhere, whatever it was.

"Well," Roger said, dropping down into his station's chair, "are we headed back to Belle Terre to tell them about our find?"

Sunn looked at Roger. He'd stopped and taken the time for a shower. Dar was doing that now and Sunn had plans to do so shortly. He felt, as Roger and Dar had felt, that he needed to wash the smell of death off of himself. But first he had needed to check on all the ship's systems and set up some long-range system-wide scans. If that big black thing was anywhere near, or coming back this direction, he wanted to know about it.

"Nope," Sunn said. "We got a black monster from the sky to track."

"You're kidding, right?" Roger asked.

"Nope," Sunn said again. "I'm not giving this planet a clean bill of health until I know more about what sucked that energy away from it. Or at least try to find out."

"We got time?" Roger asked.

"We've got at least another two days," Sunn said, "before we have to head back for the big explosion."

"You don't think Kirk has found a way to stop it yet?"

Sunn laughed. "Knowing what I know of James Kirk, it wouldn't surprise me. But just in case, I want to give him and the colonists some good news. And as much information as we can. Don't you?"

"Actually, I do," Roger said. "This wouldn't be such a bad place to settle if you spent some time cleaning out those buildings."

"Couldn't agree more," Sunn said. "Good ground for crops, lots of water, and clean air. Even without the cities it would be a good planet." He pushed himself to his feet. "Watch the scans I have set up. I need a shower."

Two hours later, after studying the information they had gotten from the records of the dead race, they lifted off, this time not in search of a planet, but in search of a giant black monster that had terrorized one.

Countdown: 4 Days, 13 Hours

The ten colony ships and four Starfleet ships were in tight formation near the small moon everyone called the Needle. Kirk studied the formation, trying to see anything wrong with it. But nothing was obvious, at least visually.

They had ten minutes until the big push that would send the Needle accelerating toward Belle Terre and the Quake Moon. This was only step two. The big step would be in a few days, when all the ships had to turn and push this small moon into line with the Quake Moon. Kirk wasn't that worried about this phase. If something went slightly wrong here, they could adjust as the moon hurtled inward toward Belle Terre. But in turning the moon right before the explosion, they only had one chance. And if they did that wrong, nothing would be left of this colony.

"All ships' tractor beams are reading green and attached," Sulu said. "Standing by."

"Hope we don't tear that thing apart," McCoy said from his position on the rail behind Kirk's chair.

"Spock's got the tractor beams balanced," Kirk said, "don't you Mr. Spock?"

"There is a six point four percent chance the small moon will be torn apart by the thrust. That is the best I could do, Captain."

"Good enough," Kirk said.

"I hope," McCoy said.

Kirk glanced around at where his Chief Engineer Scott stood. "Scotty, everything ready to go?"

"Ready and waiting, Captain," Scotty said.

"Good. Keep her that way. Uhura, patch me in to each colony ship's captain, one at a time."

"Yes, sir," Uhura said.

Over the next few minutes he checked in with every ship, making sure each was ready and completely informed on what they were going to do. Every colony ship's captain looked tired and harried. Getting their ships loaded and ready for another long, deep space trip was no easy matter, even when done slowly. But having to do it quickly, and with limited supplies was asking them to do the impossible.

"Thirty seconds," Spock said after Kirk had talked to the last person.

"Open a channel to all ships for Mr. Spock," Kirk ordered.

"Channel open, Captain," Uhura said.

"On Mr. Spock's mark, Sulu," Kirk said.

"Understood, sir," Sulu said.

"Ten seconds," Spock said to all the ships.

Kirk watched the small moon in front of them. Very shortly that small moon would be traveling at a far, far greater speed.

"Five seconds," Spock said.

The time seemed to stretch. Kirk glanced at each of his crew. As always, they were calm and poised, ready for anything. This crew had been through far too much together to let something like this excite them too much.

Finally Spock said to all the ship's captains, "One-quarter impulse. Now."

The *Enterprise* again shook slightly around them as the ship's engines shoved against the small moon.

"Tractor holding," Sulu said.

"Engines are doin' just fine, sir," Scotty said.

"Mr. Spock?" Kirk said to his science officer. "Are we on track?"

"Affirmative, Captain," Spock said without looking away from his scope.

"Good, now let's just hold it for one minute longer."

"Sixty-four seconds longer, Captain," Spock said.

"The *Yukon* reports trouble, sir," Uhura said.

"Damn," McCoy said softly.

The *Yukon* was one of the big Conestogas. It was already mostly full of colonists. "Get me Captain Battersey," Kirk ordered, "on screen."

The Conestoga's Captain Battersey came on, her wrinkled face staring at something in front of her for a moment before she looked up. Battersey was one of the more experienced and level-headed of the colony captains—she'd been instrumental in stopping a nasty bit of sabotage on the trip out. She and her husband had taken this assignment with the intent of staying on Belle Terre and retiring.

"Our tractor beam is failing, Captain," Battersey said.

"How long can you hold it?" Kirk asked, glancing at Sulu, who was monitoring all the ship's tractor beams.

"Thirty seconds, maybe," Battersey said. "But I wouldn't push that."

Sulu nodded, glancing back at Kirk.

"Spock?" Kirk asked, turning to his science officer.

"Without the *Yukon*'s tractor beam, the balance of force against the moon will be shifted. There is a high probability of tearing the moon apart."

Kirk nodded. They had to shut down and shut down fast. At this point this little moon was the only hope they had.

"Channel open to all ships," Kirk said.

"Open, sir," Uhura said.

"All ships?" Kirk asked, just to confirm. The last thing they needed was one ship not getting the word.

"All ships," Uhura confirmed.

"On my mark, everyone cut engines. Then on my command five seconds later release your tractor beams."

Kirk forced himself to take a deep breath to give each ship's captain a moment to get his people ready.

"Ready? Now!"

Kirk waited the five seconds then said, "Cut tractor beams!"

"All ships stopped," Sulu reported. "All tractor beams disengaged."

Kirk glanced up at Captain Battersey still on the screen. "Let me know as soon as possible when you can finish repairs. I'll send over my chief engineer."

"Thanks, Captain," Battersey said. "We can use the help."

The image on the screen went back to the small moon.

"On my way, Captain," Scott said, heading for the door.

"That was too close," McCoy said.

"That it was, Doctor," Kirk said. He took a deep breath, then turned to Spock, who was still studying his screens. "I assume, Mr. Spock, that the shove we gave the Needle wasn't enough."

"Correct, Captain," Spock said, without looking around. "In six hours and ten minutes we are going to need the ships that are currently present, plus four other colony ships, to push the moon for exactly two minutes and seven seconds at one-quarter impulse."

"That will put this moon on the proper path?"

"Exactly," Spock said.

"Good," Kirk said.

"I think you just might be expecting the impossible," McCoy said. "I don't think some of these colony ships can maintain that level of stress on their ships for thirty seconds, let alone over two minutes."

Kirk knew McCoy was right, but at the moment they had no choice. "We'll cross that bridge when we come to it, Doctor."

"Actually, Captain," Spock said, "the doctor is correct."

"Well I'll be," McCoy said, clearly surprised at Spock's comment. "Wish I had that recorded."

"How's that, Mr. Spock?"

"If the next attempt fails," Spock said, "we will be unable to change the course of the moon enough to get it into the correct position."

Kirk didn't like the sound of that at all. "So what do you suggest, Mr. Spock?"

"More ships, sir," Spock said. "With more ships we can decrease the amount of speed each ship needs to apply, thus reducing the amount of strain on the tractor beams and engines."

"Okay," Kirk said. "But what if one fails even at the lower speed?"

"We would then be able to adjust with the remaining ships at a higher speed to compensate. Or possibly create a backup system for each ship."

"And that will increase our chances of success?"

"Yes, sir, it will."

Kirk glanced at McCoy who only shrugged. "How many colony ships would you suggest we use, Mr. Spock."

"All of them."

McCoy laughed. "I can tell you that the governor isn't going to like this."

"All of them?" Kirk asked, staring at his science officer. "Why? Explain."

"All ships involved with this course change, and all available ships staying with the moon for at least the last forty-eight hours, would increase our chances of putting this small moon into the correct position at the correct speed on the Quake Moon by almost seventy percent."

"That much, huh?" Kirk said.

"And thus having the rupture occur and saving the planet," McCoy said.

"That is the plan, Doctor," Spock said.

Kirk stared at the expressionless face of his science officer for a moment, then turned to Uhura. "Inform the colony ships they can return to Belle Terre for the moment, but to be back here, in position, in five hours. And patch me through to Governor Pardonnet. He's not going to like this."

"I'd say that's an understatement," McCoy said, "if I've ever heard one."

Chapter Fourteen

Countdown: 4 Days, 13 Hours

PARDONNET STOOD in the small communications room of the town hall and tried to catch his breath. Luckily no one else was in the room. He couldn't believe what he was hearing from Captain Kirk. He was asking that the entire evacuation of the colony be finished in less than six hours. Four full days ahead of when the plan was to be finished.

"Impossible," Pardonnet said. "Just impossible. Do you know what is left to do, Captain?"

"I don't actually care at this point, Governor," Kirk said, his face hard and angry on the small communications screen. "Get your people on the ships within five hours. Otherwise you're dooming this planet and your people. That simple."

"But if this doesn't work," Pardonnet asked, "what then? We won't have the supplies to make it back to Federation space."

"Governor, face facts," Kirk said. "You don't have the supplies now, even if you had the entire time to load everything back on board. If this fails, we'll face getting you and all the colonists to safety then."

"How?" Pardonnet demanded.

"One problem at a time," Kirk said, his voice cold and low. "Right now there's still a good chance of saving this planet, of saving this colony. And if we do that, your worry about getting back to Federation space doesn't matter, now does it?"

Then Kirk smiled, a humorless smile that Pardonnet didn't much like at all. "What are your priorities, Governor? Retreating in failure or fighting to save your new home?"

Pardonnet's first inclination was to scream at Kirk, but somehow he managed to not do that.

He took a long, slow breath, staring into the intent eyes of Kirk. The truth of what the captain had said had cut deep. The colonists had voted almost unanimously to fight for the planet, to take the chances needed to save Belle Terre. It wasn't his position to get in the way now.

The colonists had decided to fight. He had wanted them to decide that way. This was only a change in the battle plan. Nothing more.

"All right, Captain," Pardonnet said, keeping his voice low and even. "The colonists will be loaded and the ships in position in five hours. Will that be satisfactory?"

"Perfectly, Governor," Kirk said, leaning back and nodding. "It's the right decision. Kirk out."

Pardonnet sat staring at the blank screen for a moment. He had just promised Kirk the evacuation of all the colonists could be finished in five hours and he had no idea if that was even physically possible. A large number of colonists were already back on board the ships, but he had no idea how long it would take to get the rest there. Sixty-two thousand people was simply a lot of people to move, especially quickly.

He snapped the communications link back on and called his ship. Captain Chalker answered.

"Tell all ship's captains that every colonist must be on board their ships in five hours. Initiate emergency evacuation procedures. People first, then food supplies, and then if there's time get personal effects. Contact me if there are any problems."

"Yes, Governor," Captain Chalker said without even a question.

Pardonnet cut the connection and stared at the unit. He had about twenty people to get the word to in all the different branches off the colony scattered around the world. But first he'd better get it started here, in the main colony area first.

Pardonnet stood and headed for the door. Five hours to do the impossible. Captain Kirk was known for being able to pull off the impossible.

Pardonnet strode into the other room, shoulders back, ready to work. It was time to see if he could do it too.

Countdown: 4 Days, 10 Hours

Lilian Coates came back off the mountain, flashlight in hand, into what was now a partial ghost town, partial beehive of activity. It seemed if anyone was moving, they were running. Something clearly had changed and she hadn't heard about it.

Over the last three hours she'd climbed the side of the hill in the forest above the colony, calling out

Reynold's name every hundred steps. She had heard nothing, and ran into no other searchers.

Now she was back to check if Reynold had returned to their home. The lights were still on in and around many of the domes, but even this late at night the place felt too quiet, too deserted.

There didn't seem to be anyone left here. Everything was going on down below in the main colony area.

She quickly checked her house for Reynold, called his name once again, then went down toward the center of the colony. At the beam-up point at least a hundred people were waiting. Around them were cases of clothes and other personal effects.

She stopped the first person she met, a bald man with large eyes and a worried look. "What's happened?"

"Problems with the moons," he said. "That's all I know. Evacuation has been moved up. Only two hours left. You'd better get your clothes and get to a beam-out point."

The news slammed her in the stomach like someone had punched her.

She couldn't breathe.

Tears filled her eyes.

That couldn't be possible.

What about her son?

The other children?

"I'm sorry," the man said. "But I got to go. My wife's waiting to beam up."

He turned and headed into the remaining crowd, not once looking back.

She slumped to the ground and sat, trying to get her breath back, watching the crowd move steadily toward the beam-up platform. They were vanishing almost as fast as they could move into position.

It was happening.

It was real.

Everyone was leaving.

She pushed herself up and headed into the center of town toward the town hall. If the governor was anywhere, he'd be there. He couldn't let this happen. He'd been up there on the hillside helping search for Reynold himself. They couldn't just leave her son on this planet, alone.

She forced the thought away before it overwhelmed her. She wouldn't leave Reynold.

That much she knew for sure.

The governor was standing, talking to a group of three men when she entered the building. There were a few dozen other people working at a frantic pace in other parts of the large area. When she was about halfway across the room he looked up and saw her. The look of recognition was instant and he went white, as if he'd suddenly remembered there were still six lost children.

As she got closer he excused himself and the other men stepped quickly away. The governor squared his shoulders and stepped toward her.

"What about the children?" she asked, her voice loud and carrying on purpose. She wanted everyone close by to hear what she was saying. "Are you going to just leave them?"

"Lilian," Governor Pardonnet said, "we have no choice. If we leave now there's a chance we can save this planet and many more lives."

"And sacrifice six children in the process?" Lilian shouted. She so wanted to smash the man, hit him, blame him for Tom's death, for losing Reynold. She needed something, someone to blame.

"I'm not sacrificing anyone," Pardonnet said, his voice cold and low and cutting. The man had power in his voice and right at that point he was turning the full force of it on her. "We've spent valuable time and resources over the past two days searching for your son and the rest of those children. At this point there is nowhere else to look." He took a deep breath and looked her directly in the eye. "If there was, do you think I'd be in here?"

His words snapped her anger like a twig underfoot in the forest. The large room was deathly silent as everyone stared at them. She looked at him, then slumped into a chair, fighting back the tears. "I know," she said.

He sat down beside her and put his hand on her shoulder. Around them the rest of the room suddenly broke into motion again as everyone went back to what they were doing.

"I'm sorry about Reynold," Pardonnet said. "I honestly am."

"Why the rush?" Lilian asked, getting the tears under control. She didn't have time to cry. "What happened? Is the moon about to explode?"

"No," Pardonnet said. "Not yet anyway. But every colony ship is needed to help get the ramming moon into position to stop the explosion."

"And there will be no time for the ships to come back here?" Lilian asked. "In four days?"

"Kirk and his crew don't think so," Pardonnet said. "Our best chance of saving this colony is to fight for it in space. And that's what we're doing."

Lilian nodded. Even in her anger the reason made sense. She pushed herself to her feet. "Good luck to you, Governor."

She turned and started back toward the front door. She had long ago gone past simple tired and into complete exhaustion. But she had to keep searching. Keep pushing forward. There was nothing else left for her to do.

"Wait!" Pardonnet said. "I gather you're going to stay and continue to look?"

"Wouldn't you if it was your only son?"

He nodded. "I would. So there are a few things you need to know, both for your own protection and if you find your son and the others."

She stopped and looked up into his eyes. The man truly did care for her, and for his colony. That much was clear. He was just doing the best he could with a nasty set of circumstances.

And so was she.

"What is it?" she asked.

"Do you have a watch?"

She felt her wrist to make sure it was there, then nodded.

"Note the time now," the governor said. He waited until she did as he said, then went on, talking fast. "In exactly one hundred and five hours, if our plan succeeds, this continent will be blanketed with a very short burst of high radioactivity followed shortly by extreme shock waves. During that time you need to be under cover. As much and as thick as you can find. This building has a basement that might work. Understand?"

She nodded and glanced at her watch one more time to make sure she had the time fixed in her head. "One hundred and five hours. Thank you, Governor."

"Good luck to you," he said.

"From the sounds of it," she said as she started again

for the door, "you and everyone else is going to need it as much as I am."

Countdown: 4 Days, 10 Hours

McCoy waited at the screen in sickbay as Uhura put his call to the surface through. He was like Jim in that he was getting tired of the waiting so much. He never really had been that good at waiting, but lately it seemed he was growing more and more impatient. Jim figured it was age-related. More than likely, he was right. Neither of them were getting any younger, that was for sure.

After a moment the face of Dr. Audry came on the screen. Clearly she had had very little sleep, if any, since the last time McCoy saw her. He could imagine that there was just too much to do, with far too few hours to do it. He wished he could be there helping. But his place was on the *Enterprise* at the moment. Waiting.

Dr. Audry smiled. "Dr. McCoy, good to see your face. I bet you're checking up on our little green beasties, aren't you?"

McCoy laughed. "Exactly." That bacteria was far, far too valuable to the Federation to let it perish at this point. He had no doubt that Dr. Audry and the others could save it, but he couldn't help but call and check.

"Well, I have good news to report," Audry said. "We have managed, even with the accelerated schedule, to get major samples on every colony ship."

"Great," McCoy said. The news was like a weight off his shoulders. He hadn't realized he'd been worrying about the bacteria so much.

"In fact," Dr. Audry said, "I was just about to try to contact you to ask if we could transport some storage containers to the *Enterprise* as well?"

"I don't think we're planning on being back any-where near transporter range before all the fireworks start," McCoy said.

"I figured as much," Audry said. "So we've loaded the containers destined for the *Enterprise* on two of the colony ships. You can have them transported to you when we get into position near your ship."

"Of course," McCoy said. "I'm going to feel safer having major samples of this bacteria in every ship, in-cluding this one."

"I agree," Dr. Audry said, laughing. "Who knows where this bacteria just might come in handy."

McCoy laughed also. The bacteria was going to help agriculture all over the Federation and Dr. Audry knew that. They just had to make sure it got saved.

"Contact me when the ships carrying the *Enterprise* samples are in range," McCoy said.

"Glad to," Dr. Audry said. "Talk to you in a few hours."

With that Dr. Audry cut the connection.

McCoy sighed with relief. He would feel better hav-ing samples on board the *Enterprise*. He stood and headed for the cargo bay. He was going to need a safe place to store the samples and a controlled environ-ment. Better to get that set up now before the samples got here.

Besides, it would give him something to do besides just wait.

Countdown: 4 Days, 10 Hours

Sunn had spent the last four hours with Roger and Dar, working over the records they had recovered from the Elah. From everything thing they could tell, the

"Blackness" had come in from outside the system, passed very near the planet without really touching it, and then moved on, all at a constant speed.

"I'll bet that whatever it was didn't even notice it was near a planet," Roger had said.

"Killed by an indifferent god," Dar had said.

Whether it knew what it was doing or not, something about the Blackness sucked every tiny bit of energy off the planet. That had left the Elah, an advanced culture, without one scrap of energy in anything. No transportation, no communication, no lights and heat. It had taken them and basically tossed them back into their equivalent of the stone age.

Sunn was convinced that if that had happened to man, humans would have simply climbed back. Roger had agreed. No way would something like this have stopped the human race.

But for some reason, the Elah culture believed that this Blackness was some sort of god, and that taking their energy was the sign that it was time for them to move to their next existence.

So with the arrival of the Blackness and suddenly having every scrap of their energy taken from them, almost all of the Elah had simply curled up in the buildings and starved to death.

There were signs that a few of the Elah had tried to go on. Roger, with scans from the buildings, had found signs of a few camps of Elah among the buildings. It seemed that in this one city along about two hundred had managed to stay outside after the Blackness left. Roger had called them the nonreligious ones. But clearly not enough had not believed in the sign of the Blackness, because those that tried to stay outside and start over had soon died off.

As Dar had said, "These aliens had never heard of the old cliché, *When the going gets tough, the tough get going.*" The going got tough for their entire civilization and they had just all rolled over and died.

But they had left a few records.

The Elah had traced and recorded, with star charts, the exact time and path of the Blackness as it approached and then entered their system. They gave no hint as to what it was, how big it was, or anything else. It was simply referred to as the Blackness. But in their ancient records, they had accounts of it coming from that direction before.

So Sunn figured that was where it would be now. He dropped into his captain's chair and glanced at Roger. "Course laid in?"

"Ready when you are."

"Dar?"

"Ready to chase the darkness," Dar said.

"That's Blackness," Roger said.

"Whatever," Dar said, laughing.

"Let's do it," Sunn said.

The *Rattlesnake* turned and, slick as could be, jumped to warp. They had less than four days to find this thing and report back to Kirk about the planet. Four days to find a Blackness in the depths of space.

But luckily, space wasn't black. It just looked that way.

Chapter Fifteen

Countdown: 4 Days, 5 Hours

KIRK FACED Governor Pardonnet on the main screen. "Good work, Governor. All the colonists on board?"

"All but the six missing children and Lilian Coates," Pardonnet said.

"Oh, no," McCoy said softly behind Kirk.

Kirk immediately flashed to the image of Lilian Coates standing on the beach while the children played near her. He hadn't realized one of the missing children was her boy. And with her husband dead, it was no wonder she had decided to stay behind and keep looking. She was a strong woman. If anyone could find them, she could.

"The other children's families?" Kirk asked.

Pardonnet nodded. "On board, but not easily. They all had other children to take care of."

"We'll see if we can pull a ship away at some point to go back before the final explosion," Kirk said. "If she can find those kids, we'll get all of them off of there."

"Thank you, Captain," Pardonnet said.

Neither man said a word for a moment; then finally Kirk said, "Stand by for instructions. We're going to do the next push just before the Gamma Night hits."

"Understood," Pardonnet said, and cut the connection.

The screen went back to showing the entire colony fleet in a very tight formation around them. They were all following the small moon like a pack of hungry dogs after a lame rabbit.

"Status, Mr. Spock," Kirk said, turning his mind away from the kids and to what needed to be done.

"All ships are in position. All tractor beams are connected and holding. Two minutes, six seconds remaining."

"Good," Kirk said.

Spock and Scotty had worked up a very intricate set of maneuvers for this burn to get the small moon up to speed. Instead of starting with all ships at one-quarter impulse, as they had tried last time, they would start at one-eighth impulse and work upward. Each colony ship was tied to another colony ship's tractor beam. If one ship's beam or engine started to fail, the other would simply take up the slack as needed, before the failure occurred.

This burn would need to last for exactly three minutes and forty-six seconds. And would end almost at the very moment the Gamma Night started. They wouldn't really know if they had succeeded until ten hours later.

Ten long hours of the entire colony fleet coasting in space behind the small moon. He wasn't looking forward to those hours at all.

"One minute," Spock said.

Kirk nodded. They'd been through this routine twice before. It was becoming familiar.

"Uhura, open a channel to all ships for Mr. Spock. Mr. Sulu, stand by."

"Open, Mr. Spock," Uhura said.

"Sure hope this works this time," McCoy whispered as he stepped down beside Kirk's chair.

"It has to, Bones," Kirk whispered back.

"Thirty seconds," Mr. Spock said to all the ships. "Stand by for one-eighth impulse power on my mark."

Kirk sat and watched the ships on the screen. At the moment every one of them, including all the Starfleet shuttles, was hooked to the rough surface of the small moon by a tractor beam. But in reality, they were hooked to it with a lot more than that. All their hopes, their dreams of a new home, rode on this small moon. Everything these people had was attached like a tractor beam to the ability of this moon to rupture the Quake Moon.

He never would have imagined that the success of this entire wagon train to the stars could come down to one small moon and their ability to move that moon to the right spot, at the right time, and at the right speed.

"Five seconds," Spock said.

The silence filled the bridge.

"One-eighth impulse. Now!" Spock ordered.

Kirk could feel the slight bump as the impulse engines kicked in. But at this push, the *Enterprise* wasn't even straining.

"The tractor beams of two ships failed instantly," Sulu said.

"Spock?" Kirk asked, turning to his first officer.

"The other ships are compensating, Captain," Spock said.

"Workin' like a charm," Scotty said from the engineering station. He was beaming at the success of his and Spock's plan of having a backup for every ship.

"Just keep an eye on it," Kirk said. "Last thing we want to do is tear this moon apart now."

"Aye, Captain," Scott said.

One minute later another ship's tractor beam failed and again the backup ship took up the slack.

With one minute remaining in the burn, one of the Conestogas had to drop back owing to engine overheating. Again Scotty and Spock's system filled the gap. It was becoming very clear that they had needed every colony ship after all. This clearly wouldn't have worked otherwise, especially at a higher speed.

"Thirty seconds to engine shutdown," Spock announced to all the ships. "Stand by for my mark. Release tractor beams ten seconds after engine shutdown."

Kirk stared at the small moon on the screen and all the ships pushing it up to speed. In all his years of sitting in this chair, he'd tried a lot of crazy stunts. This one had to be right near the top of the list, that was for sure. Ramming one moon into another moon to stop an explosion. How crazy was that?

"Five seconds," Spock said flatly.

The seconds went past slowly. Finally Spock said, "Engine shutdown. Now! Release tractor beams in ten seconds."

"We did it!" Sulu said.

At that moment the screen went fuzzy. The small moon and the rest of the ships disappeared into a haze of static. The Gamma Night was upon them.

"Release tractor beam, Mr. Sulu," Kirk ordered.

"Released, sir," Sulu said.

"Well, Mr. Spock," Kirk said. "Is Sulu right? Did we do it?"

"I won't know exactly for ten hours, Captain."

"I was afraid you'd say that," Kirk said.

He stared at the fuzzy screen. All the colony ships were drifting along with them. And with the small moon.

None of the ships could really move safely, or needed to. They would all maintain the formation behind the moon, adjusting only if something happened.

"This is going to be a long ten hours," McCoy said, staring past Kirk at the fuzzy images on the screen.

"Ten hours is always exactly ten hours, Doctor," Spock said. "Nothing more, nothing less."

Sulu laughed.

All McCoy could manage was a shake of the head and a mutter—something about green blood that Kirk couldn't quite hear.

Kirk got to his feet. At least at the moment his two friends weren't arguing. That would have made the ten hours even longer than it was already going to be.

Countdown: 4 Days, 3 Hours

Lilian Coates came out of her home and looked at the faint light of sunrise in the sky. The morning air was crisp and fresh, biting at her face. Last night, after talking to the governor, she had decided she needed a few hours' sleep if she was going to be looking for Reynold alone. The worst thing that could happen to her would be to trip in the dark and break a leg, with no one around to find her.

She had set an alarm for right before dawn, slept a few hours, made herself some breakfast, taken a shower, then changed clothes for the first time in more days than she wanted to think about. Now, as the sun was coming up, she was refreshed and ready to go again.

Around her the silence was like a hand holding the air out of her mouth. The row of empty dome homes felt to her like a row of tombstones. And down the hill she could see some of the empty main colony compound. She had felt alone after Tom died on the way here. But then she had Reynold and all the other colonists and friends around her. Now she really was alone.

Alone on a planet with six lost children she somehow had to find by herself in the next four days.

The task seemed impossible.

With one more look at the empty colony below and the row of dome homes stretching away from her through the trees, she headed down the hill toward the stream that flowed below the main colony compound. It had been searched, she knew. But so had every place else around here. Maybe there was something along that stream that someone had missed.

Just as she had done for days, every one hundred paces she called out Reynold's name.

The emptiness of the planet echoed her call back to her. The echo wasn't the answer she was looking for.

Countdown: 4 Days, 2 Hours

The sun was coming in bright, filling the mouth of the cave with light, when Reynold woke. The others were still asleep in their sleeping bags, but that didn't matter. The sunlight was all that mattered. He was going home now. Not even Danny could talk him out of it.

"Hey!" he shouted, his voice echoing in the cave. "The sun is up!"

He climbed out of his bag and started rolling it up to

put it away. Beside him Danny sat up and rubbed his eyes. "What are you doing?"

"Going home," Reynold said.

Danny looked over at the mouth of the cave, then smiled. "All right!"

Within minutes they were all up and ready to go. With Danny leading the way, as always, they crawled through the small opening and the brush that covered it and stood in the trees outside.

Reynold had forgotten how good the sun felt.

"Sure is quiet," Diane said.

"Real early in the morning," Danny said. "We can be home in just over an hour, in plenty of time for breakfast."

Reynold liked the sound of that.

With a shout, they started off down the hill toward home. He was really looking forward to seeing his mom again.

Chapter Sixteen

Countdown: 3 Days, 20 Hours

GOVERNOR PARDONNET had tried to sleep during the ten hours of Gamma Night, but had finally given up. The nightmares had chewed at him like rats on a dead body. First there was the image of a moon floating like a balloon in front of his face. Back and forth, in and out, constantly blocking his vision. Every time he'd try to reach for it, to shove it out of the way, it would explode.

Then another moonlike balloon would take its place.

Back and forth. In and out, until he reached for it and it would explode.

Each time it exploded he woke up. Sweating.

But it wasn't that dream that had sent him scrambling from the bed. No, it was the faces of six children.

Six children calling out to him.

Begging him not to leave them, floating around him like the balloons, in and out, back and forth.

Finally, when he could stand it no longer and reached for one, the child's head exploded.

He had woken up screaming and shaking and sweating even more.

Now, after a shower and breakfast, he stood beside Captain Chalker, waiting for the end of Gamma Night, trying to push the memory of the last nightmare as far back into his mind as he could.

There was another full hour to wait and Captain Chalker wasn't much of a conversationalist. But standing here, doing nothing, waiting, was far, far better than being alone with his thoughts.

And his nightmares.

Countdown: 3 Days, 19 Hours

Kirk stood beside Dr. McCoy, staring at the fuzzy images on the screen as they slowly cleared and became distinct. Gamma Night had passed for another twenty hours.

The other colony ships were all still in formation around the *Enterprise,* following closely behind the small moon as it plunged inward toward Belle Terre and the Quake Moon.

"All ships are reporting in fine," Uhura said, smiling, clearly relieved.

"Spock?" Kirk said.

Spock glanced away from his board. "The moon is on trajectory, Captain. We will need to make another twenty-second correction in forty minutes, however."

"Great!" Kirk said, feeling the relief relax him a little. Not knowing if their last critical maneuver right before Gamma Night had worked or not had bothered him for ten hours.

"Any chance of a ship breaking away," McCoy asked, "and going back to Belle Terre?"

Kirk knew what Bones was asking. Lilian Coates and those six children were still there. "Spock? Enough free time available for one ship to break free?"

"I don't think it would be prudent, Captain," Spock said. "We have, over the next twenty hours before the next Gamma Night interference, exactly seventeen short course and speed corrections to effect on the moon. One ship leaving formation will seriously reduce the chances of success."

"We're talking seven lives here, Spock," McCoy said, clearly angry.

"There are over sixty-two thousand lives at risk in these ships and their future at stake, Doctor," Spock said. "The choice is logical."

Kirk had to agree. And he had to stop this discussion. "Besides, Bones," Kirk said, "we don't know for certain that Lilian Coates and the six children will not survive if we succeed."

McCoy stared first at Kirk, then at Spock. Then with a grunt turned and headed for the door.

Kirk watched him go for a moment. He understood exactly how the doctor was feeling. He felt the same way. But Spock was right. Maybe after the next Gamma Night there would be time. But for the moment, they had to focus on getting that small moon into the right position.

Going the right speed.

At the right time.

There was no room for error and no being late. They couldn't even spare one shuttle. For the moment, Lilian Coates and those children were going to have to fend for themselves.

Kirk dropped down into his chair. "Uhura, open a

channel. to all ships. Mr. Spock, tell them what you need them to do. Let's get ready for the next push."

Countdown: 3 Days, 19 Hours

Sunn strode back onto his bridge and glanced at Roger, who shook his head negative. They had been speeding at warp six for seventeen hours, sensors at full out, searching for anything that might resemble the big Blackness that had passed Nevlin.

Their results? Nothing.

Sunn was truly starting to believe they were on a wild-goose chase, as the old expression went. He wasn't even sure why he was even trying. Maybe because he had discovered the olivium in the moon and Kirk and his people had discovered it was going to blow up. Maybe he was being overly cautious this time. But he knew that if they went back now, Kirk would ask about the Blackness and he wanted to have some answer.

But if they didn't get that answer pretty soon, they weren't going to get it. There was just over three and a half days until the Belle Terre moon exploded. He wanted to be back and reporting to Kirk at least a half a day before that. So that left three days.

At full warp, they were just over one day away from the Belle Terre system right now, and getting farther away by the minute. He figured they had ten more hours safely; then they'd turn around and head back.

Ten hours to find a large blackness in the openness of space. They were going to have to get very lucky.

He glanced at the course heading. Leaving Nevlin, they had set a course directly following the path the Blackness had come from one hundred years earlier. Dar had been the one to suggest this direction, since the

Elah culture had an ancient record of a blackness coming from the same direction as the one that wiped them out. Dar figured that maybe that whatever the Blackness was, it originated from this direction. Or if nothing else, it was following a very long pattern.

Sunn knew it was a long shot, but so was chasing after something that had passed a planet one hundred years earlier. This way seemed slightly less a long shot.

Sunn watched the images of stars sweeping past in warp on the main screen, then suddenly got an idea. Maybe the Elah civilization wasn't alone in its problems with the Blackness.

"Dar," Sunn said, "scan for planets on this course that the Blackness would have come close to."

"How close?" Dar asked.

"As close as the Nevlin pass," Sunn said. "Inside the system at least."

"Assuming that thing flew in a straight line," Roger said. "We're a lot of light-years away from where that line started."

"Let's just assume," Sunn said. "Humor me for the moment."

"I'll let you know if I see a system that fits that exact bill," Dar said.

The three of them sat in silence as the time and distance clicked away. Sunn wondered how Kirk was doing in his fight to save the Quake Moon. With luck, the planet they had found wouldn't matter, other than as an interesting record of something that happened in this part of space. There were a lot of planets that had once held lost civilizations. If Belle Terre survived, maybe the colony would send an expedition there at some point, to learn what they could from those long-gone people. At least that way the entire race wouldn't have died in vain.

Chapter Seventeen

Countdown: 3 Days, 19 Hours

REYNOLD SAT on his bed, the tears gone now. An hour before, he and Danny and the rest had come down off the hill, but no one was here anymore. They had all gone.

Danny checked his house.

Diane had checked hers.

Their parents had all left them.

Danny had been wrong. The moon was going to explode and everyone had left without them.

All of them had cried.

Even Danny, who always acted so tough and know-it-all. Even Danny cried.

They had run down into the main part of the colony, calling for anyone.

The colony was empty. It was the spookiest place he'd ever been, so he'd come back up here to his house, running all the way. He didn't know where the rest of them had gone. He didn't care anymore.

He was never going to talk to Danny again.

Reynold came back to his room and stood there, looking around. There was nowhere else Reynold wanted to go. He couldn't even think of anyplace else to go.

He sat on his bed and looked at the picture on his dresser of his mom and dad and him at the amusement park on Earth. Before they came here.

Before Dad got killed.

They had all been smiling. It still made him smile. It had been a fun day and he liked looking at the picture. He took it now and lay down on his bed. Maybe the cave and his mom being gone was all a bad dream and if he just slept it would all go away.

His bed felt good after sleeping on the ground so long. Really soft.

He kicked his shoes off because Mom always got mad at him when he got on his bed with his shoes on. And she was going to be mad enough at him when she came back. He didn't want her yelling at him about his shoes on the bed, too.

He knew she would never leave him. Even though he'd run away, she would never leave him. He knew she would come back. She would understand why he did it. But boy was she going to be mad.

With the picture against his chest he lay down and closed his eyes, trying not to think about all the empty buildings in the colony down the hill. Instead he tried remembering that day on Earth at the amusement park.

It had been a fun day.

Countdown: 3 Days, 16 Hours

To Kirk the routine was growing very old, even as it got more and more critical. Every half hour or so for the last six hours, Spock had directed all the ships to push the moon at an exact speed, for an exact amount of time. At least a dozen tractor beams had failed, plus two ships' engines, but so far the system of dual colony ships for every tractor beam attached to the moon was making it work.

The little moon called the Needle was gaining speed and passing the eighth planet, headed toward Belle Terre. It still had a long way to go, and some pretty good turns ahead of it, but for the moment it was right where Mr. Spock wanted it to be.

Scotty and the other engineers from the Starfleet ships had spent most of the last six hours beaming from one ship to the next, helping the colony ships keep their very tired engines working. At one point Mr. Scott had reported in that he didn't think the supply of bubble gum was going to hold out.

Kirk had told him to start using the baling wire.

Now Spock had just finished yet another short eighteen-second push successfully.

"Stand by," Spock told all the ships. "Next maneuver in thirty-seven minutes, ten seconds."

Uhura cut the connection with the other ships.

"I assume it went as well as planned, Mr. Spock?"

"It did, sir," Spock said, without looking up from his station.

"I then assume you don't need me at the moment?" Kirk said. His stomach had been rumbling for the last hour and he figured it was time to do something about it.

"For what, sir?" Spock said, glancing up.

"For—" Kirk glanced around, then laughed. "Never mind. I'll be getting some lunch. You have the bridge."

"As you wish," Spock said, then went back to work.

Kirk headed to the door. This was going too smoothly for his comfort. Yet at the same time, he was very glad it was. It was just a minor problem that in the middle of this emergency, he didn't know what to do with himself. He had no doubt that that would change shortly.

Countdown: 3 Days, 14 Hours

Lilian Coates limped into her home, kicked off her shoes, and went directly for a glass of water. Her blouse was soaked in sweat from the warm day, and she had scratches on both her arms and face from clawing her way through brush. Her feet hurt worse every hour, but so far it wasn't bad enough to slow her down. For five straight hours she'd looked and called along the stream below the main compound.

Nothing.

Now she was back here, in her home above the abandoned colony compound. Because all the buildings and streets were so new, it felt odd to have it all be abandoned. Not at all like ruins or a ghost town. This place felt as if people should come out of the doorways at any moment. But she knew no one would. She was on her own.

She allowed herself two full glasses of water, then headed back for the bathroom. A quick shower and a change of clothes and shoes and she would head back out. There was over a half day left of daylight. She couldn't waste it.

She passed the open door of Reynold's room and was all the way into the bathroom before what she had seen registered in her mind.

It couldn't be!

She was starting to hallucinate.

But at the same time she knew it wasn't a dream.

She scrambled back to his room and stood there in the doorway, staring at her sleeping son, in shock.

He really was lying there on his bed, taking a nap just as he did most afternoons.

He had come back.

Almost as if he had never left.

Before she realized it, she was on his bed, hugging him and crying.

He was crying, too, while he kept saying, "Mom, Mom, I'm sorry."

Over and over.

Countdown: 3 Days, 11 Hours

Sunn must have been dozing slightly in his chair when Dar said, "Got one!"

"Got what?" Sunn asked, coming up out of his chair, trying to get his thoughts back on track as quickly as possible.

The screen showed that they were still in warp and moving at a high rate of speed. Had Dar found the Blackness?

"A Class-M planet the Blackness might have passed," Dar said. "Dead ahead."

"Bring us out of warp and into standard orbit," Sunn said, "and don't waste any time about it."

Sunn sat back down and watched the screen as Roger took the *Rattlesnake* out of warp and swung it down into orbit faster than he'd ever done it before. Far faster than standard regulations called for, that was for sure. But way out here, who was going to care about regulations?

The planet on the screen was a brownish color, with swaths of blue and white. Clearly a desert planet with very small oceans, unlike most Class-M planets. More often than not planets habitable by humans had far more water than land.

"Evidence of a large civilization," Dar said, studying his screen. "Pre-spaceflight, it would seem."

"Scan for power sources," Sunn ordered.

"Nothing really," Dar said. "Hydroelectrical power near some larger populated areas, nothing much else. But there are signs this civilization used to be space-flight-capable."

"How do you know?" Sunn asked. There was really no way Dar could tell that from this high, even with the best scans.

"Easy," Dar said. "Look!" He pointed to the main screen that was now showing an object coming up in the distance.

"What is it?" Roger asked.

"Looks like it used to be a large space station," Dar said. "Completely dead."

Sunn stared at the alien-designed station floating larger and larger on their main viewer. This was exactly what he was afraid he'd find. And what he hoped not to find at the same time.

"How the heck has that thing stayed in orbit?" Roger asked.

Sunn had been wondering the same thing.

"It's stationed at a neutral gravity area between the planet and one of its moons," Dar said. "Should stay there for another few hundred years unless something bumps it."

"Take us in closer to the station," Sunn ordered. "See if we can find out what happened."

"That Blackness sucked the energy out of it," Roger said.

"We don't know that yet," Sunn said.

"Anyone want to make a small wager?" Roger asked.

Neither he or Dar took Roger up on that proposition.

Chapter Eighteen

Countdown: 3 Days, 11 Hours

It had taken a few minutes for Lilian to calm down enough to get Reynold calmed down. Then she got him to explain what he and the other kids had done. He spent the next few minutes holding her hand and telling her about the cave and about how they all thought that their parents wouldn't go back to Earth without them.

Then, with his hand still firmly grasping hers, they had gone up the street in search of the other children. They found them all, asleep in their own homes, on their own beds.

The children broke into tears when they saw her. She hugged them all until they calmed down. And told them that their parents really hadn't left them. Their parents had just been needed on the ships.

Then, when they were all together, she explained what had happened, how their parents had all searched and searched for them, how even the governor and hundreds of others had helped search.

The kids were all worried that they were in really big trouble when they heard about the governor, but she managed to convince them that he had just been worried like everyone else. Then she told them why everyone had gone so soon and how they were all in the ships trying to save the planet, because no one wanted to go back to Earth.

What she hadn't told them was her worry about getting back on the ships. She hadn't bothered to ask the governor or anyone else how she should go about contacting them. But there had to be a way.

"Okay," she said after they all had eaten a lunch she fixed in her kitchen. "Everyone is going to go take a quick shower in their own home, then get into clean clothes and come back here. I'm going to need all of your help on something."

"What?" Reynold asked.

"Is it going to be fun?" Danny asked, his eyes brightening up for the first time since she had found him in his bedroom.

"It will be fun, and an adventure," she said. "We have to go down into the main part of the compound and find a communications set."

"So we can talk to our parents?" Diane asked.

"Exactly," Lilian said. "If we find one, you can talk to them. So anyone know where a communications board might be?"

She asked that question in hope that one of the kids had seen a communications room with one of their parents. But they shook their heads no.

"It's scary down there," Diane said. "No one's there."

"We're all going to stay together," Lilian said, hugging Diane. "So there won't be anything to worry about. And I'll stay right with you. Okay?"

Diane nodded, but didn't look at all convinced.

"Now everyone, off to the showers, then come right back here. Clean clothes and socks. Then we'll take you to talk to your parents."

Reynold headed down the hall and the rest went through the front door at a run, trying to see who could be first. She had managed so far to turn it into an adventure for them. She just hoped they could find a communications set. Or that someone had thought to leave one.

She wished she had been in good enough shape to think to ask for one. But beating up on herself for that now was just a little too late.

Now she had all six of the children's lives in her hands. She had to stay calm and clear-thinking. There was still plenty of time left.

Countdown: 3 Days, 11 Hours

Sunn and Dar crawled through the old airlock and onto the alien space station wearing spacesuits. Sunn hated the restrictive suits, but in this instance they had no choice. Not only did they have to cross some open space, but the atmosphere in the old station had long ago frozen. From what Dar could tell, just over one hundred years before. Same time frame as when the Elah had lost all their power.

The corridor and doors were huge in comparison with the *Rattlesnake*'s. The ceilings were at least eight feet, and much wider than anything standard in Federation space. And Dar and Sunn could walk side by side through the doors. The station had the look of a very early space program. Every inch of space seemed to be used for something mechanical.

"Bet these people were big," Dar said after they had looked around for a few minutes.

"Let's see if we can find out," Sunn said, moving off toward where Dar had figured the main control room was for the station.

Sunn moved slowly, making sure his gravity boots held him firm to the alien decking. He didn't want to take any more time here than absolutely necessary. If he discovered that the Blackness had been responsible for this, they would take the *Rattlesnake* and head at full speed for Belle Terre. Captain Kirk could draw his own conclusions at that point with the information Sunn would give him. If the colonists needed the planet they had found, they would face dealing with this Blackness then. At this point, Sunn was hoping they wouldn't.

It didn't take them long to discover the true size and look of the station aliens. One frozen body was lodged against the ceiling. It was vaguely humanoid. Long, wide, camel-like nose, massive humps on the back, huge hands, cloven feet without shoes. The eyes were frozen open but Sunn couldn't see their color. Clearly a race that had evolved on an arid planet.

He and Dar studied it for a moment, then moved on through the wide door and into the control room. A half dozen more of the aliens were dead in there, lodged in one position or another against bulkheads or massive chairs.

Dar moved over to a panel, brushed a light dusting of frost off, and then said, "Computer access here."

Sunn had been studying the one who looked to be in charge. He had bright gold bands on his massive chest that wrapped around the humps on his back and then up and over his forehead. Clearly some sort of uniform.

"Get it fired up and downloaded," Sunn said. "I want

to get out of here. But make sure you don't leave any sign we were here."

"Try my best," Dar said.

With one more look at the gold-wrapped alien, Sunn moved over to help Dar. At least this race, from what he could tell was going on down on the planet, was making a comeback from losing all its energy, if that was what happened here. They hadn't all just sat down and given up like the Elah had. Maybe in another fifty or one hundred years, they'd be back up here in orbit, giving their long-dead brothers a decent burial.

Last thing they needed then was to discover aliens had been on board in the meantime.

After a few minutes, Dar said, "Primitive, but I got it all. Downloaded to the *Rattlesnake*'s computer."

"Great," Sunn said.

Dar quickly unhooked his equipment, then moved over beside Sunn. Sunn glanced around them, giving the gold-wrapped alien one last look. When these people got back into space, all they'd see was a little disturbed frost on one panel. Not enough to clue them into anyone else being here.

Sunn tapped the communications link in the side of his helmet. "Roger, we're headed back."

"You got it," Roger's voice said. "I'll be waiting."

Thirty minutes later Sunn was sitting in his captain's chair, watching the playback of the Blackness coming at the station, right up to the point where there was nothing.

Just as it had happened on Nevlin to the Elah. Only this time they had a recording of it. And as far as Sunn was concerned, the big mass of Blackness was one of the scariest things he'd ever seen. And not just because he'd seen what it could do to entire planets.

"Any idea what that thing was?" Sunn asked.

"Not a clue," Dar said. "Not one stinking clue."

Sunn nodded. "All right, I've seen enough. Get us back to Belle Terre. Top speed."

"Think Kirk and the Starfleet people are going to want to see this?" Roger asked, laughing.

"I have no doubt about that," Dar said.

Neither did Sunn. Not one doubt at all.

Countdown: 3 Days, 8 Hours

For over three hours, Lilian and the children had searched colony buildings looking for communications equipment.

Nothing.

They had found where some had been, in a room in the main town hall. But clearly the colonists had planned on never coming back here, or having a here to come back to. So they had taken everything they needed to start again. And that included the communications equipment, of course.

After she and the children had found the empty room in the town hall, she had made it into a game for the kids to keep searching. It wasn't until three hours of having no luck that finally Danny stopped outside the last building they had looked through. "We're never going to get to talk to our parents, are we?"

Diane and the other boys started crying, so Lilian had gathered them around. "We're just going to have to wait until they get the moon stopped and come back for us."

"What happens if they can't stop it?" Danny asked, also on the edge of tears.

"Then one of the ships will check on us and beam us off the planet before anything happens," Lilian said.

"Really?" Diane asked.

"Really," Lilian said. "Remember I said that even the governor was searching for all of you. He's not going to let the moon explode with us here. No way."

She just hoped she was sounding as brave and sure as her words. She actually had no idea if the governor would come back for them or not. She clearly remembered his words, and the number of hours he had told her to remember. There were still eighty of those hours left.

A very long time.

"Okay," Danny said, sounding half convinced.

"Tell you what," Lilian said, noticing that the light was slowly getting dimmer. "We can search more tomorrow. Right now let's go back to my home and decide where we're all going to sleep."

"If I get my bed and blankets from my house," Diane said, "can I stay with you and Reynold?"

"Of course you can," Lilian said. "Everyone is sleeping over tonight. It will be fun."

That cheered them up some. At a run they headed back up the hill toward home, racing each other to see who could get there first. Lilian followed behind, a little slower, trying to figure just what she was going to do if no one came back to check on them. She had no idea at all.

Ahead of her the kids laughed, the sound echoing down through the trees and empty buildings. It was a great sound, one that she had thought she might never hear again. But at the moment she had Reynold's life and five other children's lives in her hands. Having no idea what to do just wasn't acceptable.

Countdown: 2 Days, 23 Hours

Kirk stared at the small moon on the screen. And the massive fleet of colony ships hovering behind it. He was getting very, very tired of staring at that surface, yet there was over two more days of doing just that. Sometimes the most critical of missions was the most trying. This was one of those times.

"Cut engines now," Mr. Spock ordered all ships.

Kirk motioned that Uhura should cut the link to the other ships. In a few seconds it wouldn't matter if she cut the link or not. Gamma Night was almost on them again, and would cut all communications anyway. Ten hours of drifting, out of touch with everything.

Mr. Spock glanced up from his station as the main screen went fuzzy with the Gamma Night. "The small moon is on course."

"Good," Kirk said. But he knew it hadn't really been that good a thirty-six-second push at one-eighth impulse. Three ships had lost engines before the thirty-six seconds was up. Two others had lost tractor beams. Without the backup ships for each colony ship, they would have had disasters.

This fleet was just plain tired. Most of these ships needed complete overhauls that they were never going to get way out here. They had never been intended for this kind of wear and tear right after taking such a long flight. It was amazing more of them weren't breaking down.

Yet they couldn't break down on the final push. During that last shove on the small moon, they didn't have the luxury of having half the colony ships as backup. All of them would have to be pushing, and for longer than thirty-six seconds, to make that small moon impact the Quake Moon in the right spot, at the right speed. Scotty and his crew were doing everything they could to keep ships running, but there was no doubt that the last push was going to be a problem.

Around him the bridge was quiet. Over the last hours he'd talked to the governor about trying to get a ship out of formation and back to Belle Terre to check on Lilian Coates and the children. They just hadn't be able to spare even one ship so far. But Kirk was going to try to do just that during the next period between Gamma Nights.

Kirk also wondered what had happened to Captain Sunn and the *Rattlesnake*. If anyone could find a useable planet and make it back here, Sunn could. Kirk hadn't expected to hear from Sunn yet, because he was sure Sunn was far out of ship-to-ship communication range. Even if Sunn did find a suitable planet, Kirk hoped they didn't need it. But the problems coming up on the last big push, when all the ships would be pushing without backup, worried Kirk a great deal. Having a backup planet, and the *Rattlesnake* helping push, would be a very, very good thing. If Sunn could just get back here in time.

"McCoy to Captain Kirk." McCoy's voice came over the comm line from sickbay.

"Go ahead, Doctor," Kirk said. "Problem?"

"Got a patient that needs some food and rest is all," McCoy said.

"And who would that be?" Kirk asked. He hadn't been informed of anyone in sickbay.

"I'm talking to him," McCoy said.

Kirk laughed. "Yes, Doctor. On my way."

He stood and, with one more glance at the fuzzy image of the small moon on the screen, headed for dinner and a good night's sleep. There just wasn't anything else to do at the moment.

Part Four

LONG LAST DAY

Chapter Nineteen

Countdown: 1 Day, 3 Hours

GOVERNOR PARDONNET stared at the tired face of Captain Kirk as Kirk said exactly what Pardonnet was afraid Kirk would say. "I'm sorry, Governor. We just can't spare a ship to jump to Belle Terre."

"Not even one of the shuttles?" Pardonnet asked.

"Not even a shuttle," Kirk said, shaking his head. "You know we're using everything that has power and can be rigged with a tractor beam. The next push is in eleven minutes. Our longest time between pushes during the entire twenty hours before the next Gamma Night is sixteen minutes."

Pardonnet sighed. That was exactly what had happened last time during the twenty-hour period between Gamma Nights. And it was going to happen again. Lilian Coates and those children, if she had found them, were alone on Belle Terre for now. And that was haunting Pardonnet, giving him nightmares.

"Governor," Kirk said. "I promise you that after the last big push *Enterprise* will do a sweep of the planet. We'll get her and the kids off of there before anything happens."

Pardonnet nodded. Kirk had promised this before, but both of them knew the timetable. The last Gamma Night was going to release them just one hour before the small moon needed to be hitting the Quake Moon. Then they had to do the last, big push of the small moon. If the maneuver worked, there would be less than thirty minutes to find Lilian and the kids, beam them off, and get the ships out of danger from the explosion. A thousand things could go wrong in that short amount of time.

"Are long-range scans of the area possible yet, Captain?" Pardonnet asked. They were twenty hours closer than the last time Pardonnet had asked Kirk that question. But he had to ask. It just hadn't occurred to him, or from what he could discover, anyone else, to leave something for Lilian Coates to reach them with. He had no idea if she'd found the missing children, or if she was even still alive.

"Not yet," Kirk said. "Probably not until we come out of Gamma Night for the last hour."

Pardonnet nodded. He could tell Kirk didn't like the idea of Lilian and six children on Belle Terre any more than he did. But it just didn't look as if there was anything either one of them could do about it.

"Thanks, Captain," Pardonnet said, and cut the connection. Around him the ship readied for another short push against the small moon that was hurtling sunward. Even though they were doing these maneuvers in small increments, at only one-eighth impulse, it still wore heavily on all the ships, and took time each push to get ready.

Captain Chalker was busy; so were the crew. Pardonnet felt just about as useless as he'd ever felt. Right now his colony and all the people that had followed him vast distances to Belle Terre were at risk, and he could do nothing but sit and watch and wait. There was nothing for him to govern, nothing to lead. Every ship and every ship's crew had to fight this fight. And that was out of his jurisdiction completely.

He started to say something to Captain Chalker, then stopped himself. Quickly he turned and headed off the bridge. If he was going to bother someone, it was better he did it down in the mess area. At least there he wouldn't get in the way of those who were trying to save all their lives.

Countdown: 1 Day, 1 Hour

Lilian glanced at her watch, then up at where Captain Kirk had sat on the sand dune what seemed like an eternity ago. Had it really been so long ago? There was no doubt the world had changed a great deal since then. And it was only a few weeks old for her then. She had changed, too. Gotten stronger. Around her the children played in the sand, just as they had done that day.

She kicked off her shoes and let the coolness of the sand comfort her. The ocean air was fresh, the afternoon breeze light and just cooling enough. A perfect Belle Terre afternoon. She hoped the governor and Captain Kirk managed to save Belle Terre. It had to be one of the prettiest places in the entire sector.

She glanced at her watch. Twenty-seven hours left. Twenty-seven hours until this planet would be bathed with radiation.

If it didn't get destroyed.

She was counting on the radiation and hadn't let herself think of the other possibility much at all. Pardonnet had told her to get under something right at the explosion hour. She hadn't given it any thought at the time, because of the search for the children. She could have crawled under a blanket for all she was concerned at that point.

Now was different.

Now she had six children to save. For the past two days, she couldn't find anything she felt safe putting the children under to protect them from radiation. At best, the town meeting hall had a storage area underground. She'd take them there and do what she could to make it tight.

If she had to. She was hoping she wouldn't have to. Almost counting on it. Kirk, Governor Pardonnet would come back for them. They had to.

She stood, her back to the ocean, watching the six kids play. Reynold seemed fine, but the others alternated between being very upset that they weren't with their parents, and treating all this as a grand adventure. She tried to keep it on the adventure side as much as possible, telling them their parents were working hard to save the planet and they all just had to be patient. Everyone would all come back very soon.

Sometimes she said that almost as much for herself as the children.

She glanced up at the empty sand dune where Captain Kirk had sat all those days ago. It was empty, just as everything else in this colony was empty. Couldn't one of the ships have come back? How hard would that have been? She knew the governor wasn't going to forget her and the children. Something must be keeping them from coming back.

But she couldn't imagine what that might be, for the life of her. So until they came back, she was going to make it as easy on the children as she could.

And search like crazy for a place to shelter them when the time came.

If the time came.

Countdown: 23 Hours

Sunn sat in his command chair, staring at the stars as they flashed past on the screen. He loved this, and had always been able to just sit watching for hours. They had just had a great exploration trip. Successful. This was why he'd left Texas, why he'd gone into space in the first place. He just loved exploring, finding new places. And since space was so big, there were certainly a vast amount of new spaces to find. Enough to keep him more than busy the rest of his life.

He glanced at their location and their speed and did the quick calculation. At this speed it would be twelve hours until they were in communications range with the *Enterprise,* eighteen hours until they actually got to Belle Terre.

Assuming the engines kept together.

As Roger had told him a number of times over the last day or so, they were pushing the old *Rattlesnake* too hard. But Sunn knew the *Rattlesnake* was up for the task.

Eighteen hours would get them to Belle Terre at least three, maybe five hours before everything blew. Sunn just hoped Kirk had the situation under control. The planet they had found was a good alternative, but not a great one. Belle Terre was better, if Kirk could save it.

"Well, well," Dar said, "what do we have here?"

Sunn glanced at Dar. "What?"

"I think I just accidentally found what we were looking for?"

Sunn's stomach twisted and he came up out of his chair. "The Blackness?"

"I think so," Dar said, smiling.

"What is it?" Roger asked. "Can you tell?"

"Only way I even found it was wondering what was causing a blockage of my long-range scanners. On my sensors it's just a big black empty area of space."

"Moving?" Sunn asked.

Dar stared at his screen for a moment, then nodded. "Sure is. Subwarp, but still pretty fast."

"How long is it going to slow us down to take a closer look?"

Dar shook his head. "Twenty minutes at most. But I don't think we want to do that. We don't know how far the range is on that thing."

Sunn glanced at Roger, then Dar. They had been sent on a mission to find a planet. They had found one, but that Blackness out there was the planet's big question mark. This was their chance to at least give the colonists and Captain Kirk more information to base a decision on.

"We went searching for that," Sunn said. "Now that we've found it, I at least want to get some closer sensory data."

Roger shook his head.

"Not too close, huh?"

"Not too close," Sunn agreed. "Roger, take us to what Dar thinks is a safe distance."

"I think we're fine right here," Dar said.

Sunn laughed. "Can we get decent long-range scans of whatever it is from here?"

"No," Dar said.

"Then take us to a point where we can," Sunn said. "And put the damn thing on screen."

"Got it," Roger said.

"There's nothing to see," Dar said. "At least with our eyes and on our sensors."

The screen changed to a starfield as the *Rattlesnake* dropped out of warp. It took Sunn a moment to see the Blackness, but then he did. It blocked an area of stars, leaving the picture with an empty hole where there should be stars.

He sat back, watching, as whatever it was got closer. He had had lots of times in his years in space when his stomach wrapped up in a knot of fear. This was another of those times. It had never stopped him from acting and making decisions, but he was always aware of the fear.

"I think we're just about close enough," Dar said.

"Agreed," Sunn said. "All stop."

"Stopped," Roger said.

"Anything?" Sunn asked Dar.

"I can't seem to—"

Suddenly, every light, every screen, even the image of the blackness and stars, flickered, like a candle in the wind.

The next instant Sunn was sitting in pitch darkness.

Complete silence.

His hands gripped the armrests on his chair as he slowly floated upward.

Blackness.

Total blackness.

"Seems this was just a little too close," Roger said, his voice filling the dark.

For the first time in Sunn's life, the fist of panic in

his stomach threatened to overwhelm him. He just floated there, holding onto the armrests of his captain's chair, listening to his own breathing, because he knew anything else he could do at the moment would be wrong.

Of course, if the Blackness had stripped all the power out of the *Rattlesnake,* as it seemed as if it had, there was nothing right they could do.

Chapter Twenty

Countdown: 21 Hours

"MRS. COATES," Diane said. "I lost my bracelet. I think it's in the cave. Can we go look for it tomorrow?"

Lilian stared at the dark-haired, nine-year-old Diane. Outside it was starting to get dark, and Lilian had just started dinner for the kids. Then Diane had asked the simple question about her bracelet and Lilian felt the relief flow through her. The cave.

Why hadn't she thought of that before? They could be in the cave when the explosion happened. Of course.

"Mom, are you all right?" Reynold asked.

Lilian realized that she had almost spilled the bowl of rice in her hand. She sat it down and smiled. "More than all right. And Diane, of course we can go back to the cave. As soon as it gets light."

"I don't want to go back there," Reynold said.

Lilian patted her son's hand. "It will be fun. Just

trust me. And I'll be with you this time. Don't you want to show me where you all hid?"

"I suppose," Reynold said.

"I found the caves," Danny said proudly.

"How far are they from here?" Lilian asked.

"It took us two hours to hike home," Reynold said, holding up his watch. "I timed us."

"Well," Lilian said. "I'm looking forward to seeing them. We'll take a picnic lunch and have fun. What do you all say?"

All the children agreed.

She relaxed and watched them eat. Now, at least, if the governor couldn't get back to pick them up, she and the children had a place to hide from the radiation. She would just make sure they were all inside when the Quake Moon exploded. Maybe then they'd have a chance.

It was the cave that had gotten them all into this fix. Just maybe it would be the cave that would save them.

Countdown: 20 Hours

Sunn watched as the flame of the small fire flickered, sending strange orange shadows over the mess area. For the last three hours, bundled up against the creeping cold, they had struggled to find any way to get some energy back into the *Rattlesnake*.

They had tried everything they could think of, including setting up a bike and pedaling a generator to charge a battery. The battery wouldn't hold the charge, and the generator didn't have enough power to work even an emergency subspace beacon.

Nothing they tried worked.

The Blackness, whatever it was, had taken every tiny

bit of the ship's energy. The only thing they had left were some old-fashioned matches that Sunn had kept in his cabin in a drawer. It had taken him, Roger, and Dar twenty minutes of floating weightless in the dark, forcing open hatchways, to find his quarters and light that first match.

The light had been a savior. The yellow flickering flame, Dar and Roger's faces in the dark, his cabin with his unmade bed, were all gifts to stop his growing insanity in the darkness.

He had had no idea just how black total blackness could be. It had seemed to close in around him, smother him. Even though he knew the *Rattlesnake* inside out and backward, it had suddenly, in pitch darkness and weightlessness, seemed alien and different.

He never wanted to be in that type of darkness again.

Out of his socks, they put together some small torches to get them back to the supplies, where they figured out better, slower burning material.

But even with the flickering flame to see by, and the emergency air opened slowly into the control and engine rooms, they had been unable to get even the slightest spark from anything on the ship. Even the portable energy source they had taken onto the alien space station had been sucked dry.

The *Rattlesnake* was dead. Nothing more than a floating hunk of metal, slowly losing its heat to the cold of deep space.

After Dar had finally given up, and Roger agreed, Sunn had moved them to the mess area. It was the only place on the ship where there was a port looking out to the stars. It was colder there, but if he was going to die, he wanted to at least do it looking at the stars he loved.

They couldn't see the Blackness out that port. More

than likely it was long gone by now, leaving them behind just as it had left entire races in the past.

What was that thing?

Sunn had no doubt he would never find out now. Just one of the many mysteries of space. He was just sorry he wasn't going to get to search out more of those mysteries. He so loved doing that.

They managed to build a fire in the middle of where Sunn had eaten many meals over the years, lighting the fire under one of the bolted-down tables. The slight spin of the ship created just enough gravity to hold the fire against the bottom side of the table.

He wanted the fire, even though he knew it would take their air faster. At this point Sunn knew it didn't much matter what killed them. They were either going to freeze to death, or die from lack of oxygen. He wasn't sure which, and he didn't want to ask Dar to figure out what would come first.

Death was death. What did it matter how it happened, as long as it happened in space? He had never had any illusions that someday he would die in space. He just hadn't expected it to happen so soon.

Or in this fashion. He and Roger and Dar were going to die the way the Elah had done. Those people had gathered inside, around fires, and waited to die.

They were doing the same thing.

And yet he couldn't think of another option. Maybe this was how the Elah had felt?

"What do you think James Kirk would do in this situation?" Dar asked.

Sunn thought about it. He had no idea.

"Even the great James Kirk will someday die," Roger said. "It happens to all of us."

"Some of us sooner than later," Dar said.

Sunn smiled at his two friends in the faint light of the fire. Even in an impossible situation, they were still joking. All the years together had been fun, at least for him. He just hoped they felt the same way now.

He stared at the flames as his mind slowly seemed to pull back from his cold body.

Think, dammit! There had to be a way out of this.

No power, no ability to communicate or keep up environment controls. No power at all and nothing around them but deep space.

There had to be a way out.

There had to be.

He'd think of it, right after a short nap.

Beside him Dar snored lightly, his breath coming hard.

Roger's eyes were closed and frost had formed on the lids.

They were dying and there wasn't anyone coming to the rescue.

With one last look at the stars he loved so much, he closed his eyes.

Just a short nap. That was all he needed.

Sunn, Dar, and Roger faced the stars, side by side, as they all had been for years.

A short time later the flame under the table went out and only the light of the stars shone on the explorers.

Chapter Twenty-one

Countdown: 1 Hour

KIRK STARED at the screen as the fuzziness cleared and the Gamma Night passed them. All the colony ships were still in place behind the small moon. Everything looked to be in perfect position, as far as he could tell visually.

"Well, here we go," Scotty said.

"Let's just hope we go the right direction," McCoy said from his spot holding on to the rail.

Kirk nodded. One hour until, with luck, they crashed the small moon into the Quake Moon.

One hour to save this colony.

"All ships reporting ready," Uhura said.

Kirk glanced around at where his science officer studied his panel. "Up to you, Mr. Spock. Lieutenant, open a channel to all ships."

"Open," Uhura said.

"Attention," Spock said. "All ships connect your

tractor beams to your assigned position. Any ship experiencing a problem, report at once."

The silence on the bridge seemed to get intense. Kirk glanced around at each of his officers. None of them said anything.

Then Sulu said, "Tractor beam connected. Standing by."

Again the silence gripped the bridge as Spock waited until all ships had a chance to carry out their orders.

Kirk stared at the ships on the main screen. Somehow, they had to make this work. There was just too much riding on it.

"No reports of problems, Mr. Spock," Uhura said.

Spock nodded. "On my mark," Spock said to all the colony and Starfleet ships, "engage engines at one-quarter impulse and hold that speed for exactly six minutes and twelve seconds. Stand by."

Kirk knew that many of the colony ships would never be able to sustain such a push, but at this point none of them had a choice. They had to try.

"Five seconds," Spock said.

Again the silence on the bridge weighed down even the air. Kirk sat forward in his chair, his full attention on the screen in front of him.

"Engage engines," Spock ordered. "One-quarter impulse, now!"

"One-quarter impulse," Sulu said as around them the *Enterprise* seemed to groan and shake.

Kirk could feel the rumbling and vibration through his chair. He had no idea what it was doing to those colony ships. But he had a hunch it wasn't good. At one-eighth impulse, many of the tractor beams and engines of the colony ships had failed over the last few days. This push was factors greater strain on them.

And needed to be maintained far, far longer.

On the screen the scene looked no different. The entire wagon train to the stars was grouped in a small cluster, all pushing on a small moon. Conestogas mixed with smaller ships. A pathfinder ship beside the coroner ship. An industrial ship side by side with the hospital ship. A very strange sight indeed as they all pushed for the very life of the colony.

"One minute," Sulu shouted over the growing noise.

Kirk was glad that minute had gone by quickly. He checked around the bridge. McCoy nodded at him, but said nothing. All the others concentrated on their stations.

So far no ships had reported problems. So far, so good. But he knew a ship's captain wouldn't report a problem unless he had no choice. Every engineer, every captain knew how important this last push was. They were all going to drive their ships to the breaking point and beyond before giving up. He was going to do the same to the *Enterprise* if need be.

"Two ships reporting imminent tractor-beam failure," Uhura reported.

Uhura was only telling the bridge crew. Spock was getting the same reports through his earpiece.

"Both ships cut tractor beam and engines," Spock said. "Drop out of formation. *Republic,* increase your speed to twenty-seven percent full impulse."

On the screen Kirk watched as two of the smaller private ships suddenly dropped back and out of sight. They would immediately head out of the system to a point a safe distance away that had been agreed upon. With luck, within the hour every ship would be holding at that point outside the Belle Terre system.

Spock had worked up an elaborate system of replacement balances if a ship couldn't sustain its task. Most of the pickup would fall on Starfleet ships, for obvious reasons. The *Republic* was a Starfleet cutter. This kind of strain had to be tearing it apart almost as much as the colony ships.

"Two minutes," Sulu said.

Only four minutes and sixteen seconds to go. A lifetime, as far as Kirk was concerned.

"The *Lakota* is about to lose one of its engines," Uhura said, glancing quickly at Spock.

Kirk stared at the *Lakota* on the screen. It was one of the big Conestogas, carrying thousands of colonists. Losing one of the two big mule engines would send the ship into a possibly fatal spin.

"*Lakota*," Spock said, "Cut tractor beam and fall back. Mr. Sulu, increase the *Enterprise* speed to twenty-nine percent impulse. Now!"

On the screen the *Lakota* dropped away as the noise around them and the rumbling of the *Enterprise* increased at the extra strain. Kirk hoped the *Lakota* had enough engines left to get out of the range of the coming explosion. If not it was going to have to be towed, and after all this, there just might not be enough power left in any ship to tow anything.

"Three minutes," Sulu said.

Almost halfway.

Around him the *Enterprise* was shaking as if some giant had a fist around it and was trying to break it open. Scotty was working intently at his engineering board, his fingers flying, doing everything in his considerable powers to keep the ship working. But the shaking was rocking Kirk right down to his bones. He couldn't imagine what it was doing to all the ship's systems.

"How long can this ship hold up?" McCoy shouted

over the rumbling as he held tightly onto the railing as if it were the ledge over a high canyon.

"As long as it needs to, Doctor," Kirk shouted back.

"The *Macedon* is losing its tractor beam," Uhura reported.

"*Macedon*, cut your tractor beam and fall back," Spock ordered at once. "*Beowulf*, increase to point two-eight percent impulse power."

Kirk watched as the corporate ship *Macedon* vanished from the screen. Even though they had lost ships, there were still so many he couldn't tell where the others had even been.

"Four minutes!" Sulu shouted over the rumbling and shaking of the *Enterprise*.

This was like some sort of strange race. Could enough of the ships manage to hang on until the finish line? Two more minutes and he'd know the answer to that question. They all would.

The seconds ticked past as Kirk watched the screen intently, waiting for something to happen, hoping against hope that nothing would.

"The *Norfolk* and the *Mable Stevens* are both losing engines," Uhura shouted over the rumbling.

Kirk spotted Governor Pardonnet's ship the *Mable Stevens* among the remaining ones, then glanced back at his first officer.

"Both ships fall back," Spock ordered. "Mr. Sulu, increase to point three impulse."

The bridge shook so hard now that Kirk had to hold on to the arms of his chair to keep from being bounced out. And the rumbling was almost deafening. Smoke was slowly filling the bridge and Kirk had no doubts that damage reports were pouring in from all over the ship.

"Five minutes!" Sulu shouted.

Only one minute and twelve seconds to go. An eternity, especially the way the *Enterprise* was being pounded. This was a great ship, but Kirk doubted it could hold up to this kind of punishment much longer.

Kirk glanced over at where Scotty was madly working over his controls. "Can she hold, Mr. Scott?"

"She has no other choice, Captain!" Scotty shouted back without looking up.

Kirk nodded.

"Five minutes, thirty seconds!" Sulu shouted.

Less than one minute left!

Suddenly on the screen Kirk saw what he'd been hoping to not see. One of the mule drives on the Conestoga *Northwest Passage* exploded.

The crew of the big ship managed to get the other engine off almost at once. But almost wasn't fast enough. Not when the physics of spaceflight were concerned.

Slowly, then faster and faster, the big ship started to spin.

"*Impeller,* increase to point three impulse now!" Spock ordered.

The big ship was gaining speed in its spin, and was slowly heading inward toward the small moon. There were thousands of people on that ship.

Kirk slammed his hand on the comm link on his chair. "Kirk to *Northwest Passage!* Captain Burch, come in!"

"Burch here," the voice came back. "We released our tractor beam a fraction too late and the force is pulling us toward the moon. We can't correct the spin."

"They'll hit in less than thirty seconds," Sulu shouted over the roaring and shaking.

"There are thousands of people on that ship, Jim!" McCoy shouted.

Kirk stared at the spinning Conestoga. There was no way he could let thousands of people die just to save this planet. No way at all. They had come this close. Maybe they were close enough to make it all work. But at the moment all his choices were gone.

He slammed his fist on his communications link. "Kirk to all ships!" he shouted over the rumbling and shaking. "Cut engines, then cut tractor beams on my command and fall back. Ready? Cut engines now!"

Around him the rumbling almost instantly stopped, leaving the intense silence of suddenly missing loud noise.

"Engines at full stop," Sulu said.

"Cut tractor beams," Kirk ordered the fleet.

"Tractor beam cut," Sulu confirmed.

"All ships have released their tractor beams and are pulling back," Spock said.

"Mr. Sulu, match the spin of the *Northwest Passage* and get a tractor beam on her at once."

"We do not have the power to stop the ship alone," Spock said, stating the facts flatly as he always did. Even when those facts meant the death of thousands of colonists.

"I understand," Kirk said as on the screen all the ships started to fall back away from the moon, leaving the big, spinning Conestoga all alone.

Kirk punched his comm link again. *"Impeller! Republic,* help us with the *Northwest Passage.* We're going to pull that ship out of there."

"Copy that," Captain Merkling came back.

Sulu quickly took the *Enterprise* in closer to the moon and the big Conestoga. A black scar on the side of the big ship clearly indicated where the mule engine had exploded. Luckily, the explosion didn't seem to have damaged the ship itself. Scotty's design of putting the big engines on the outside of the ship had worked this time.

"Tractor beam ready," Scott said.

"Eighteen seconds until impact," Spock said.

"Attach it, Mr. Sulu."

"Done," Sulu said.

"Slow their spin and get that ship stopped. One-quarter impulse!"

Suddenly the noise was back, as loud and pounding as before. Sparks exploded out of one panel and smoke again started to fill the bridge as the *Enterprise* strained against the huge dormitory ship.

Strained to stop the forward momentum of a huge mass far larger than the *Enterprise.*

Kirk glanced around at Mr. Spock.

"The ship will still collide with the moon in twelve seconds," Spock shouted.

Kirk punched his comm link. *"Impeller? Republic? Where are you? Get tractor beams on this ship!"*

"Both are connected and pulling!" Sulu shouted.

Kirk again glanced at Spock, who looked up from his instruments and shook his head.

"Go to one-third impulse!" Kirk shouted to Sulu and the two captains of the other Starfleet ships.

"One-third!" Sulu shouted.

Around Kirk the ship felt as if it was going to shake apart. In all his years aboard a starship, he'd never stressed one this hard before. And to save thousands of lives, he was going to push it even harder if he had to.

"The *Northwest Passage* is slowing!" Sulu shouted.

"It will still collide with the moon in eight seconds!" Spock shouted back.

On the main screen there almost didn't seem to be any distance at all between the rough surface of the small moon and the skin of the big ship.

"Forty percent impulse. Now, Mr. Sulu!"

The engineering panel in front of Mr. Scott exploded, sending him toppling backward. McCoy instantly was at his side on the ground.

Fire sprang up from two panels and it was everything Kirk could do to hold on to his chair as he stared through the smoke at the main screen. He didn't want to watch the big ship collide with the moon, but he couldn't not watch.

Then suddenly it was over.

The noise, the shaking, everything suddenly stopped.

The *Enterprise* shot away from the moon and the Conestoga, making the moon and ship seem as if they had instantly disappeared from the main screen.

"Our tractor beam failed," Sulu shouted, then realized he no longer needed to shout.

Scotty, with a loud groan and McCoy's help, pushed himself back to his feet and moved back toward his station.

"You all right, Scotty?" Kirk asked.

"I've been better, Captain," Scott said. "I don't know why the tractor beam failed, though." He bent over his panel.

"Mr. Sulu, get us back close to that moon."

"No need, Captain," Spock said as he turned from his station. "The *Northwest Passage* did not collide with the moon. We managed, with the last pull, to stop its forward progress. The *Impeller* has it in tow and is moving away slowly."

"Thank heavens," McCoy said as both Sulu and Chekov cheered.

"And the moon?" Kirk asked. "Did we miss?"

"The final push was cut short by exactly eighteen point four seconds," Spock said. "From the optimum line and speed, we missed by three point six percent."

"Enough with the numbers, Spock," McCoy said. "Is the Needle going to hit the Quake Moon or not?"

"It will, Doctor," Spock said. "The question is now, whether the collision will obtain the desired results."

"How soon until the collision?" Kirk asked.

"Thirty-eight minutes and twelve seconds," Spock said.

"Lets make sure all ships are on their way to the safe point," Kirk said. "Then Mr. Sulu, take us into a standard orbit over the main colony location on Belle Terre. We have some children to rescue."

McCoy patted him on the back. "I was hoping you were going to say that."

"Doctor, I was hoping I was going to get the chance to say that."

Chapter Twenty-two

Countdown: 35 Minutes

As THE LAST DAY had progressed, getting closer and closer to the time the governor had warned her about, Lilian Coates became angrier and angrier. Why hadn't someone come back for them? How could they just leave children to die like this? None of it made any sense.

She had timed their arrival at the cave for just one hour before the time, just to keep them out in the open long enough for a ship in orbit to find them. But when it came down to the last hour, she had no longer believed a ship was coming. She decided then that she was going to have to keep these kids safe as best she could, and hope someone returned afterward. If there was a planet to return to.

Lilian Coates had watched as the children had slid one at a time through the brush and the small hole into the rocks. It was no wonder no one had found them.

214

The small mouth of the cave was impossible to see, even up close. No doubt a dozen searchers had walked right by it.

The kids had made it inside just fine, but she was another matter. On her stomach, she had inched her way forward, the rock pressing against her back and shoulders. At one point she felt as if she was stuck completely, her hands stretched out in front of her, her face pressed into the dirt of the tunnel entrance. It was the most suffocating experience she'd ever had. The weight of the mountain above her smashing her into the ground.

For an instant she almost panicked, then made herself calm down. She had to get inside and get this entrance blocked. The children's lives depended on her.

"You need help, Mom?" Reynold had asked from inside the cave, his flashlight shining on her face.

"Can you pull on my arms?" she had replied. "Reynold on one arm, Danny, you on the other."

She could feel the young, strong hands of the two boys grab her arms and then pull. At the same time she used her feet to push and instantly had been pulled through into the darkness of the cave.

"Thanks," she had said to the two boys, giving them a hug as she stood. With a flashlight in hand, she moved inside, letting the kids excitedly show her for a few minutes where they had slept and where Reynold had built a fire just like his dad had shown him how to do.

Then she and the children had found enough rocks to fill up the entrance hole completely. Danny asked why and all she had said was because she wanted to.

She glanced at her watch. Only thirty minutes until the time Governor Pardonnet had warned her about.

"This cave looks like it goes back farther," she said.

"A long ways," Danny said.

"Yeah," Diane said. "I found some really neat caves with really high ceilings back there, too. You want to see?"

"I sure do," she said.

They loved the idea of showing her more of the cave. With Danny leading the way, and Reynold staying close to her, they climbed over some rocks and moved farther into the mountain.

She figured that if she could keep them back there for at least the next hour, just to be sure, they would be safe.

Assuming all the ships had survived and stopped the main explosion. If not, it wasn't going to matter how far down in the caves they were.

Countdown: 27 Minutes

"What do you mean there are no life signs down there?" Kirk asked.

"Exactly that, Captain," Mr. Spock said. "I find no human life signs within a hundred-mile radius of the main colony."

"Well, do a finer scan and cover every inch again. They have to be there somewhere."

Spock nodded and turned back to his science station.

Kirk stared at the image of Belle Terre on the main screen. Was it possible that the kids and Lilian Coates were dead? If so, what had happened? This planet wasn't a very dangerous place. It was a very beautiful planet. He just hoped that in twenty-seven minutes it would still be beautiful. Or at least still here. The Needle was streaking at the Quake Moon, and in just over twenty minutes this would all change, one way or another.

The bridge seemed quiet and half empty after all the excitement of the last hour. McCoy had gone to sickbay to treat the injured from around the ship. Nothing serious, just burns and bumps, a number of them on Chief Engineer Scott, who was already back in Engineering, trying to find out why the tractor beam failed when it did. He took its failure almost as a personal insult.

"Governor Pardonnet is asking to speak to you, Captain," Uhura said.

"Put him on."

The governor's tired face filled the screen. He and everyone else on all the ships knew what had happened. They all knew that the Needle was close to being on target and now all they could do was wait and find out if close was enough.

"Did you find them, Captain?" Pardonnet asked.

"Not yet," Kirk said. "We're doing a very close scan of the entire area."

"Captain," Spock said, "my second scan has come up negative as well. The only logical conclusions are that either they are not down there, they are somehow shielded, or all of them are dead."

Pardonnet heard Spock's report. "That's not possible," the governor said. "Look again."

"Oh, I guarantee you," Kirk said, "we'll look as long as we can. Have all other ships arrived at the safe point?"

The governor nodded. "They have."

"Good," Kirk said. "Then we'll look until the very last possible moment."

Pardonnet nodded. "Thank you, Captain," he said softly, and cut the connection.

Kirk stared at the beautiful image of Belle Terre as it replaced Pardonnet's face on the screen. The governor clearly cared about his people. Kirk admired that about the man. There were a lot of things Kirk liked about Pardonnet.

"Spock, expand your search area," Kirk ordered. "Maybe Lilian Coates and those kids managed to get farther away than we give them credit for."

"We have exactly twelve minutes before we have to leave the area, Captain," Spock said.

"Then get searching," Kirk said. "I want those kids and Lilian Coates on this ship when we leave."

Twelve minutes later, that wasn't to be.

Chapter Twenty-three

Countdown: 1 Minute

LILIAN COATES had kept shining her flashlight at the roof of the cave as the children showed her some of the new rooms. Then, with less than a minute on her watch until the moment the governor had warned her about, she found an area of the cave roof that looked very solid and smooth. Might not be the safest place, but the best she could do.

She had the children gather there, then told them to all sit and be ready to cover their heads. Their parents might be blowing up the Quake Moon very soon.

They were both excited and afraid at the same time. Excited that their parents were out there, saving the planet. Afraid of what might happen.

She felt the same way, except far more afraid than anything else.

Two minutes after the time the governor had warned

her about, the ground under them started to shake. Slowly at first, then harder and harder.

Reynold grabbed her arm.

"Cover your heads," she shouted as dust filled the air around their flashlight beams.

Rocks fell, pounding into the ground as everything kept shaking and shaking.

A couple of the children screamed.

"Stay down!" she shouted. "Keep your heads covered."

Pebbles and dust fell on them.

Then, slowly, just as it had started, the shaking stopped.

All the children were crying and coughing. Dust swirled around them, stopping all their flashlight beams within feet of the light, making the area between them glow in an eerie fashion.

"It's all right!" she said, trying to calm them. "It's all over."

But she wasn't sure of that herself. That seemed much worse than the governor had warned her about. Had the full explosion happened and they rode it through?

"Can we leave?" Diane asked between coughs and sobs. "I don't like it in here anymore."

"We have to wait a few minutes," Lilian said. "Until some of this dust settles. Then we can go."

She didn't want to tell them she was worried that the shaking might just have trapped them in here if a rock or part of the roof had come down in the wrong spot. If that was the case, no one was going to find them. Ever.

She had the children gather around her in a tight circle, flashlights pointed inward. In a few minutes they were laughing about how silly they all looked in the dust. That was why she so loved children. They had the ability to move on and forget.

She didn't. All she could think about was getting out of this cave and seeing if there was a world outside to go to.

And maybe someday giving Governor Pardonnet a piece of her mind for leaving her and the children like this.

At that moment the ground under them shook again.

The children screamed and the dust swirled even harder around them.

Countdown: 1 Hour

The bridge of the *Enterprise* was deathly silent as his crew watched the big screen. Kirk imagined that every inch of every colony ship was the same way as here. People gathered around images of a small moon moving closer and closer to a large one. What was about to happen would dictate the future for over sixty thousand people. For most of them, this would be the most important moment of their lives.

The two moons were a strange sight. The Quake Moon was the size of a large melon, while the Needle was the size of a marble rushing at the melon.

Kirk glanced around at his crew, then back at the screen. No one was talking.

Everyone just watched and waited.

In what seemed like slow motion, the tiny Needle touched and then plowed into the face of the larger Quake Moon.

Rock and dust blew outward into space like water moving away from a rock hitting the calm surface of a lake. Kirk knew that the smaller moon was hitting just off center on one of the old plugs that used to release the pressure from inside the Quake Moon. The hope was that the impact would vaporize part of the plug and jar the rest of it lose, without rupturing the entire moon.

The shape of the smaller moon seemed to hold for the longest time, a round bullet smashing into the rough skin of the Quake Moon. Kirk suddenly had a worry that the surface of the Quake Moon was so hard, it would simply vaporize the Needle without allowing it to do much damage. But Spock had checked all of that. He believed this had a good chance of working.

Then the smaller moon vanished completely in the explosion of rock and dust.

Kirk stared, fascinated. He'd seen a lot of things in his years in space, but nothing like this before. And never had he been responsible for crashing two moons.

"Did it work?" McCoy asked, turning away from the screen to glance at Spock.

Spock said nothing.

"You'll know if it worked, Doctor," Kirk said, not taking his gaze from the expanding cloud of rock and dust on that moon's surface. "Trust me."

At that moment the expanding explosion seemed to instantly change shape. Now the collision and explosion results were no longer in the slow motion of low gravity. A massive hunk of red-hot rock shot from the explosion site into space, directly out of the center of the cloud. For an instant it appeared as if the smaller moon had hit and then bounced.

But Kirk knew that wasn't possible. This hunk of rock was trailing a long, intensely red plume of flame behind it. It was as if the moon had suddenly ignited an old-fashioned rocket from its side.

The massive hunk of rock that was streaking away

from the moon was the remains of the plug. Just as they had hoped to do in the first attempt, this collision had pulled the plug.

It was the most beautiful sight Kirk had ever seen.

Blue and red and orange material shot from the hole in the surface of the Quake Moon, expanding and cooling almost instantly as it reached open space.

The wave of color seemed to spread from the Quake Moon, flickering through the rainbow and then vanishing to the blackness of rock and dust.

"The pressure has been released," Spock said. "The Quake Moon itself seems to be maintaining its integrity."

Kirk glanced back at McCoy and smiled. "It worked, Doctor."

Sulu, Chekov, Uhura, and Scotty all joined the doctor in shouts of joy. Kirk just sat and watched as the Quake Moon fountain of color continued. He imagined those same shouts of joy were being repeated by over sixty thousand people at this very moment.

"You need to warn the colony ships to secure for impact," Spock said. "Thirty seconds."

Kirk nodded.

"Impact, what impact?" McCoy shouted, the smile gone from his face

"Uhura, open a channel to all ships," Kirk said.

"Open," Uhura said.

"Our little stunt seems to have worked," Kirk said to all the captains. "Secure for impact from the quantum shock wave in twenty seconds. Kirk out."

"Turn us directly at the Quake Moon, Mr. Sulu," Kirk ordered.

"Turned, sir," Sulu responded in a moment.

On the screen the moon was still spewing colors into

space, but not as fast or as strong. The pressure inside that moon was clearly almost gone. Now, after they rode out the quantum shock wave caused by the olivium release, they could return to Belle Terre and see what they now faced.

"Impact in three seconds," Spock said. "Two. One. Quantum wave passing now!"

The *Enterprise* rattled for a moment, then went silent again.

"Was that it?" McCoy asked, prying his fingers from what looked to be a death grip on the railing.

Kirk laughed. "That was it. Not much, compared to what we've been through, was it?"

"I can't take much more of this," McCoy said. "I'm just too old."

"A few ships are reporting minor damage, Captain," Uhura said. "Nothing serious."

"Good," Kirk said, staring at the now small fountain of color still pouring from the hole they had created in the side of the Quake Moon. "Take us back to Belle Terre, Mr. Sulu. Let's see what we have left to work with."

"At least there's a planet still there," McCoy said.

"That's a start," Kirk said.

Chapter Twenty-four

Countdown: Terminated

GOVERNOR PARDONNET slumped in a chair behind Captain Chalker on the bridge of *Mable Stevens* and just stared at the screen. The quantum shock wave had knocked them around a little, but not seriously. And the *Mable Stevens*'s engines had been repaired. On the screen, the last sputtering of matter shot from the hole they had punched in the Quake Moon.

And beyond that, Belle Terre still existed.

It was a beautiful sight. The best he'd seen since they had first arrived here weeks ago.

His mind couldn't completely accept the fact that they had won this battle. He had worked so hard to get used to the idea of taking this colony back to Federation space that he couldn't even think what needed to be done next. He knew there had to be thousands of things that needed immediate attention, but for the life of him, he couldn't figure out what one of them was.

He just kept staring at the beautiful sight of their planet, whole and floating there in space.

"The *Enterprise* is heading back to Belle Terre," Chalker said, glancing back at Pardonnet. "What would you like to do?"

"I suppose follow it," Pardonnet said.

Chalker laughed. "Thought you might say that."

Pardonnet forced himself to stand and take a long, deep breath. He had to get focused. The problems were far from over. From what he remembered about this success, it came with a price. Belle Terre was going to be affected with extreme weather for at least the next few years. And the large continent had been bombarded with bad radiation and might not even be habitable at all.

He was this colony's leader. It was going to be up to him to face these problems with his people, and solve them. But compared with the problems of trying to go back to the Federation, these were going to be a pleasure to face.

On the screen the image of Belle Terre grew slowly larger as the ship sped toward it. At least there was still a planet to have problems on. He and every colonist owed Captain Kirk and the *Enterprise* crew a gigantic thank-you. Without them this colony would never have gotten here, and now been allowed to stay. They owed Kirk everything at the moment, and Pardonnet wasn't going to forget that.

"Eight minutes until orbit," Chalker said.

Pardonnet stared at the image of Belle Terre, letting the feelings of success fill him completely. From this distance it didn't look changed much. But he knew it was going to be. At this moment it just didn't matter. It was still there.

Then he remembered the children and a wave of sadness covered the joy. He couldn't imagine how Lilian Coates and the children could have survived being on the planet's surface during such an event. But he vowed search parties would look again as soon as possible. And someday the answer to what happened to them would be known.

But first he had a colony to rebuild and sixty-two thousand people to get into homes again, on their new planet. And then there were the problems caused by now being the richest colony ever because of the olivium. He thought he'd been busy the last three weeks since they arrived. The next few were going to be even worse.

And he was going to love every minute of it.

Countdown: Terminated

Kirk stared at the still-beautiful images of Belle Terre. The planet looked, at least from orbit, basically the same. Earthlike and serene. But he could see even from this distance some differences. The main continent was covered at the moment in clouds that looked dark, almost black. And the color of the oceans seemed to have changed from a gentle light turquoise to a dark, angry blue.

"Spock, what's happening down there?"

"The change in the location of the Quake Moon is causing numerous earthquakes of varied intensity. The atmospheric disturbances are violent in many areas, with winds over one hundred miles per hour."

"That doesn't sound good," McCoy said.

"Understatement there, Doctor," Kirk said.

Spock went on with his report. "There are many fires spread over vast portions of the main continent, choking the atmosphere with smoke. A dozen volcanoes have suddenly become active. Much of the animal life and vegetation on the main continent has been destroyed by the radiation burst from the explosion. The island chains on the protected side of the planet are still intact, but experiencing small earthquakes and violent weather."

"Radiation?" Kirk asked. "How bad is it now?"

"Acceptable levels," Spock said.

"How long are these weather conditions going to last?" McCoy asked.

"Unable to ascertain that information without more study," Spock said. "But intermittently for at least the next few years. It is possible that many of the conditions will not return to a milder state for centuries."

Kirk nodded. "Well, at least there's still a planet here."

"And it is habitable," Spock said.

"By whose standards?" McCoy asked. "Earthquakes, dead continents, volcanoes, and extreme weather don't sound habitable to me."

"Better than limping back to Federation space on crowded, damaged ships," Kirk said, staring at the planet on the screen. "At least here they can still build the colony they hoped for. It's going to be a little harder."

"How about the main colony area?" McCoy asked. "Did the buildings remain standing?"

Spock studied his board for a moment, then said, "Some did, some did not. Difficult to ascertain from this distance."

Kirk turned to Sulu. "Start a scanning search pattern for any sign of those children and Lilian Coates around that main colony area. Include below-surface areas in case they took cover somewhere. Mr. Spock, you help him."

He hadn't liked the fact that they had not been able to find any signs of the children before the moon collision. He wanted to know what had happened to them and he wasn't going to let this drop until he did.

"The nature of the minerals in the rock formations around the main colony blocks normal scanning procedures," Spock said.

"Then adjust the sensors," Kirk said. "Those children and Lilian Coates have to be down there somewhere. Or at least their bodies do. I want them found."

"Understood," Spock said. "But it will take some time to adjust the sensors to scan through those rock formations. At least an hour."

"Just do it," Kirk said. "Get Scotty to help you."

"Captain," Uhura said, "Governor Pardonnet's ship is entering orbit. He would like to talk to you."

"Put him on," Kirk said.

McCoy stepped down and stood beside Kirk's chair so he too could be in the conversation.

"Captain Kirk," Governor Pardonnet said the moment his face came on the screen. "I would like to thank you and your crew on behalf of all the colonists."

Kirk nodded his head slightly. "Governor, we accept your thanks, but we only helped. All the ships were important to the success. And every colonist risked their lives to get it done. I think the thanks go to all of them, also."

Pardonnet laughed, the light coming back into his eyes. "I agree, Captain. But thank you anyway."

"You are more than welcome," Kirk said, also laughing.

Then Pardonnet's face grew serious. "Captain Chalker tells me you are already running a search for the lost children?"

"We are," Kirk said. "We'll let you know if we find anything at all."

"Good," Pardonnet said. "When do you estimate we can return to the surface?"

"We don't know the answer to that just yet," Kirk said. "We're going to first need complete weather studies and ground conditions. Then you and your people should have enough information to make a good decision as to how to proceed. And where to start your colony over."

"Good thinking, Captain," Pardonnet said. "I'll get my people working on getting ready, and studying the weather. There's a lot to do, isn't there?"

"That there is, Governor," Kirk said. "But at least there's still a planet to do it on."

Kirk cut the connection.

"These people are in for a hard fight," McCoy said.

"That they are," Kirk said. "And with all the olivium in that moon, we're going to be right here with them for a while. I have a hunch they're going to need us."

"Captain!" Sulu shouted. "A human form just appeared on the ground above the colony."

"What?" Kirk asked, glancing up at Spock who confirmed what Sulu said with a nod.

"Why would anyone beam down into that mess right now?" McCoy asked. "That storm must have winds of over eighty miles per hour."

"Maybe one of the children's parents wanting to get back to the search," Kirk said. Anything was possible, especially when it came to desperate parents.

"I don't think so, Captain," Spock said. "Another form has just appeared. They seem to be children. Possibly crawling out of some sort of cave that was blocking our sensors."

"McCoy, you're with me," Kirk said as he jumped and headed for the lift door at full speed. "Spock, get those sensors calibrated for seeing through that rock. And then get the transporter ready for beaming through. Make it fast!"

Countdown: Terminated

Lilian Coates had managed, through a series of small earthquakes, to get the kids back through the cave and near the entrance. The dust wasn't settling much, and they all kept stumbling over rocks and banging shins. She had also banged her head on a low rock so hard she thought she was going to pass out. She had managed to go on, but right now she had a headache that wouldn't stop.

At the cave opening the wind from outside was swirling the dust in the front area like a mixing bowl, choking them, and causing a high-pitched whining sound.

She knelt down at the opening and could tell at a glance, even with the wind and dust blasting at her face, that she wasn't getting out anytime soon. Part of the entrance had collapsed, leaving a small opening.

"I can get through that, Mom," Reynold said, squatting down beside her.

"So can I," Danny said. "You want us to go out and take a look?"

That was exactly what she wanted them to do, but she wasn't sure if she should let them. She could tell that a hard wind was blowing out there. And it seemed to be raining. But staying in here wasn't going to get them rescued. Someone had to go out there and she couldn't, so it had to be the children.

She moved back from the opening. "Reynold, you have that rope I asked you to bring?"

"Sure do," he said, digging in his pack.

He handed it to her and she took it, letting the nylon line uncoil onto the ground. Quickly she made a loop and tied it around Reynold's waist. Then she made another loop about six feet farther back along the rope and tied it around Danny's waist.

"Now promise me, boys," she said, "you will not take this rope off."

"Promise, Mom," Reynold said.

"Yeah, I promise, Mrs. Coates," Danny said.

She nodded. "Here's what I want you to do, so listen carefully."

Both boys nodded.

"How come they get to go?" Diane asked.

"You are all going to take turns," she said, smiling at Diane. "Reynold and Danny are just the first ones. Okay?"

Diane nodded.

"Good," Lilian said. She figured that their best chance of being found was by being out in the open. If anyone was looking, they would see two boys standing on the hillside.

She turned back to face the two boys. "I want you both to crawl out just beyond the opening. Then I want you to look around, see what it looks like out there. Then call as loud as you can for help and come back in. Understand?"

Both nodded.

"Be careful," she said.

Reynold got on his hands and knees and wiggled into the hole, pushing his way through.

Danny was right behind him.

With the two boys in the opening, the wind was blocked for a moment, letting the dust in the air slow some.

Lilian tied the rope around her own waist and held on to it with both hands, playing out just enough to keep the rope slack behind Danny. There was no telling what the earthquakes and weather were doing out there, and she wanted to make sure she could get the boys back in the cave no matter what happened.

She and the other four children all crouched around the opening, peering through as Reynold and Danny reached the outside and stood up.

The wind again slapped them and she had to fight to keep the rope fairly tight. Neither boy seemed to want to move away from the opening of the cave. That was good, but she didn't know what that meant. What was happening out there?

Then Danny started back inside, followed quickly by Reynold. When they reached her she could tell they were both wet and scared. Very, very scared.

"The trees are all knocked down," Reynold said, clearly breathless. "The forest is mostly gone and it's raining really hard."

Danny nodded. "We couldn't see very far at all, and the wind is so strong I thought it would pick me up."

"Yeah, me too," Reynold said. "Real scary."

Lilian nodded. It seemed that the tame weather of Belle Terre was now a thing of the past.

"I want to go now," Diane said.

The other three said the same thing, so Reynold gave Diane his loop and Lilian made sure it was tight around her waist. Then Josiah took the next loop. They were both acting brave, but Lilian could tell they were both scared about what Danny and Reynold had said.

"Don't stay out there too long," she said as they started through the opening.

The two children made it outside without problems and stood up. Lilian kept the rope tight, just as she had done with Reynold and Danny, as the wind again smashed into her face through the opening.

Then she heard Diane scream, loud and long and hard. A scream that carried over the wind and cut through the swirling dust.

"Diane!" Lilian shouted, trying to see what had happened through the small opening and the wind and dust. She couldn't see anything at all. Both children had moved away from the opening out there.

She started to pull back on the rope, but it was suddenly slack. The end came back untied.

Every nerve in her body panicked.

She dove into the opening. Maybe she could make her way out to get them, if she squeezed really hard.

Then in front of her the smiling face and broad shoulders of Captain Kirk filled the small cave opening, blocking the wind.

"Lilian Coates, I presume?"

She stared at him for a moment, not believing what she was seeing.

Then every ounce of energy left her.

She put her face down in the dirt and just lay there, trying to catch her breath, trying to let herself believe this was finally over.

She'd kill Captain Kirk later for scaring her. Right now, besides not being able to get to him, she just didn't have the energy.

Chapter Twenty-five

Countdown: Terminated

KIRK SAT in his captain's chair, watching the main screen and relishing how good a few full nights' sleep felt. Belle Terre floated lazily below them, still beautiful from a distance. Too bad that wonderful beach he'd sat on wasn't available anymore. It might be again, someday in the future, after the weather calmed down. But right now the beach was a cold, windy place with angry waves and blowing sand. Resting right here on the bridge was a much, much better place to be.

Around him everyone went about their duties quietly, giving him time to think and just relax.

Over the last few days, since what everyone was calling the Quake Moon incident, the colonists had been preparing to slowly move back to the surface. He'd pretty much stayed out of their decisions, figuring mostly that it was none of his business. The governor was a good leader. Young, but getting more experienced by the day. Kirk was going to let him make his own mistakes, as long as those mistakes didn't threaten the overall safety of the colony.

Yesterday, McCoy and Dr. Audry had discovered that the natural bacteria they had saved on every ship would help the ground on the main continent grow crops again quicker. Kirk had found that fascinating, the planet helping itself. Typical of the ways of the universe.

Lilian Coates and the children had all gotten back aboard their ships safely. The kids had asked a lot about how their parents had saved the moon from exploding. McCoy had spent time telling them, as he gave each child a checkup, how their parents had been heroes, and would never have left them on the planet normally.

With luck, the children would all be healthy and come through the event all thinking it was a big adventure. If that happened they would have Lilian Coates to thank. She had clearly saved them, in more ways than one. Kirk found her fascinating.

There was only one loose end that Kirk couldn't figure out. What had happened to the *Rattlesnake* and Captain Sunn? He could find no record of Sunn telling anyone which direction he was headed. And yesterday the *Enterprise,* using a high-boost frequency, had tried to contact the *Rattlesnake* without success.

Sunn and his small crew had simply vanished. Kirk knew that ships vanished all the time in space, but not a ship doing a mission for him. That ate at him. And in a few weeks, if Sunn didn't make it back, Kirk was going to see if they could go find the *Rattlesnake.*

But first, they had a colony to protect and help get settled again on its new home. They had been lucky during this entire problem that the Kauld hadn't interfered. More than likely they had figured the Quake

Moon would do all the work for them by chasing the humans away. But again it hadn't worked out the way the Kauld may have wanted, and that made Kirk smile.

On the main screen the image of Belle Terre floated peacefully, the Quake Moon just beyond it. Kirk knew that planet was a long way from peaceful, and taming it was going to take decades. Plus the contents in and around that Quake Moon were going to change this area of space forever when news got back to the Federation.

Kirk smiled and leaned back, letting himself relax. It was all going to be a challenge.

He loved challenges.

Pocket Books
Proudly Presents

STAR TREK®
New Earth

ROUGH TRAILS
(Book Three of Six)

L. A. Graf

Available from Pocket Books

Turn the page for a preview of
Rough Trails . . .

"She's away!"

Without benefit of an antigrav, the crate tipped gracelessly over the lip of the shuttle's hatch and fell free. Chekov leaned to the extent of his safety cable and watched the container tumble toward the ocean of airborne dust below, wondering how much chance they had of it landing anywhere near the drop target. The high-pitched shriek of its sonic beacon was swallowed up so quickly by the howl of Llano Verde's winds that he suspected if it went too far astray, it would never be found again.

Behind him, Plottel's voice, muffled by a filtration mask already several wearings too old, intoned blandly, ". . . and three and two and one . . ."

The crate's parachute ripped into existence with a *whhuf!* Chekov could imagine but actually couldn't hear over the roar of the dust storm outside. Fluorescent orange billowed into violent bloom, snapping the crate out of reach of the maelstrom only briefly before relaxing back into its descent. Almost immediately, wind tipped the parachute sideways and began dragging the crate sharply lateral of its original drop path. Storm-blown dust and sand swarmed the crate, the lines, the 'chute like famished ants. Once the air sealed behind the drop, Chekov couldn't even tell where the supplies had torn their way through. Swallowed by this wounded and angry planet, just like the sonic beacon. Just like everything else.

"Heads up, C.C."

Kevin Baldwin didn't have to give a jerk on Chekov's safety line to get his attention, but he did it anyway. Baldwin's primary source of amusement seemed to be irritating everyone around him. The sudden assault on Chekov's balance while hovering ten klicks above Belle Terre's surface launched his heart up into his throat. He grabbed at the sides of the hatch with both hands, but clenched his teeth before gasping aloud. That instinct let him preserve at least a modicum of dignity. Backing calmly away from the opening, he tried hard to ignore Baldwin's laughter as he disconnected the lifeline and shouldered out of its harness.

The hatch rolled shut with a grinding squeal that made Chekov's teeth hurt. Dust in the mechanism, sliding between the parts. Dust in everything—the air, the floor, his hair, his clothes. When Reddy, the shuttle's pilot, had promised they'd be above the ceiling of the dust storms, Chekov had assumed that meant they'd be flying in clear air. Instead, it meant Reddy kept the shuttle just high enough to avoid clogging the intakes on the atmospheric engines; Chekov, Baldwin and Plottel could stand in the open hatch under the protection of goggles and filtration masks, but didn't have to wear the kevlar bodysuits required by stormgoers on the surface. Not much of a trade-off, considering he'd still have to buy a new set of clothes the minute he set foot in Eau Claire. Or, at least, he would if he wanted Uhura to be seen with him in public.

Swiping uselessly at the front of his trousers, Chekov finally settled for patting himself down to dislodge the uppermost layers of grime. "I never thought I'd hear myself say this." He stepped sideways out of his own dust cloud. "But there's too damned much olivium on this planet."

Plottel and Baldwin shucked their breath masks before the light above the hatch had even cycled from red to green. "Maybe." Plottel didn't smile as he crossed the cargo shuttle's deck to dig a battered canteen out of a locker. "But if it weren't for all that damned olivium, Starfleet wouldn't have stuck around, and we'd be deprived the pleasure of your company on this little flight."

Chekov watched him fill his mouth with water, rinse and spit into a disposal pan, then pass the canteen on to Baldwin. "And if Starfleet weren't here, there'd be no one in-system with rations to spare for your emergency supply drops."

"If Starfleet weren't here—" Baldwin discharged a mouthful of water at Chekov's feet, creating an anemic slurry of mud, dust, and olivium. "—we wouldn't be in this mess to begin with."

Chekov nodded once, lips pursed, then went back to beating the planet out of his clothes.

This was an exchange they'd had, in various permutations,

at least twenty times since the cargo shuttle kicked off from the orbital platform above Belle Terre. Chekov had given up pointing out that, while Starfleet's actions might have directly led to the gamma-ray burst that most everyone called the Burn, it was only because of Starfleet that the planet still existed at all. Allowing the Burn had actually been the best in a very short list of options. While it all but defoliated most of a hemisphere, the colonists had been ferried out of harm's way. When house-sized segments of Belle Terre's largest satellite slammed into the face of her smallest continent, there was no one there to kill, no homesteads to lay waste. The combined Starfleet and colony ships, led by the *Enterprise,* had salvaged half a planet and an entire colony from otherwise certain destruction.

And the colonists had yet to forgive them.

From the moment they left Earth's gravity well, the Belle Terre colonists had bristled with fierce independence. They made their own rules, picked their own battles, all but spat upon Starfleet's offers of help and personnel—even when that help saved them from the numerous disasters that had plagued the colony expedition practically from the word go. Even now, when extended dust storms threatened the small continent of Llano Verde with starvation, the *Enterprise*'s sacrifice of its own rations to assemble relief supply drops was accepted with palpable resentment. The fledgling colony had nothing to spare for its own members, but the *Enterprise*'s continued humanitarian support was interpreted as an implied criticism of Belle Terre's ability to take care of itself.

This flight to the surface was no different. The volume of olivium dust laced through Llano Verde's soil after the Quake Moon impacts made transporter travel there impossible, and Captain Kirk had issued a moratorium on Starfleet personnel hitching free rides on civilian-operated shuttles. Which put Chekov in a bit of a bind. He'd been left on the orbital platform three weeks ago when the *Enterprise* set out to patrol for pirate traffic, keep an eye out for the Kauld—aliens who had attacked the expedition—and search for the missing vessel *Rattlesnake.* Chekov was officially cut loose, on leave, grounded. Sometime in the next two or three months, the light courier *City of Pittsburgh* was due at Belle Terre to pick up Chekov, John Kyle, and two other *Enterprise* crewmen for reassignment to the newly commissioned science vessel *Reliant*. Until *City of Pittsburgh* arrived, Chekov, Kyle, and the others were expected to rest, relax, and comport themselves in a manner that wouldn't aggravate the Belle Terrans any more than was inevitable. In general, this translated into long stretches of profound boredom as far away from the colonists as possible. Chekov spent the time trying to get used to seeing himself with executive officer's bars on his shoulder and answering to the title "lieutenant commander." He hadn't felt so small and ill suited to a uniform since being named *Enterprise*'s chief of security two years before.

Which was why he was once again violating Kirk's prohibition to join Sulu and Uhura for dinner in Eau Claire, the continental capital of Llano Verde. The two had been stationed there with Montgomery Scott and Janice Rand for several weeks, cut off from chatty communiqués by Gamma Night and olivium-contaminated dust, not to mention swamped with work and colonial frustrations. Long months away from shipping out to his new assignment, Chekov was lonely, insecure, and painfully bored. Part of him feared he'd never make the kind of lifelong friends on the *Reliant* that he had on the *Enterprise*; another part half-hoped their reunions would somehow prove him too indispensable to let go. He would be allowed to serve under Kirk on board the *Enterprise* forever.

In reality, he knew all he would get out of the trip was a good dinner and a few precious hours of socializing before he returned to his restless and unrelaxed days on the orbital platform.

Chekov had made an end run around Kirk's moratorium by refusing to be shuttled surfaceward like so much cargo. He knew about the weekly runs to air drop emergency supplies across Llano Verde. Showing up in the bay just before Orbital Shuttle Six kicked off, he offered to help the civilian laborers pitch the crates toward their assigned drop points in exchange for a shuttle ride down to Eau Claire. It wasn't just a chance to "pay" for passage, it was also a chance to be useful, sweat off some of his frustrations, and leave a positive impression on the colonials. Or so he'd thought. Vijay Reddy, the pilot, suggested that Chekov leave the heavy lifting to the laborers and ride up front with him. Not about to be coddled out of honestly paying his way, Chekov insisted on remaining in back to work alongside Baldwin and Plottel. Since neither of the laborers objected, Chekov assumed they were perfectly happy to have an extra set of hands.

By an hour into the flight, he'd figured out where he really stood. When he wasn't dragging a crate—without help—forward from the cargo hold, he was supposed to either lend his back to shoving the crates through the airlock, or sit out of the way on one of the armless benches welded into the bulkhead. His comments weren't welcome, and neither was his presence. They spoke to him only when forced to, and made no effort to censor their bitterness toward Starfleet when they talked between themselves. For his own part, Chekov swallowed most of the angry comments that sprang to mind. Another hour or so and they'd be on the surface. He would part ways with them in Eau Claire, and contemplate Kirk's wisdom in recognizing from the outset that the colonists needed as much physical and emotional space as Starfleet could give them.

A little communications panel high on the bulkhead chirruped with incongruous cheer. Unlike communicators or even crystal-based radios, intercom systems based on hardwire connections still functioned perfectly despite all the olivium radiation Belle Terre could throw out. The wall speaker, however, buzzed from the weight of the dust coating its tympanum. "Dave, how many crates have we got left back there?"

Plottel touched the container on which he sat as though silently acknowledging it in his count, then craned his neck to check the deck behind him. "Three up front, another twelve in the hold."

"And who's scheduled to get most of them?"

Baldwin set down the canteen and reached out to steady the cargo manifest dangling near the hatch door, squinting at its dust-fuzzed display panel. "Four go to Desert Station. Everyone else gets two or three."

"Okay." Reddy paused, caught up in some piloting duty, and Chekov felt the subliminal shift in mass that meant they'd changed heading without slowing down. "Hold out one from the Desert Station drop. They'll have to make do with three."

"Sedlak isn't gonna like us changing the manifest like that," Baldwin warned.

Invoking the continental governor's name injected a startling level of annoyance into Reddy's voice. "Sedlak isn't here. We've got an extra drop on the list for the northeast side of Bull's Eye—a group of herders who got stranded by the storm."

"What the hell were they doing out on a day like this?" But Plottel was already scrubbing at his goggles to clear them, getting set for another round of labor.

"They went out three days ago, before the dust got so bad. The ranch they're attached to didn't get word down to Eau Claire until yesterday, and the spaceport wasn't able to punch through the dust to the orbital platform until just now. Otherwise, we could've just put additional shipments aboard." The speaker snapped, nearly drowning out Reddy's grumbling sigh. "Now we're going to have to shortchange somebody. It might as well be Desert Station."

Ironically, if a Starfleet officer had made the same suggestion, there would have followed ten minutes of defensive resistance before any action could occur. As it was, Baldwin and Plottel started untangling their safety harnesses while Chekov was still stealing a single swallow of water from Baldwin's abandoned canteen.

"Is there any way to contact Eau Claire?" Chekov asked as he scooped his own harness up off the filthy deck. He'd given Uhura the original arrival time, and didn't want to leave her pacing the spaceport, wondering what had become of him.

"Don't worry about Eau Claire—they're used to this." Plottel was either trying to reassure him, or head off any fretting before it began. "The spaceport won't even consider us late until we're three hours past our scheduled ETA."

Chekov repressed a sigh. "It wasn't the spaceport I was worried about," he said, but without much expectation of being listened to. "Is there any way to contact anyone on the planet?"

" 'Fraid not," Baldwin said, wrenching the hatch open on the sea of roiling dust outside. "Nothing gets through that dust out there, not unless it's falling through." His grin was wide enough to see around the edge of his dust mask as he gestured toward the open door. "Feel free to take the message down yourself, C.C., if you want to. We won't try to stop you."

And they might even help me on my way, Chekov thought,

remembering Baldwin's previous push. He reached for the nearest lifeline and clipped it on a little more quickly than dignity allowed. Even the howl of Belle Terre's dust storm wasn't loud enough to drown out the resulting shout of mocking laughter.

"Uhura to Sulu. Come in, Sulu."

Uhura had said the phrase so often over the past five weeks that by now the words slid out of her mouth without the slightest effort—or attention—on her part. She pressed the correct transmission key on her experimental communications panel, paused for the appropriate time afterward to allow a reply to come through, but no longer really listened for an answer to her call because no answer had ever come. "Auditory feedback fatigue" had been the official term for it back at Starfleet Academy. Out here, on the nebulous fringes of known space, people just called it communications burnout. It was a condition most often seen in the crew of disabled ships who spent so long listening for an answer to their distress calls that they missed hearing it when it actually came.

"Uhura to Sulu. Come in, Sulu."

Uhura had recognized the syndrome in herself about two weeks ago and been horrified. Her entire career in Starfleet was based on her ability to listen. She knew she had a keener ear than many other communications officers, and she prided herself on her ability to thread out a signal buried in electromagnetic noise, or hear the barest scratch of a message through the resounding silence of subspace. Finding herself adrift in a numb haze of not listening, not even sure how many hours she had spent repeating the same six words without paying attention to them, had shaken her professional confidence right down to the bone. Could something as simple as futility really overcome all those years of training and experience?

"Uhura to Sulu." She fiddled with the gain on the transmitter to keep herself alert, watching the transmission histogram on her monitor spike into alarmed red then fade back to green as the computer compensated for the adjustment she'd made. The reception histogram, which was supposed to display the frequencies of Sulu's response to her hail, remained a dull flat-lined gray, just as it had since the first day she started hailing him.

A burst of irritation momentarily clawed a hole through Uhura's boredom. There was absolutely no reason this experimental communications system shouldn't be working. The pall of olivium-contaminated dust that hung over the island subcontinent of Llano Verde during its long, dry winter was known to attenuate every known kind of subspace and electromagnetic transmission. But the dust had created a dense surface layer in the planet's stratified troposphere, permanently trapped beneath cleaner and colder air above it. The knife-sharp boundary between those air masses should have been able to amplify and reflect back any signal that managed to reach it—every computer model and Starfleet expert Uhura had consulted agreed on that. So while Janice Rand worked on augmenting the city's short-range communications using olivium's natural crystal resonance, Uhura had designed a long-distance communications system that relied simply on punching a strong signal up to the top of the dust layer and letting nature take care of the rest. All she had to do—in theory—was calibrate the system by noting which electromagnetic frequencies created the best reflections at different points on the subcontinent. With computers varying her output signal nanosecond by nanosecond as she spoke, and a special receiver carried in the experimental shuttle Scotty had designed and Sulu was test-flying around Llano Verde, the whole project should have taken about two days to complete.

In theory.

"Uhura to Sulu. Come in, Sulu."

"Commander Sulu's flight plan said he was going all the way to Mudlump today, down on the south coast," a familiar voice said from right behind her. "Could he really answer you from there even if he heard you?"

Uhura sighed and turned to face the stoop-shouldered man behind her. His green-hazel eyes were puffy, his thinning reddish hair badly needed a trim, and his colony uniform was rumpled and coffee-stained. He looked exactly like what he was: not a rugged settler, but one of Belle Terre's too-few and too-overworked technical experts, hired on long-term contracts to help the colony through its initial growing pains. Despite her own tribulations, Uhura managed to summon up a sympathetic smile. No one could fault the colony's initial strategic plan for not taking a planetary catastrophe like the

Burn into account, but that didn't make life easier for continental government employees like Chief Technical Officer Neil Bartels.

"The transmitter I sent with him is automatically programed to reply on whatever frequency it just received." She accepted the steaming mug he held out for her, grateful for the bracing combination of Belle Terre spices and artificial caffeine concentrate. After several weeks of conferring over technical specifications and borrowing circuit-testing equipment, they'd fallen into the habit of sharing a cup of afternoon tea before the last and dullest stretch of the day. Uhura privately suspected that Bartels would have been even happier to spend his break discussing his numerous technical problems with Montgomery Scott, but the chief engineer had spent the last few weeks out at the spaceport as Sulu ran his shuttle through its paces. "Any reply from it should get bounced and amplified by the atmospheric boundary layer exactly the same way mine did on the way to him. That means it will arrive right back here."

Bartels lifted an eyebrow at her over his steaming mug of tea. "Even if his Bean is jumping really fast at the time?"

It was a measure of Uhura's stress level that the nickname the irreverent Llano Verde colonists had given Sulu and Scotty's antigravity vertical flight vessel could no longer spark even a flicker of amusement. "That's why I'm using a range of simulcast frequencies," she said, rubbing at the frown lines that seemed to have engraved themselves permanently into her forehead. "I tried to stuff in as much bandwidth as the system could handle without getting any negative interference on the carrier wave. I'm not sure it's really enough to compensate for Sulu's movement over an extended broadcast, but if he lets me reply every so often—"

"Assuming he ever hears you."

Uhura winced. The disadvantage of chatting with fellow technical specialists was their clear-eyed grasp of the crux of a problem. She knew exactly how to extrapolate reflectance angles to all parts of the subcontinent once she had a minimum set of established values, and she'd even figured out how to correct the system for daily meteorological variation of the boundary layer. But she still had no answer for the fundamental question of why Sulu had never, not even once, heard any of her experimental hails.

"Have you talked to the weather people lately?" she asked. It wasn't an attempt to change the subject, although Bartels' puzzled look told her he hadn't followed her train of thought. Llano Verde had gotten its name from its previously lush semitropical climate. At some point, those Burn-disrupted rains were going to return, washing the olivium dust out of the atmosphere for a while and making the need for Uhura and Rand's new communications systems much less urgent. "When are they predicting that the dust season will end?"

The technical officer sighed and drained the rest of his tea. "Depends on who you ask," he said. "The computer modelers think we'll get spring monsoons in the next month or two, but the hydrologists keep saying they don't have the field data to support it." He ran a hand along the top of her console, brushing off dust and shaking his head ruefully. "I'm not sure how rumors spread so fast through the Outland without any real communications system, but I've already got half the continent begging me for flood-control dams while the other half is yelling for irrigation channels."

Uhura's tea suddenly tasted acrid on her tongue, as if her taste buds had just noticed how foreign those native spices were. She swallowed the last of it with difficulty. "I'm sorry. I know I should have had this system up and running for you weeks ago—"

"Hey." Bartels reached out to pat her arm in a half-gentle, half-awkward way that struck Uhura as oddly familiar. It took her a moment to realize that it was the same inept manner in which Chief Engineer Scott dealt with the human aspects of his job. "I wasn't blaming *you,* Commander. We weren't the ones who called up Starfleet and demanded an overnight fix for Llano Verde's transportation and communications systems. Governor Sedlak tried to tell Pardonnet that even Starfleet technology couldn't solve the mess the Quake Moon made of this continent, but he just wouldn't listen. And no one else has made any more progress than you—"

Uhura shook her head in disagreement. "Mr. Scott and Commander Sulu have the latest version of the Bean running almost full-time. All they have to do now is work out a navigation system that doesn't depend on making constant contact with the orbital platform—"

"Just like all you have to do is find the right frequency to bounce off that dust layer. It's like they say in the Outland—

you've got to swallow a whole lot of dust before there's room in your throat for any water."

Uhura smiled at the colony technical officer, appreciative both of his support and the unique way he had phrased it. "I've never heard that saying before."

Bartels snorted. "That's because you don't have Outlanders tracking radioactive dirt into your office two or three times a day to tell you exactly how they think you should be doing your job." He swept up the empty mugs with a clatter, as if the mere thought of his constituents had flogged him back to work. "Come to think of it, don't bother to get that system of yours working anytime soon," he advised her as he left. "I hate to think how many more irate citizens I'd hear from if they could just pick up a comm and call their complaints in."

When he first felt the deck jolt beneath him, Chekov was struggling to back his way out of the cargo hold while towing five hundred kilos of malfunctioning grav-sled. It strained to keep its belly even ten centimeters above the decking, and every irregularity reached up to trip it, knocking it off course and killing its momentum. He'd cursed and kicked his way through moving a dozen other crates in exactly the same way. While his patience decreased with every repetition of the battle, he wasn't about to complain. So when the deck thumped against the soles of his feet and made him stumble, Chekov wrote it off to the grav-sled bottoming out yet again, or Plottel and Baldwin indelicately rolling one of the crates in the forward compartment.

Then his sense of balance attenuated in a moment of free fall, and the liberated grav-sled slewed sideways like a drunken bear. Whatever official safety procedures he'd once learned for handling grav-sleds flashed out of existence as he danced aside to avoid being crushed against the remaining crates in the hold. When full weight returned an instant later, Chekov was already halfway up one of the access ladders with his feet pulled up out of the way. The sled slammed back down to the deck, and the wall of crates it had bumbled against teetered but refused to fall.

Plottel and Baldwin were nowhere to be seen in the forward hold. The hatch to the outside whistled dolefully, adding more dust to the mosaic already filling the shuttle floor. A flash of what he at first took to be ochre landscape rolled into view through the opening, followed by an equally dismal patch of khaki sky. Chekov hadn't thought they were close enough to the surface to see beneath the pervasive clouds. Then he realized it wasn't ground he saw, but the eerily sharp demarcation between the "clear" airspace of safe shuttle passage and the roil of Llano Verde's dust storm. There was something odd about the orientation of that boundary, something that clashed with Chekov's own internal sense of balance. Either the edge of the dust storm had become vertical rather than horizontal, he thought, or Reddy was turning the shuttle in a banking turn so tight that centrifugal force had overcome the usual pull of gravity.

Keying the airlock closed on the jarring view, Chekov went forward to look for the rest of the crew in the cockpit.

"I tell you, there was nobody." Plottel's filtration mask hung from one hand while he combed the fingers of the other through his dust-caked hair. "We should have been right on top of them, and I couldn't see a soul."

Nodding in terse reassurance, Reddy waved everyone away from the back of his seat as he made delicate adjustments to the board. "Give me a minute to see if I can get back to our original coordinates."

Chekov leaned between Plottel and Baldwin, stealing a glance at the controls and then up at the viewscreen. It looked as if the shuttle was making a tight circle around their drop coordinates, but he could see that Reddy was actually keeping his helm at dead center. He wondered if they'd gotten caught up in some freakish dust-storm squall. "What's going on?"

"They're dead."

Plottel cuffed Baldwin across the top of his head. "Nobody's dead." But his own voice was too angry, his eyes too frightened to carry much conviction.

"What happened?" Chekov asked again, a bit more sternly this time.

No sharp comments about meddling Starfleet officers now. Reddy leaned aside slightly to open up Chekov's view of the panel, his hands never ceasing their rapid play on the controls. "The coordinates for those stranded herders put us inside the Bull's Eye crater, not on the outside rim like I thought. Most of the crater interior is water. I didn't want to waste the drop by putting the cargo in the lake . . ." His voice trailed off, and the shuttle gave another convulsive buck.

"So you went below the dust to get a visual on the ground?" Chekov asked incredulously.

"Yes." Reddy never took his eyes off the viewscreen. Chekov wasn't sure why, since dust now skated across it in waves so sheer and fast, they might have been plunging through a sea of gauzy curtains. He couldn't believe the pilot had really thought they'd have a chance of seeing people on the ground in this mess. "There was a clearing in the dust. I thought it looked big enough—"

"—for us to fly in and out of," Chekov finished. "But it wasn't."

"No," Reddy admitted. "And now we have to find it again."

Chekov frowned and helped himself to the copilot's chair, trying to make sense of the readings flickering across that side of the control panel. The altitude sensor put them at five thousand meters up, while the ground detector insisted they were within skimming distance of the surface. One velocity indicator had them flying at a steady two hundred kilometers an hour, while its backup flashed the warning for stalling speed. Chekov glanced across at Reddy, his frown deepening.

"Olivium contamination," the pilot said before he could ask. "Bull's Eye is one of the Quake Moon's impact craters. Radiation levels are a thousand times greater there than on the rest of the planet."

Chekov hear Baldwin snort from behind his seat. "Yeah, that nuclear stuff will only kill you. It's the subspace crap that messes up the instruments."

"So the only way to relocate your clearing is by dead reckoning?" Chekov glanced up at the forward screen, set to full transparency now that external visual sensors were rendered useless by the olivium. It didn't make much difference. "We need to pull above the ceiling of the storm."

"What we need is to make sure those lost herders get their supplies!" Plottel fisted one hand on the back of Reddy's chair. "They're counting on us to keep them alive!"

Chekov unleashed all his frustration with the colonists in a single fierce glare. "We need to pull up! A downed shuttle and crew of dead people won't help those herders, or anyone else on this planet."

"We can't."

Chekov shot a startled look at Reddy. "What?"

The pilot's dark face was stiff with restrained panic. "We can't pull up. We're losing thrust."

Swallowing the sour taste of dread in his mouth, Chekov stretched in front of Reddy to punch at the blast controls for the atmospheric engines. The gut-sinking surge in acceleration that should have followed the thruster fire never came. Instead, coarse juddering slammed through the shuttle's frame, and Chekov's adrenaline spiked along with the temperature gauge before he could slap off the engines.

"The intakes are clogged." He searched the console for some encouraging reading with growing alarm. All he saw was olivium-sparked incoherence. "Can we recalibrate our sensors?"

Reddy forced a quick reboot through the main shuttle computer, then shook his head stiffly. He looked almost too tense to breathe.

Chekov dug behind himself for the seat restraint, settling back to belt in. "We have to slow our descent." He didn't even turn to look back at Plottel and Baldwin. "Get back and strap down."

"Using what?" Baldwin wanted to know. He sounded near to tears.

Plottel made a calming little noise, and Chekov heard him tug the other man toward the cockpit doorway. "We've got the safety harnesses," Plottel said evenly. "Come on, Kev."

They passed out of hearing, and just that quickly out of Chekov's thoughts. The faint spasm of guilt following his silent dismissal didn't last long—his years in Starfleet had taught him not to tangle up his concentration with things outside his control. That meant Plottel and Baldwin, Sulu and Uhura, any chance of a career on board the still-distant *Reliant*—

Wind caromed against the shuttle with a sound like wild banshees. Chekov gripped the edge of the console, his stomach lurching up into his throat. "Inertial dampers are failing." It wasn't a guess.

"Everything's failing." Reddy fought to bring their nose up, might have been succeeding, all his efforts drowned in the pounding of wind and sand. "No attitude thrusters, no antigrav backup—"

Of course not. Not on a shuttle this battered by countless trips down through the dust storms of Belle Terre. Chekov tried again to boot up the sensor displays on the copilot's console, blowing a glitter of accumulated dust off the controls and wishing cargo shuttles had anything resembling a survivable glide ratio. The front windshield writhed with sun-stained browns and reds. Hints of horizon, flashes of what might be water. Not sure what inspired his sudden urgent certainty, Chekov reached over to grab Reddy's sleeve. "Raise shields."

The pilot spared him a single sideways glance. "We're not a starship. The only thing these shields are good for—"

"Raise shields!" Instinct, faster than thought. Without waiting for Reddy's understanding, he pushed the shield generator to maximum. They'd been falling stern-first, dragged down by the weight of engines and emergency supplies. Now their rear kicked upward, hard enough to throw them both forward into the dual panel, fast enough to make the shuttle echo with the groan of metal fatigue.

With an abruptness that made his gut clench, the shuttle broke clear of the dust and hurtled into shockingly transparent air. Chekov didn't have time to wonder if this was the same clearing that had first lured Reddy to the surface, because their trajectory was taking them straight down into it. And at the bottom, far too close, he saw the glitter of raw, reflected sunlight. His instincts had been right—they were only seconds away from contact with the surface.

Dust-swarmed inertial dampers struggled against the violent shifts in mass, but couldn't entirely save them from the impact. It came with a weird sluggishness, as if the ground had somehow oozed around their shields instead of crashing into them. Then silvery curtains of water geysered up over the windshield, and all view of this world was drowned.

OUR FIRST SERIAL NOVEL!

STAR TREK®
STARFLEET: YEAR ONE

A Novel in Twelve Parts®

by
Michael Jan Friedman

Chapter Eleven

"I know," said Matsura, "this comes as a surprise to you." He glanced at his fellow captains, Dane included. "To *all* of you."

In their places, Matsura would probably have been surprised as well.

He was an Earth Command officer by training as well as inclination, not one of the research types Clarisse Dumont had foisted on the Federation's new Starfleet. And at that moment, with every Earth colony in the Oreias system threatened by a mysterious fleet of alien marauders, his military skills were needed more than ever.

But this one time, Matsura felt compelled to pursue a different course of action.

"Listen," he told the others, "I may be on to something. I was studying the Oreias Seven colony back on the *Yellowjacket* a little while ago, and I noticed there were two hills at the edge of the colony."

"Wait a minute..." said Shumar. "There were two hills outside the Oreias Five colony as well."

"I'm aware of that," Matsura replied. "I got the information from your first officer a few moments ago."

"Two hills," Stiles repeated quizzically. "And that *means* something?"

"It sure as hell might," said Shumar.

"So what did you see when you went to examine the terrain for yourself?" asked Cobaryn.

"I'm not sure," said Matsura.

Zipping open the front of his uniform, he delved into an interior pocket and pulled out a handful of what he had found. They were fragments of something, each piece rounded, amber-colored, and brittle.

"I did some digging with my laser," Matsura told the others, "and this is what I came up with. The hill was full of it."

Cobaryn held his hand out. "May I?"

Matsura deposited his discovery in the Rigelian's silver-skinned palm. Then he watched Cobaryn's ruby eyes glitter with curiosity as he held the material up to the light.

"Any idea what it is?" asked Shumar.

Cobaryn made a face. "Something organic, I would guess."

"I'd say so too," Shumar chimed in. He glanced at Hagedorn. "Can we bring up a scanner?"

"Absolutely," said Hagedorn.

Before two minutes had elapsed, one of the *Horatio*'s security officers produced the device Shumar had requested. Shumar hefted it, pointed its business end at the stuff in Cobaryn's palm, and then activated it.

"What is it?" asked Matsura.

Shumar checked the scanner's readout. "It's a polysaccharide." His brow creased. "One that we found in great abundance in the hardest hit area on Oreias Five."

"So we have a pattern," said Matsura.

"So it would seem," Cobaryn responded.

"Though it's one we don't understand yet," Hagedorn pointed out.

"True," Shumar conceded. "But if one of the other colonies is near a couple of hills, and the hills happen to have this stuff inside them, there's a good chance that colony will be a target soon."

Stiles scowled. "And if it is? You think we ought to sit in orbit and wait for an attack?"

Shumar shook his head. "No, because the aliens might go back to Oreias Five. Or Oreias Seven, for that matter."

"So what *should* we do?" asked Dane, who, in Matsura's memory, had never posed so earnest a question before.

"We use our five good ships to hunt the aliens down," said Shumar, "just as Captain Stiles proposed. That's the best approach to keeping *all* the colonies from harm."

"But at the same time," Matsura added, "Captain Shumar and I pursue our hill theory...and see if we can figure out why the aliens decided to attack Earth colonies in the first place."

Cobaryn smiled. "A reasonable strategy."

Hagedorn regarded Matsura. "You're certain about this? I could always use an experienced hand on my bridge."

"Same here," said Stiles.

Clearly, thought Matsura, they didn't think his services would prove critical to the research effort. Still, he shook his head. "Thanks," he told his former wingmates, "but you'll do fine without me."

Hagedorn seemed to accept Matsura's decision. "Suit yourself. We'll hook up with you when we get back."

"After we've plucked the aliens' tailfeathers," Stiles chipped in.

But Matsura had engaged the triangular ships, and he knew it wouldn't be as easy as Stiles was making it out to be. Not by half.

"Good luck," said Matsura.

It was only inwardly that he added *You'll need it.*

Alexander Kapono had been overseeing the spring planting on Oreias Eight when he was called in from the fields.

As he opened the curved door to the administrative dome, he felt a breath of cool air dry the perspiration on his face. It was a welcome relief after the heat of the day.

"What is it?" he asked Chung, one of his tech specialists.

Chung was sitting on the opposite side of the dome behind his compact communications console, a smaller version of the one used on the bridges of Earth Command vessels. "You've got a message from Starfleet."

"Captain Dane?" asked Kapono.

Dane had said he would be in touch when they figured out what had prompted the attack on Oreias Five. However, the administrator hadn't expected to hear from the captain so soon.

The technician shook his head. "It's from a Captain Matsura. He says he's on his way to take a look around."

"Doesn't he know Dane did that already?"

"He says he wants to visit anyway."

The administrator grunted. "I guess he thinks he's going to find something that Dane missed."

Chung chuckled. "I guess."

To Kapono's knowledge, Earth Command captains had never worked this way. It made him wonder if Dane, Matsura, or anyone else in Starfleet had the slightest idea of what he was doing.

Cobaryn peered over his navigator's shoulder at a pattern of tiny red dots on an otherwise black screen. "Are you certain?"

"As certain as I can be, sir," said Locklear, a man with dark hair and blunt features who had navigated an Earth

Command vessel during the war. "This is almost identical to the ion concentration that led the *Horatio* and the *Gibraltar* to the aliens."

The captain considered the red dots. They seemed so innocent, so abstract. However, if Locklear was right, they would steer the *Cheyenne* and all her sister ships into a clash as real as flesh and blood.

"Contact the other ships," Cobaryn told his navigator. He returned to his center seat and sat down. "Let them know what we have discovered."

"Aye, sir," came the response.

The fleet had spread out as much as possible to increase its chances of picking up the enemy's trail. However, it would only take a few seconds for the *Cheyenne*'s comm equipment to span those distances.

"They're responding," said Locklear. "The *Horatio* is transmitting a set of convergence coordinates."

During the Romulan War, Hagedorn had led Earth Command's top *Christopher* squadron—the one that had secured the pivotal victory at the planet Cheron. It made sense for Cobaryn to defer to him in tactical matters. Anything else would have been the height of arrogance.

"Chart a course," the Rigelian told his navigator.

"Charting," said Locklear.

"Best speed, Mr. Emick."

"Best speed, sir," his helmsman returned.

Cobaryn sat back in his chair and regarded his viewscreen, where he could see the stars shift slightly to port. They were on their way to a meeting with their sister ships.

And after that, if all went well, they would attend a different kind of meeting...along with their mysterious adversaries.

Bryce Shumar wiped some sweat from his sunburned brow and considered the hole he was standing in—a ten-foot deep burrow that descended into the heart of a tree-covered mound of red dirt.

Oreias Eight's sun was a crimson ball of flame, its sky an immense vast blue oven. The colonists who had come to watch Shumar work—a collection of children and their caregivers, for the most part—didn't seem to mind the relentless heat so much.

But then, they had had a few months to get used to it. The captain had been on the planet's surface less than half an hour.

Training his laser pistol at the unusually thick tree root at his feet, he pressed the trigger. The resultant shaft of blue energy pulverized the root and dug past it into the rocky red ground below.

"Why don't I take over for a while?" asked Matsura, who was sitting on a grimy shelf of rock at the level of Shumar's shoulders.

The former Earth base commander cast a glance at him. It was true that his wrist was getting tired from the backlash of all his laser use. However, he hated to admit that he was in any way less physically capable than Matsura, who was a good several years his junior.

"I'm fine so far," said Shumar.

"You sure?" asked Matsura.

"Quite sure," the older man told him. Setting his jaw against the discomfort in his arm, he continued his task.

Suddenly, the ground seemed to collapse beneath the onslaught of his laser beam and Shumar felt his feet slide out from under him. Before he knew it, he was sitting in a drift of loose red soil...

With something hard and amber-colored mixed into it.

"Hey!" cried Matsura, dropping down from his perch to land on a ledge of dirt that was still intact. "Are you all right?"

Shumar took stock of his situation. "I'm fine," he

concluded, though not without a hint of embarrass-
ment.

The younger man reached down and picked up a
molded piece of amber-colored material about a third of
a meter long. "Look at this," he said.

Shumar's eyes narrowed as he considered the object.
It was the substance they had been excavating for, but in
aggregate form.

"Same stuff?" asked Matsura.

"Looks like it," Shumar told him.

He poked through the dirt with his fingers and dug out
another fragment. This one had a molded look to it as
well, and it was even bigger than the first piece. As he
brushed it off, he came to a conclusion.

"It's part of a shell," he said.

"How do you know?" the other man asked him.

"It's too regular to be a random accretion," Shumar
pointed out. "And it's not strong enough to be part of an
internal skeleton."

Matsura nodded. "So how do you think it got in here?"

Shumar frowned. "Good question."

"If the shell belonged to an animal," the younger man
speculated, "the thing could have burrowed in here and
died."

"But, remember," said Shumar, "we found evidence of
similar remains in and around all those other mounds. So
burrowing would have to have been an instinctive behavior for this animal."

"And it would have to have been in existence on Oreias Five and Oreias Seven as well."

Shumar nodded. "Which means it was transported
here by an intelligent, spacefaring civilization."

Matsura looked thoughtful. "For what purpose?"

For what purpose indeed? Shumar asked himself.

He turned the piece of shell over in his hands, watching it gleam with reflected sunlight . . . and an alternative

occurred to him. "On the other hand," he muttered, "maybe it wasn't an animal at all."

"What do you mean?" asked Matsura.

But Shumar barely heard the man's question. He was still thinking, still following the logic of his assumption. Before he knew it, the mystery of the Oreias system had begun to unravel itself right before his eyes.

"Are you all right?" Matsura prodded, concern evident in his face.

"I've never been better," said Shumar. He turned to his colleague, his heart beating hard in his chest. "Have you ever heard of Underwood's Theory of Parallel Development?"

Matsura shook his head. "I don't think so."

"It encourages us to assume, in the absence of information to the contrary, that species develop along similar lines. In other words, if an alien has a mouth, it's likely he's also developed something along the lines of a table fork—even if his mouth doesn't look anything like your own."

"And if you find buried shells...?" asked Matsura.

"Then you have to ask yourself why *you* might have buried them—or more to the point, why you might have buried *anything*."

Suddenly, understanding dawned in the younger man's face. "Then that's it?" he asked. "That's the answer?"

Shumar smiled, basking in the glow of his discovery. "I'd bet my starship on it."

In fact, that was *exactly* what he would be doing.

Aaron Stiles shifted in his center seat. "Anything on scanners yet?" he inquired of his navigator.

Rosten shook her head. "Nothing yet, sir."

The captain frowned. It had been clear from the increasing integrity of the ion trail they had been following that the enemy wasn't far off. It could be only a matter of minutes before they picked up the triangular ships and got a handle on the odds against them.

Not that it mattered to Stiles how many aliens he had to fight. This time, there was no retreat. One way or the other, he and his comrades were going to put a stop to the attacks.

"Sir?" said Rosten.

The captain glanced at her. "You have them?"

"Aye, sir," his navigator assured him.

Stiles got up from his seat and went to stand by Rosten's console. Studying it, he could see a series of green blips on the otherwise black screen. He counted six of them.

Good odds, he thought. *Excellent* odds.

He returned to his seat and tapped the communications stud on his armrest. "Stiles to Hagedorn."

The captain of the *Horatio* responded a moment later. "I know," he said over their radio link. "We just noticed them. I'll contact the others."

"Bull's-eye formation?"

There was a pause on the other end. "You know me too well, Captain. Bull's-eye it is. Hagedorn out."

Stiles smiled grimly to himself, then turned to his weapons officer. "Power to all batteries, Mr. Weeks."

"Power to all batteries," Weeks confirmed.

"Maintain speed," the captain told his helm officer.

Urbina checked her instruments. "Full impulse."

Darigghi came over to stand by Stiles's side. "It would appear a confrontation is imminent," he observed.

The captain resisted the temptation to deliver a sarcastic comeback. "It would appear that way."

"I realize I was not very helpful in our last clash with the aliens," the Osadjani went on. "If there is something more I can do this time, please let me know."

Stiles looked up at Darigghi. It wasn't at all the kind of statement he had expected from his first officer.

"I'll do that," the captain assured him.

Darigghi nodded. "Thank you."

Stiles leaned back in his chair. Maybe a leopard could change its spots after all.

"Navigation," he said, "any sign that we've been spotted?"

"None, sir," Rosten replied. "It'll be—"

The captain waited a moment for his navigator to finish her sentence. When she didn't, he turned to her—and saw that she was focused on her monitor, her brow puckered in concentration.

"Lieutenant?" he prompted.

Rosten looked up at him. "Sir," she said, "I've received a message from Captain Shumar and Captain Matsura. They're asking all of us to return to Oreias Eight."

Stiles felt a spurt of anger. "Are they out of their minds? We're on the brink of a battle here!"

His navigator's cheeks flushed. "Yes, sir."

The captain hadn't meant to chew her out. It wasn't *her* fault that Shumar and Matsura had gone insane.

"Sorry," he told Rosten. "I should know better than to shoot the messenger."

The woman managed a smile. "No problem, sir."

"Why are we being recalled?" asked Darigghi.

Rosten shrugged. "They say they've discovered something that makes it unnecessary to confront the aliens."

His teeth grinding angrily, the captain opened a channel to the *Horatio* again. "This is Stiles," he snapped. "Did you receive a message from Shumar and Matsura?"

"I did," Hagedorn confirmed.

"And what do you think?"

"I think we've worked hard to track the aliens down. I also think we've got an opportunity here to end their activity in this system."

"Then we're on the same page."

He had barely gotten the words out when another voice broke into their radio link. "This is Captain Cobaryn."

Stiles rolled his eyes. "Go ahead," he said.

"I cannot imagine that the recommendation we received sits well with you. After all, we are close to engaging the enemy."

"Damned right," Stiles replied.

"Nonetheless," said the Rigelian, "I trust our colleagues' judgment. I do not believe they would have sent such a message unless the value of their discovery was overwhelming."

"Same here," a fourth voice chimed in.

Stiles recognized the voice as Dane's. It was just like the Cochrane jockey not to follow protocol and introduce himself.

"Ever heard the one about the bird in the hand?" Stiles asked. "Right now, we've got the aliens where we want them. We may never get another shot like this one."

"This isn't just Shumar talking," Dane reminded them. "It's Matsura too. He knows how you feel about stamping the aliens out."

"And despite that," said Cobaryn, "he is asking us to turn around."

Try as he might, Stiles couldn't ignore the truth of that. If it had just been Shumar trying to rein them in, he wouldn't even have considered complying. But Matsura had an Earth Command officer's mentality.

For a moment, no one responded, the only sound on their comm link that of radio buzz. Then Hagedorn spoke up.

"I hate to say this," he said in a thoughtful, measured voice, "but it sounds like we don't have much of a choice in the matter. If there's a chance to avoid bloodshed, we've got to take it."

Stiles felt his stomach muscles clench. They were on the verge of completing their mission, for crying out loud. They were *this* close to showing the aliens that Starfleet wasn't an organization to be taken lightly.

But he couldn't argue with Hagedorn's logic. Even in

war, one had to seize the bloodless option if it became available.

Stifling a curse, he said, "Agreed. *Gibraltar* out."

And with a stab of his finger, he severed the link.

He was about to give Urbina instructions to come about when Darigghi saved him the trouble. As the captain looked on, doing his best to contain his bitterness, he saw the stars swing around on their viewscreen.

One thought kept going through his mind, over and over again: *Shumar had damned well better know what he's talking about.*

Hiro Matsura could feel a bead of perspiration trace a stinging path down the side of his face.

"Let me get this straight," said Stiles, who was studying the amber-colored shell fragment that Matsura had just handed him. "You dug this out of a mound of dirt and decided to call us back from an imminent confrontation with the enemy?"

He didn't sound impressed. But then, Matsura reflected, Stiles hadn't heard Shumar's theory yet. Neither had Hagedorn, Danc, or Cobaryn, who looked a little befuddled themselves as they stood by a gutted mound in the blazing light of Oreias.

"It wasn't just what we found," Shumar responded patiently. "It's what it all represents."

"And what *does* it represent?" asked Hagedorn, who seemed inclined to exercise patience as well.

Matsura picked up another of the orange-yellow fragments that he and Shumar had laid on the ground beside the ruined hill. This piece was more rounded than some of the others, more obviously designed to fit the anatomy of a living creature.

"We asked ourselves the same question at first," he told Hagedorn. "What was it about these shells that compelled someone to bury them? And who did the burying?

Then Captain Shumar came up with an explanation."

Shumar picked up on his cue. "There's a scientific theory that alien species exhibit remarkably similar behavior, even when they're separated by many light years."

"I believe I've heard of it," said Hagedorn. "Underwood's Theory of Parallel Development, isn't it?"

"Exactly right," Shumar confirmed. "And with Underwood's thinking in mind, I asked myself why I would have buried these shells—why I would have buried anything, for that matter."

"To honor the dead," Cobaryn blurted. He looked around at his fellow captains. "I am quite familar with human customs," he explained.

"Captain Cobaryn is right," said Shumar, smiling at his colleague's enthusiasm. "We demonstrate our respect for our deceased friends and relatives by burying them."

Dane looked perplexed. "But I don't see any bodies lying here. Just a bunch of shells."

"True," Matsura conceded. "But maybe that's where the resemblance to human customs ends. Maybe this species sheds its shells, like certain insects on Earth—and feels it has to bury them, because their shells were once a living part of their anatomy."

"And if it's true," said Shumar, "that these shells have some spiritual value to this species, is it any wonder that it would object to offworlders intruding on its burial grounds?"

"In other words," Cobaryn added, following his friend's logic, "the aliens who attacked Oreias Five and Oreias Seven...did so because we encroached on their sacred property?"

"It looks that way," said Shumar.

The captains exchanged glances as they mulled what Shumar and Matsura had told them. No one was outwardly incredulous.

"Makes sense, I suppose," said Dane, speaking for everyone.

"But we're not certain this is the answer," Hagedorn reminded them. "We have no conclusive proof."

"Scientists seldom do," Shumar pointed out. "Often, they have to go with what their instincts tell them. And right now, my instincts are telling me we've hit the mark."

The sun beat down on the six of them as they absorbed Shumar's comment. Matsura, of course, had already accepted his colleague's explanation. He was thinking about the next step.

"So," he said, "what do we do now?"

Matsura had barely gotten the words out when his communicator started beeping. In fact, *all* their communicators started beeping.

He took his own device out, flipped it open, and spoke into it. "Matsura here," he replied.

"Captain," said Jezzelis, his voice taut with apprehension, "there is an alien armada approaching Oreias Eight."

Matsura's mouth went dry. "Exactly what constitutes an armada?" he asked his first officer.

"I count fourteen ships, sir. And according to our sensor readings, their weapons have already been brought to full power."

Matsura looked at the others, all of whom seemed to have received the same kind of news. Their expressions were grim, to say the least. And it wasn't difficult to figure out why.

With the *Yellowjacket* all but useless, they were outnumbered almost three to one. Not promising, Matsura thought.

Not promising at all.

Look for STAR TREK fiction from Pocket Books

Star Trek®: The Original Series

Star Trek: Voyager®

Star Trek®: New Frontier

Star Trek®: The Badlands

#1 • Susan Wright
#2 • Susan Wright

Star Trek® Books available in Trade Paperback

Omnibus Editions
    Invasion! Omnibus • various
    Day of Honor Omnibus • various
    The Captain's Table Omnibus • various
    Star Trek: Odyssey • William Shatner with Judith and Garfield
      Reeves-Stevens
Other Books
    Legends of the Ferengi • Ira Steven Behr & Robert Hewitt Wolfe
    Strange New Worlds, vol. I and II • Dean Wesley Smith, ed.
    Adventures in Time and Space • Mary Taylor
    Captain Proton: Defender of the Earth • D.W. "Prof" Smith
    The Lives of Dax • Marco Palmieri, ed.
    The Klingon Hamlet • Wil'yam Shex'pir
    New Worlds, New Civilizations • Michael Jan Friedman
    Enterprize Logs • Carol Greenburg, ed.

STAR TREK
THE EXPERIENCE
LAS VEGAS HILTON

Be a part of the most exciting deep space adventure in the galaxy as you beam aboard the U.S.S. Enterprise. Explore the evolution of Star Trek® from television to movies in the "History of the Future Museum," the planet's largest collection of authentic Star Trek memorabilia. Then, visit distant galaxies on the "Voyage Through Space." This 22-minute action packed adventure will capture your senses with the latest in motion simulator technology. After your mission, shop in the Deep Space Nine Promenade and enjoy 24th Century cuisine in Quark's Bar & Restaurant.

- -

Save up to $30